S0-BOZ-871

Also by Nadine Gordimer

NOT FOR PUBLICATION

and Other Stories

by Nadine ⌊Gordimer

NEW YORK · THE VIKING PRESS

First published in 1965 by The Viking Press, Inc.
625 Madison Avenue, New York, N. Y. 10022

Published simultaneously in Canada by
The Macmillan Company of Canada Limited

Library of Congress catalog card number: 65-12829
Printed in the U. S. A. by Vail-Ballou Press, Inc., Binghamton, N. Y.

"Something for the Time Being," "The African Magician," "Tenants
of the Last Tree House," and "The Pet" first appeared in *The New
Yorker;* other stories were first published in *Atlantic Monthly, Harper's
Magazine, Kenyon Review, Mademoiselle,* and *Saturday Evening Post.*

Contents

NOT FOR PUBLICATION

and Other Stories

Not for Publication

It is not generally known—and it is never mentioned in the official biographies—that the Prime Minister spent the first eleven years of his life, as soon as he could be trusted not to get under a car, leading his uncle about the streets. His uncle was not really blind, but nearly, and he was certainly mad. He walked with his right hand on the boy's left shoulder; they kept moving part of the day, but they also had a pitch on the cold side of the street, between the legless man near the post office who sold bootlaces and copper bracelets, and the one with the doll's hand growing out of one elbow, whose pitch was outside the YWCA. That was where Adelaide Graham-Grigg found the boy, and later he explained to her, "If you sit in the sun they don't give you anything."

Miss Graham-Grigg was not looking for Praise Basetse. She was in Johannesburg on one of her visits from a British Protectorate, seeing friends, pulling strings, and pursuing, on the side, her private study of following up the fate of those people of the tribe who had crossed the border and lost themselves, sometimes over several generations, in the city. As she felt down through the papers and letters in her bag to find a sixpence for the old man's hat, she heard him mumble something to the boy in the tribe's tongue—which was not in itself anything very significant in this city where many African languages could be heard. But these sounds formed in her ear as words: it was the language that she had learnt to understand a little. She asked, in English, using only the traditional form of address in the tribe's tongue, whether the old man was a tribesman. But he was mumbling the blessings that the clink of a coin started up like a kick to a worn and useless mechanism. The boy spoke to him, nudged him; he had already learnt in a rough way to be a businessman. Then the old man protested, no, no, he had come a long time from that tribe. A long, long time. He was Johannesburg. She saw that he confused the question with some routine interrogation at the pass offices, where a man from another territory was always in danger of being endorsed out to some forgotten "home." She spoke to the boy, asking him if he came from the Protectorate. He shook his head terrifiedly; once before he had been ordered off the streets by a welfare organization. "But your father? Your mother?" Miss Graham-Grigg said, smiling. She discovered that the old man had come from the Protectorate, from the very village she had made her own, and that his children had passed on to their children enough of the language for them all to continue to speak it among themselves, down to the second generation born in the alien city.

Now the pair were no longer beggars to be ousted from her conscience by a coin: they were members of the tribe. She found out what township they went to ground in after the day's begging, interviewed the family, established for them the old man's right to a pension in his adopted country, and, above all, did something for the boy. She never succeeded in finding out exactly who he was—she gathered he must have been the illegitimate child of one of the girls in the family, his parentage concealed so that she might go on with her schooling. Anyway, he was a descendant of the tribe, a displaced tribesman, and he could not be left to go on begging in the streets. That was as far as Miss Graham-Grigg's thoughts for him went, in the beginning. Nobody wanted him particularly, and she met with no opposition from the family when she proposed to take him back to the Protectorate and put him to school. He went with her just as he had gone through the streets of Johannesburg each day under the weight of the old man's hand.

The boy had never been to school before. He could not write, but Miss Graham-Grigg was astonished to discover that he could read quite fluently. Sitting beside her in her little car in the khaki shorts and shirt she had bought him, stripped of the protection of his smelly rags and scrubbed bare to her questions, he told her that he had learnt from the newspaper vender whose pitch was on the corner: from the posters that changed several times a day, and then from the front pages of the newspapers and magazines spread there. Good God, what had he not learnt on the street! Everything from his skin out unfamiliar to him, and even that smelling strangely different—this detachment, she realized, made the child talk as he could never have done when he was himself. Without differentiation, he related the commonplaces of his life; he had also learnt from the legless copper bracelet man how to make *dagga* cigarettes and smoke them for a nice feeling. She asked him what he thought he would have done when he got older, if he had had to keep on walking with his uncle, and he said that he had wanted to belong to one of the gangs of boys, some little older than himself, who were very good at making money. They got money from white people's pockets and handbags without their even knowing it, and if the police came they began to play their penny whistles and sing. She said with a smile, "Well, you can forget all about the street, now. You don't have to think about it ever again." And he said, "Yes, med-dam," and she knew she had no idea what he was thinking—how could she? All she could offer were more unfamiliarities, the unfamiliarities of generalized encouragement, saying, "And soon you will know how to write."

She had noticed that he was hatefully ashamed of not being able to write. When he had had to admit it, the face that he turned open and victimized to her every time she spoke had the squinting grimace—teeth showing and a grown-up cut between the faint, child's eyebrows—of profound humiliation. Humiliation terrified Adelaide Graham-Grigg as the spectacle of savage anger terrifies others. That was one of the things she held against the missionaries: how they stressed Christ's submission to humiliation, and so had conditioned the people of Africa to humiliation by the white man.

Praise went to the secular school that Miss Graham-Grigg's committee of friends of the tribe in London had helped pay to set up in the village in opposition to the mission school. The sole qualified teacher was a young man who had received his training in South Africa and now had been brought back to serve his people; but it was a beginning. As Adelaide Graham-

Grigg often said to the Chief, shining-eyed as any proud daughter, "By the time independence comes we'll be free not only of the British government, but of the church as well." And he always giggled a little embarrassedly, although he knew her so well and was old enough to be her father, because her own father was both a former British MP and the son of a bishop.

It was true that everything was a beginning; that was the beauty of it—of the smooth mud houses, red earth, flies and heat that visitors from England wondered she could bear to live with for months on end, while their palaces and cathedrals and streets choked on a thousand years of used-up endeavour were an ending. Even Praise was a beginning; one day the tribe would be economically strong enough to gather its exiles home, and it would no longer be necessary for its sons to sell their labour over that border. But it soon became clear that Praise was also exceptional. The business of learning to read from newspaper headlines was not merely a piece of gutter wit; it proved to have been the irrepressible urge of real intelligence. In six weeks the boy could write, and from the start he could spell perfectly, while boys of sixteen and eighteen never succeeded in mastering English orthography. His arithmetic was so good that he had to be taught with the Standard Three class instead of the beginners; he grasped at once what a map was; and in his spare time showed a remarkable aptitude for understanding the workings of various mechanisms, from water-pumps to motorcycle engines. In eighteen months he had completed the Standard Five syllabus, only a year behind the average age of a city white child with all the background advantage of a literate home.

There was as yet no other child in the tribe's school who was ready for Standard Six. It was difficult to see what could be done now, but send Praise back over the border to school. So Miss Graham-Grigg decided it would have to be Father Audry. There was nothing else for it. The only alternative was the mission school, those damned Jesuits who'd been sitting in the Protectorate since the days when the white imperialists were on the grab, taking the tribes under their "protection"—and the children the boy would be in class with there wouldn't provide any sort of stimulation, either. So it would have to be Father Audry, and South Africa. He was a priest, too, an Anglican one, but his school was a place where at least, along with the pious pap, a black child could get an education as good as a white child's.

When Praise came out into the veld with the other boys his eyes screwed up against the size: the land ran away all round, and there was no other side to be seen; only the sudden appearance of the sky, that was even bigger. The wind made him snuff like a dog. He stood helpless as the country men he had seen caught by changing traffic lights in the middle of a street. The bits of space between buildings came together, ballooned uninterruptedly over him, he was lost; but there were clouds as big as the buildings had been, and even though space was vaster than any city, it was peopled by birds. If you ran for ten minutes into the veld the village was gone; but down low on the ground thousands of ants knew their way between their hard mounds that stood up endlessly as the land.

He went to herd cattle with the other boys early in the mornings and after school. He taught them some gambling games they had never heard of. He told them about the city they had never seen. The money in the old man's hat seemed a lot to them, who had never got more than a few pennies when the mail train stopped for water at the halt five miles away; so the sum grew in his own estimation too, and he exaggerated it a bit. In any case, he *was* forgetting about the city, in a way; not Miss Graham-Grigg's way, but in the manner of a child, who makes, like a wasp building with its own spittle, his private context within the circumstance of his surroundings, so that the space around him was reduced to the village, the pan where the cattle were taken to drink, the halt where the train went by; whatever particular patch of sand or rough grass astir with ants the boys rolled on, heads together, among the white egrets and the cattle. He learnt from the others what roots and leaves were good to chew, and how to set wire traps for spring-hares. Though Miss Graham-Grigg had said he need not, he went to church with the children on Sundays.

He did not live where she did, in one of the Chief's houses, but with the family of one of the other boys; but he was at her house often. She asked him to copy letters for her. She cut things out of the newspapers she got and gave them to him to read; they were about aeroplanes, and dams being built, and the way the people lived in other countries. "Now you'll be able to tell the boys all about the Volta Dam, that is also in Africa—far from here—but still, in Africa," she said, with that sudden smile that reddened her face. She had a gramophone and she played records for him. Not only music, but people reading out poems, so that he knew that the poems in the school reader were not just short lines of words, but more like songs. She gave him tea with plenty of sugar and she asked him to help her to learn the language of the tribe, to talk to her in it. He was not allowed to call her *madam* or *missus*, as he did the white women who had put money in the hat, but had to learn to say *Miss Graham-Grigg*.

Although he had never known any white women before except as high-heeled shoes passing quickly in the street, he did not think that all white women must be like her; in the light of what he had seen white people, in their cars, their wealth, their distance, to be, he understood nothing that she did. She looked like them, with her blue eyes, blond hair, and skin that was not one colour but many: brown where the sun burned it, red when she blushed—but she lived here in the Chief's houses, drove him in his car, and sometimes slept out in the fields with the women when they were harvesting kaffircorn far from the village. He did not know why she had brought him there, or why she should be kind to him. But he could not ask her, any more than he would have asked her why she went out and slept in the fields when she had a gramophone and a lovely gas lamp (he had been able to repair it for her) in her room. If, when they were talking together, the talk came anywhere near the pitch outside the post office, she became slowly very red, and they went past it, either by falling silent or (on her part) talking and laughing rather fast.

That was why he was amazed the day she told him that he was going back to Johannesburg. As soon as she had said it she blushed darkly for it, her eyes pleading confusion: so it was really from her that the vision of the pitch outside the post office came again. But she was already speaking: ". . . to school. To a really good boarding-school, Father Audry's school, about nine miles from town. You must get your chance at a good school, Praise. We really can't teach you properly any longer. Maybe you'll be the teacher here yourself, one day. There'll be a high school, and you'll be the headmaster."

She succeeded in making him smile; but she looked sad, uncertain. He went on smiling because he couldn't tell her about the initiation school that he was about to begin with the other boys of his age-group. Perhaps someone would tell her. The other women. Even the Chief. But you couldn't fool her with smiling.

"You'll be sorry to leave Tebedi and Joseph and the rest."

He stood there, smiling.

"Praise, I don't think you understand about yourself—about your brain." She gave a little sobbing giggle, prodded at her own head. "You've got an awfully good one. More in there than other boys—you know? It's something special—it would be such a waste. Lots of people would like to be clever like you, but it's not easy, when you are the clever one."

He went on smiling. He did not want her face looking into his any more and so he fixed his eyes on her feet, white feet in sandals with the veins standing out over the ankles like the feet of Christ dangling above his head in the church.

Adelaide Graham-Grigg had met Father Audry before, of course. All those white people who do not accept the colour bar in southern Africa seem to know each other, however different the bases of their rejection. She had sat with him on some committee or other in London a few years earlier, along with a couple of exiled white South African leftists and a black nationalist leader. Anyway, everyone knew him—from the newspapers, if nowhere else: he had been warned, in a public speech by the Prime Minister of the South African Republic, Dr. Verwoerd, that the interference of a churchman in political matters would not be tolerated. He continued to speak his mind, and (as the newspapers quoted him) "to obey the commands of God before the dictates of the State." He had close friends among African and Indian leaders, and it was said that he even got on well with certain ministers of the Dutch Reformed Church, that, in fact, *he* was behind some of the dissidents who now and then questioned Divine Sanction for the colour bar—such was the presence of his restless, black-cassocked figure, stammering eloquence, and jagged handsome face.

He had aged since she saw him last; he was less handsome. But he had still what he would have as long as he lived: the unconscious bearing of a natural prince among men that makes a celebrated actor, a political leader, a successful lover; an object of attraction and envy who, whatever his generosity of spirit, is careless of one cruelty for which other people will never forgive him—the distinction, the luck with which he was born.

He was tired and closed his eyes in a grimace straining at concentration when he talked to her, yet in spite of this, she felt the dimness of the candle of her being within his radius. Everything was right with him; nothing was quite right with her. She was only thirty-six but she had never looked any younger. Her eyes were the bright shy eyes of a young woman, but her feet and hands with their ridged nails had the look of tension and suffering of extremities that would never caress: she saw it, she saw it, she knew in his presence that they were deprived forever.

Her humiliation gave her force. She said, "I must tell you we want him back in the tribe—I mean, there are terribly few with enough education even for administration. Within the next few years we'll desperately need more and more educated men. . . . We shouldn't want him to be allowed to think of becoming a priest."

Father Audrey smiled at what he knew he was expected to come out with: that if the boy chose the way of the Lord, etc.

He said, "What you want is someone who will turn out to be an able politician without challenging the tribal system."

They both laughed, but, again, he had unconsciously taken the advantage of admitting their deeply divergent views; he believed the chiefs must go, while she, of course, saw no reason why Africans shouldn't develop their own tribal democracy instead of taking over the Western pattern.

"Well, he's a little young for us to be worrying about that now, don't you think?" He smiled. There were a great many papers on his desk, and she had the sense of pressure of his preoccupation with other things. "What about the Lemeribe Mission? What's the teaching like these days—I used to know Father Chalmon when he was there—"

"I wouldn't send him to those people," she said spiritedly, implying that he knew her views on missionaries and their role in Africa. In this atmosphere of candour, they discussed Praise's background. Father Audry suggested that the boy should be encouraged to resume relations with his family, once he was back within reach of Johannesburg.

"They're pretty awful."

"It would be best for him to acknowledge what he was, if he is to accept what he is to become." He got up with a swish of his black skirts and strode, stooping in the opened door, to call, "Simon, bring the boy." Miss Graham-Grigg was smiling excitedly toward the doorway, all the will to love pacing behind the bars of her glance.

Praise entered in the navy blue shorts and white shirt of his new school uniform. The woman's kindness, the man's attention, got him in the eyes like the sun striking off the pan where the cattle had been taken to drink. Father Audry came from England, Miss Graham-Grigg had told him, like herself. That was what they were, these two white people who were not like any white people he had seen to be. What they were was being English. From far off; six thousand miles from here, as he knew from his geography book.

Praise did very well at the new school. He sang in the choir in the big church on Sundays; his body, that was to have been made a man's out in the bush, was hidden under the white robes. The boys smoked in the lavatories and once there was a girl who came and lay down for them in a storm-water ditch behind the workshops. He knew all about these things from before, on the streets and in the location where he had slept in one room with a whole family. But he did not tell the boys about the initiation. The women had not said anything to Miss Graham-Grigg. The Chief hadn't, either. Soon when Praise thought about it he realized that by now it must be over. Those boys must have come back from the bush. Miss Graham-Grigg had said that after a year, when Christmas came, she would fetch him for the summer holidays. She did come and see him twice that first year, when she was down in Johannesburg, but he couldn't go back with her at Christmas because Father Audry had him in the Nativity play and was giving him personal coaching in Latin and algebra. Father Audry didn't actually teach in the school at all—it was "his" school simply because he had begun it, and it was run by the order of which he was Father Provincial—but the reports of the boy's progress were so astonishing that, as he said to Miss Graham-Grigg, one felt one must give him all the mental stimulation one could.

"I begin to believe we may be able to sit him for his matric when he is just sixteen." Father Audry made the pronouncement with the air of doing so at the risk of sounding ridiculous. Miss Graham-Grigg always had her hair done when she got to Johannesburg, she was looking pretty and gay. "D'you think he could do a Cambridge entrance? My committee in London would set up a scholarship, I'm sure—investment in a future prime minister for the Protectorate!"

When Praise was sent for, she said she hardly knew him; he hadn't grown much, but he looked so *grown-up,* with his long trousers and glasses. "You really needn't wear them when you're not working," said Father Audry. "Well, I suppose if you take 'em on and off you keep leaving them about, eh?" They both stood back, smiling, letting the phenomenon embody in the boy.

Praise saw that she had never been reminded by anyone about the initiation. She began to give him news of his friends, Tebedi and Joseph and the others, but when he heard their names they seemed to belong to people he couldn't see in his mind.

Father Audry talked to him sometimes about what Father called his "family," and when first he came to the school he had been told to write to them. It was a well-written, well-spelled

letter in English, exactly the letter he presented as a school
exercise when one was required in class. They didn't answer.
Then Father Audry must have made private efforts to get in
touch with them, because the old woman, a couple of children who had been babies when he left, and one of his
grown-up "sisters" came to the school on a visiting day. They
had to be pointed out to him among the other boys' visitors; he
would not have known them, nor they him. He said, "Where's
my uncle?"—because he would have known him at once; he had
never grown out of the slight stoop of the left shoulder where
the weight of the old man's hand had impressed the young
bone. But the old man was dead. Father Audry came up and
put a long arm round the bent shoulder and another long arm
round one of the small children and said from one to the other,
"Are you going to work hard and learn a lot like your brother?"
And the small black child stared up into the nostrils filled with
strong hair, the tufted eyebrows, the red mouth surrounded by
the pale jowl dark-pored with beard beneath the skin, and then
down, torn by fascination, to the string of beads that hung from
the leather belt.

They did not come again but Praise did not much miss visitors because he spent more and more time with Father Audry.
When he was not actually being coached, he was set to work to
prepare his lessons or do his reading in the Father's study,
where he could concentrate as one could not hope to do up at
the school. Father Audry taught him chess as a form of mental
gymnastics, and was jubilant the first time Praise beat him.
Praise went up to the house for a game nearly every evening
after supper. He tried to teach the other boys, but after the first
ten minutes of explanation of moves, someone would bring out
the cards or dice and they would all play one of the old games
that were played in the streets and yards and locations. Johannesburg was only nine miles away; you could see the lights.

Father Audry rediscovered what Miss Graham-Grigg had
found—that Praise listened attentively to music, serious music.
One day Father Audry handed the boy the flute that had lain
for years in its velvet-lined box that bore still the little silver
name-plate: Rowland Audry. He watched while Praise gave the

preliminary swaying wriggle and assumed the bent-kneed stance of all the urchin performers Father Audry had seen, and then tried to blow down it in the shy, fierce attack of penny-whistle music. Father Audry took it out of his hands. "It's what you've just heard there." Bach's unaccompanied flute sonata lay on the record-player. Praise smiled and frowned, giving his glasses a lift with his nose—a habit he was developing. "But you'll soon learn to play it the right way round," said Father Audry, and with the lack of self-consciousness that comes from the habit of privilege, put the flute to his mouth and played what he remembered after ten years.

He taught Praise not only how to play the flute, but also the elements of musical composition, so that he should not simply play by ear, or simply listen with pleasure, but also understand what it was that he heard. The flute-playing was much more of a success with the boys than the chess had been, and on Saturday nights, when they sometimes made up concerts, he was allowed to take it to the hostel and play it for them. Once he played in a show for white people, in Johannesburg; but the boys could not come to that; he could only tell them about the big hall at the university, the jazz band, the African singers and dancers with their red lips and straightened hair, like white women.

The one thing that dissatisfied Father Audry was that the boy had not filled out and grown as much as one would have expected. He made it a rule that Praise must spend more time on physical exercise—the school couldn't afford a proper gymnasium, but there was some equipment outdoors. The trouble was that the boy had so little time; even with his exceptional ability, it was not going to be easy for a boy with his lack of background to matriculate at sixteen. Brother George, his form master, was certain he could be made to bring it off; there was a specially strong reason why everyone wanted him to do it since Father Audry had established that he would be eligible for an open scholarship that no black boy had ever won before—what a triumph that would be, for the boy, for the school, for all the African boys who were considered fit only for the inferior standard of "Bantu education"! Perhaps some day this beggar child from the streets of Johannesburg might even become the first black South African to be a Rhodes Scholar. This was what Father Audry jokingly referred to as Brother George's "sin of pride." But who knew? It was not inconceivable. So far as the boy's physique was concerned—what Brother George said was probably true: "You can't feed up for those years in the streets."

From the beginning of the first term of the year he was fifteen Praise had to be coached, pressed on, and to work as even he had never worked before. His teachers gave him tremendous support; he seemed borne along on it by either arm so that he never looked up from his books. To encourage him, Father Audry arranged for him to compete in certain interschool scholastic contests that were really intended for the white Anglican schools—a spelling bee, a debate, a quiz contest. He sat on the platform in the polished halls of huge white schools and gave his correct answers in the African-accented English that the boys who surrounded him knew only as the accent of servants and delivery men.

Brother George often asked him if he were tired. But he was not tired. He only wanted to be left with his books. The boys in the hostel seemed to know this; they never asked him to play cards any more, and even when they shared smokes together in the lavatory, they passed him his drag in silence. He specially did not want Father Audry to come in with a glass of hot milk. He would rest his cheek against the pages of the books, now and then, alone in the study; that was all. The damp stone smell of the books was all he needed. Where he had once had to force himself to return again and again to the pages of things he did not grasp, gazing in blankness at the print until meaning assembled itself, he now had to force himself when it was necessary to leave the swarming facts outside which he no longer seemed to understand anything. Sometimes he could not work for minutes at a time because he was thinking that Father Audry would come in with the milk. When he did come, it was never actually so bad. But Praise couldn't look at his face. Once or twice when he had gone out again, Praise shed a few tears. He found himself praying, smiling with the tears and trembling, rubbing at the scalding water that ran down inside his nose and blotched on the books.

One Saturday afternoon when Father Audry had been entertaining guests at lunch he came into the study and suggested that the boy should get some fresh air—go out and join the football game for an hour or so. But Praise was struggling with geometry problems from the previous year's matriculation paper that, to Brother George's dismay, he had suddenly got all wrong, that morning.

Father Audry could imagine what Brother George was thinking: was this an example of the phenomenon he had met with so often with African boys of a lesser calibre—the inability, through lack of an assumed cultural background, to perform a piece of work well known to them, once it was presented in a slightly different manner outside one of their own textbooks? Nonsense, of course, in this case; everyone was overanxious about the boy. Right from the start he'd shown that there was nothing mechanistic about his thought processes; he had a brain, not just a set of conditioned reflexes.

"Off you go. You'll manage better when you've taken a few knocks on the field."

But desperation had settled on the boy's face like obstinacy. "I must, I must," he said, putting his palms down over the books.

"Good. Then let's see if we can tackle it together."

The black skirt swishing past the shiny shoes brought a smell of cigars. Praise kept his eyes on the black beads; the leather belt they hung from creaked as the big figure sat down. Father Audry took the chair on the opposite side of the table and switched the exercise book round toward himself. He scrubbed at the thick eyebrows till they stood out tangled, drew the hand down over his great nose, and then screwed his eyes closed a moment, mouth strangely open and lips drawn back in a familiar grimace. There was a jump, like a single painful hiccup, in Praise's body. The Father was explaining the problem gently, in his offhand English voice.

He said, "Praise? D'you follow?"—the boy seemed sluggish,

almost deaf, as if the voice reached him as the light of a star reaches the earth from something already dead.

Father Audry put out his fine hand, in question or compassion. But the boy leapt up, dodging a blow. "Sir—no. Sir—no."

It was clearly hysteria; he had never addressed Father Audry as anything but "Father." It was some frightening retrogression, a reversion to the subconscious, a place of symbols and collective memory. He spoke for others, out of another time. Father Audry stood up but saw in alarm that by the boy's retreat he was made his pursuer, and he let him go blundering in clumsy panic out of the room.

Brother George was sent to comfort the boy. In half an hour Praise was down on the football field, running and laughing. But Father Audry took some days to get over the incident. He kept thinking how when the boy had backed away he had almost gone after him. The ugliness of the instinct repelled him; who would have thought how, at the mercy of the instinct to prey, the fox, the wild dog long for the innocence of the gentle rabbit, and the lamb. No one had shown fear of him ever before in his life. He had never given a thought to the people who were not like himself; those from whom others turn away. He felt at last a repugnant and resentful pity for them, the dripping-jawed hunters. He even thought that he would like to go into retreat for a few days, but it was inconvenient—he had so many obligations. Finally, the matter-of-factness of the boy, Praise, was the thing that restored normality. So far as the boy was concerned, one would have thought that nothing had happened. The next day he seemed to have forgotten all about it; a good thing. And so Father Audry's own inner disruption, denied by the boy's calm, sank away. He allowed the whole affair the one acknowledgment of writing to Miss Graham-Grigg—surely that was not making too much of it—to suggest that the boy was feeling the tension of his final great effort, and that a visit from her, etc.; but she was still away in England—some family troubles had kept her there for months, and in fact she had not been to see her protégé for more than a year.

Praise worked steadily on the last lap. Brother George and

Father Audry watched him continuously. He was doing extremely well and seemed quite overcome with the weight of pride and pleasure when Father Audry presented him with a new black fountain pen: this was the pen with which he was to write the matriculation exam. On a Monday afternoon Father Audry, who had been in conference with the bishop all morning, looked in on his study, where every afternoon the boy would be seen sitting at the table that had been moved in for him. But there was no one there. The books were on the table. A chute of sunlight landed on the seat of the chair. Praise was not found again. The school was searched; and then the police were informed; the boys questioned; there were special prayers said in the mornings and evenings. He had not taken anything with him except the fountain pen.

When everything had been done there was nothing but silence; nobody mentioned the boy's name. But Father Audry was conducting investigations on his own. Every now and then he would get an idea that would bring a sudden hopeful relief. He wrote to Adelaide Graham-Grigg: ". . . what worries me—I believe the boy may have been on the verge of a nervous breakdown. I am hunting everywhere . . ."; was it possible that he might make his way to the Protectorate? She was acting as confidential secretary to the Chief, now, but she wrote to say that if the boy turned up she would try to make time to deal with the situation. Father Audry even sought out, at last, the "family"—the people with whom Miss Graham-Grigg had discovered Praise living as a beggar. They had been moved to a new township and it took some time to trace them. He found Number 28b, Block E, in the appropriate ethnic group. He was accustomed to going in and out of African homes and he explained his visit to the old woman in matter-of-fact terms at once, since he knew how suspicious of questioning the people would be. There were no interior doors in these houses and a woman in the inner room who was dressing moved out of the visitor's line of vision as he sat down. She heard all that passed between Father Audry and the old woman and presently she came in with mild interest. Out of a silence the old woman was saying, "My-my-my-my!"—she shook her head down into her bosom in a stylized expression of commiseration; they had not seen the boy. "And he spoke so nice, everything was so nice in the school." But they knew nothing about the boy, nothing at all. The younger woman remarked, "Maybe he's with those boys who sleep in the old empty cars there in town—you know? —there by the beer hall?"

Son-in-Law

During the war they had kept him hidden from the Germans and in the first days after liberation they had had to protect him from roaming bands of zealots among their own people, because although he was a Jew he had also once been a German.

The old man, sitting in his railwayman's cap with his pipe at the window, said, "What time is he going to work today?"

The daughter handed her father his coffee. "Here—"

The old man waved to her to put it down beside him. "What time, Werner?"

"What's that?" He was spooning the contents of a pot of jam into the china jar with the bamboo handle; she would not have anything on the table in the container in which it came from the shops. Her eyes met his, blank; only the meeting belied that they were severally preoccupied. "About ten o'clock—today. I think. Perhaps I'll leave a bit early and pay a business call on the way to the office."

The old man looked out the window, marvelling. "Six o'clock every morning of my life for fifty-one years."

"But he doesn't happen to work on the railway, Papa."

"Don't eat me up, my girl."

"Offices don't open at six o'clock."

"Times have changed, that's all I'm saying."

She was putting on her flowered silk scarf, brown hat and gloves; she too had been used to getting up early all her life and the make-up on her neat middle-aged face was as fresh and clearly applied as it was when they were going out to a coffee party in the evening. She put a packet of sandwiches in her bag and kissed her father.

She looked at him briefly; with such a look, compressed, tele-

graphic, containing without so much as the twitch of the nerve
in an eyelid to betray it, all her eloquence, she had warned him
of the passing of the German patrols in the street outside. The
front door closed behind her.

When she had gone the atmosphere in the flat dropped. It
was as if, without her, there was no connection between them,
the old man could not get at him. Even the physiognomical
differences between them underwrote harmlessness, as certain
species of animals, though actually belonging respectively to the
genera of prey and victim, may coexist peacefully so long as
each does not recognize the other for what he really is. The old
man had small bright blue eyes like a light left burning in an
empty room. He did not wear his false teeth and from his pink
face drawn in to the pursestring of his mouth, his high round
cheekbones stood out in fists. He had never left home.

The other was quietly washing up. He stood helplessly, as
sedentary people do. He was bald with a big dome of sallow
brow and a frill of curly grey and black hair from ear to ear.
Among so many blue-eyed people his heavy black eyes, drooping
at the corners and underscored by scoops of shiny purple-brown
shadow were startling, as if he were perhaps designed to see at
night.

He took the old man for his morning visit to the lavatory and
left him there while he finished the dishes and hung up the
drying cloths. When the old man was ready, there was a grunting call, and he went up the passage to fetch him and settled
him in his chair again. "Papa, I'll have time to take you to the
tobacconist if you want to." The old man was gradually losing
the power of his legs and could go out into the street only in his
wheelchair.

"Not today."

He said, "I mean, I can leave out the business call."

The old man gave a dismissing gesture. Then forgetful, he
took out his tobacco pouch to make sure once again that it
contained sufficient for the day. These small rituals filled time
satisfactorily, becoming more repetitive as they reduced in variety.

He went into the bedroom. It had been the room of the old

man and his wife, before Anne-Marie and he were married and the old woman died. The two high old-fashioned beds took up the whole place. The down quilts were puffed like the breasts of birds; Anne-Marie did not leave a hairpin out of place when she left in the mornings. He sat down on his bed with a shuddering sigh and put out his hand to turn on the tiny bedside radio, barely audibly.

After a few minutes the old man called, "What's the time?"

There was the face of her gilt travelling clock: nearly ten to ten. Swiftly, while stealthily turning off the radio as he called back, he got to his feet and stood a moment, letting slow breathing sway him a little. Then he took his coat off the hanger, put on his hat, opened a drawer, and slipped a packet of peppermints into his coat pocket. Again he stood as if he had forgotten something. Meanwhile he picked up her fancy nail file where it hung on a little tree of such implements, and passed the point under each of his thick white nails with the movement of someone paring an apple

In the living room the old man had the morning paper beside him; his presentation hunter pocket-watch was lying face up on the table. He was watching the grey pigeons that materialized out of the grey sky upon the window ledge outside. "They seem to come right at your face. How they stop in time, with the glass—"

Seven to ten on the dial now, ticking as loud as a bomb on the table.

He said, indulgent of the pastimes of the old, who have nothing better to do, "Well, I must get along." And in clear, loud enunciation: "I won't be home at lunchtime today, Papa."

"I know, I know." There was the usual arrangement when the old man was left alone; the caretaker would come in to give him the lunch Anne-Marie had left prepared.

The old man picked up the hunter, put it to his scaly red ear and then in his pocket.

Five to, surely. He said, an afterthought, "Good-bye." The old man peered round through his misty glasses with a movement of the hand as if to say, never mind that now.

As the cathedral clock expanded and contracted the heart of the city to the single stroke of one she came from her office down the path towards him in her flowered silk scarf, brown hat, and gloves. She looked at the bench and he flicked his handkerchief over it before she sat down. "Did you get the fish?"

He patted the damp limp parcel to draw her attention to it and she nodded. "Soles?"

"Nothing today. Three slices of halibut. He recommended."

"What about the laundry this afternoon? You won't forget?"

"That's tomorrow. Today's Tuesday."

She gave herself a mock tap on the temple, but her face retained its look of preoccupied, sad obstinacy, a look as characteristic of her as of some breeds of dog.

She unwrapped their sandwiches. She made very good sandwiches and he was always hungry for them. They began to eat and she said, "You should leave earlier sometimes."

The pleasure of taste died out of his large face.

"Ten o'clock, and then you're home at three or four in the afternoon." She went on eating, ruminatingly, looking at him for some suggestion.

"Not always," he said. "Sometimes I go at nine."

"Half past," she said. "Once in a blue moon." She looked at him anxiously, at the same time in a quick parenthetic movement clearing her teeth of fragments with a contortion of the lip

"Old people forget. He doesn't remember from one hour to the next."

She shook her head in the authority of her childhood, girlhood, womanhood experience of her father, not only as her father, but also as her countryman, her kind.

She pressed him to have the last sandwich. "No, I had a coffee and a roll."

"Where?"

"That place next to the fishmonger."

She made a mouth. She had once been in there with him and been given a badly washed cup. She broke the bread in two and handed him half. They did not speak and their gaze, the plain, naked gaze of middle-aged people who have no admiration to seek from each other, no sexual coquetry to make for dissimulation between them, was the one that had always been their most lucid communication: the gaze with which she had warned him about the Germans, and with which, later, after the war, it was decided that he would marry her.

"The Jew will go back home now," the old man had said, not unkindly; he had always referred to him as the Jew, as he might have said "the lodger."

"What home?" she said.

And so he had stayed. "He's looking for a job," Anne-Marie told her mother. "Well, I hope so," said the old lady. The little family lived on Anne-Marie's salary as a filing clerk and the old man's pension from the railways; they couldn't afford to keep him. And yet if he didn't go, if it was true there was nowhere left back where he came from for him to go to, how could they get rid of him while their daughter was beginning to walk out with him, openly, now that he was allowed on the streets like anybody else? How could they throw out someone she went with, holding his arm in the cathedral square?

"What sort of job?" Anne-Marie asked him, when they were walking out. He told her he supposed business of some kind. What had he done before? Oh, it would be import and export, he said. Yes, that would have to be it: something where he could use his knowledge of his mother tongue. His dead wife's parents had had a big fur and hide business; apparently he had had some sort of executive position made for him there. But he was not sure about how to go about getting a job on his own, quite on his own, in a foreign country. "He's looking." "There are several possibilities," Anne-Marie kept telling the old people. It began to be assumed that he would leave the flat at a certain time every morning in pursuit of this job, and that it was decent for him to return only after an adequate amount of time had been spent in the pursuit.

Whenever they talked about marrying, they were both thinking of the parents. When they finally reached the point of making an actual date (the beginning of her annual leave for

that particular year), he said, "I don't know how they'll . . . ?"
meaning because he was a Jew. But she, out of her own silence,
was saying slowly, "Just for the meantime, we could say you've
got a job now. I mean, otherwise I'll never hear the end of it,
how can you marry and keep a wife and so on. . . . You go out
every morning, anyway."

Import and export, he told them. Just a small office—in the
office of a friend. He was his own boss. In a small way, naturally; he could come and go more or less as he pleased. Then
when you've found something, Anne-Marie said to him, they
won't know the difference. And in the meantime . . . Fortu-
nately it was a big city. The old people really only knew their own
little corner of it, the butcher, the tobacconist, a few cronies
from the railways. When people said what does your son-in-law
do? they said—with the vagueness of those who have never
been merchants of any kind themselves—he's in the import
business, he's in the city. It was understood that it was a modest
living; they all lived just as carefully as they had before there
was a son-in-law in business, but this was as the old lady understood it: Anne-Marie was not making a show of her husband's
earnings, any more than she herself would have done—she was
putting away a nice little nest-egg.

It was tricky so long as the old lady was alive because she
went about more and even in her circle of old ladies there were
some who had sons in insurance and even import and export.
But if the name of her son-in-law meant nothing to them it
merely confirmed what she already knew: that he was not much
to speak of, and a foreigner into the bargain. Once she was gone
and the old man practically bedridden, it did not matter in
what quarter, in what street, what building, endless intersection
of corridors and passages and closed doors without numbers,
leading ever farther and farther from it, that office was situated.
Yet it was necessary for it to exist somewhere. So long as the old
man lived its existence had to be proved every day.

He had never "found something" and Anne-Marie, as his
wife, never asked him how he passed those hours, every day,
when he had to be out of the flat. If the weather was bad, she

would say with a flash of anxiety, "Werner, don't forget the thick scarf, you know your chest." For a time he had been considered as taken up with the task of proving his right to *Wiedergutmachung*, the compensation the Germans paid, to those who had survived their persecution, for the loss of material possessions. He filled in forms in the evenings—"Werner has all this stuff to attend to," she would say to her parents—and spoke of his appointments at the office set up to deal with such applications. But in the end it appeared that the comfortable sums he had calculated on paper would never come to him because documents establishing his rights proved to be no longer in existence in Germany. He continued to get an occasional official letter which he would study carefully while Anne-Marie remarked to her father, "Still so much work about his German claims."

Days like this one were frequent. After she had gone back to her office, he sat in the park with the parcel of fish, waiting for the time to be able to go home. Sometimes the burden of proof of that office was depressingly heavy; how could what was nonexistent weigh so much? Just like his German claims; how could something that had become nonexistent be worth so much? The load of indigestion from her good sandwiches took on the weight of all this nonexistence in his breast. He got up and walked round the square among the pigeons, who, like him, took their sustenance from the hand of a stranger, in a public place.

He went down to the railway station to look up the time of a train he and Anne-Marie would take if they went for a day's excursion at Whitsun, five weeks ahead. In the great echoing hall of voices and footsteps, he bought a newspaper. He dropped in at the laundry to tell them what time he would call tomorrow. In the café where they knew him well, as men are known in the cafés of big cities as the one with the tweed overcoat or the one with the terrible cough, he sat and drank another cup of coffee in the stale corner whose air, at the beginning of spring, was that that had been enclosed at the beginning of winter. On the tram he found a place in one of the two entrance seats that faced each other. Between the swaying bodies of people standing, a woman looked at him, not intently but restfully, her head lolling slightly backward on her fur collar. She wore the light-coloured delicate shoes and gloves that only the well-off can afford to wear in the grimy city. Late fifties; widow with money who buys herself the best of everything but doesn't believe in wasting it on taxis. There were many such women in the comfortable private hotels up on the hill. His great eyes seemed weighted to his cheeks in their downward gaze. But he had done it many times before; he had only to lift them slowly but suddenly, and not smile, but merely let the corners droop a little more, while the dark folds beneath tautened their pleats a little, and a charming amber light swam up from some forgotten depth like a spirit that had been imprisoned in the black waters of a lake. He might perhaps have found something, here, with one of those women. But having tried out this piece of effortless effectiveness—not a thought, even—he always let it go back and die in the dark. And he was aware without thinking about it that this one thing that he could have done would soon cease to be summoned into possibility; the ladies would begin to see an old man sitting opposite them.

As soon as he got off the tram he had the sense of pleasant weariness and enervation that came to him as if, as a reward, he really had returned from a day's work. The fish parcel had seeped through pink with blood, but he was almost home, and it was quarter past four today. The old man could check it on his hunter as much as he liked. He opened the door, gained the warm fug gratefully, and called out, "Papa, better late than never! Would you like your coffee?" There was no answer and he went quietly past the old man in the chair and took off his outdoor things and put on slippers and went to set the water to boil. But when he tried to wake the old man for his coffee, he found that he was deeply unconscious. Anne-Marie wept beside the bed in the hospital all night, and by evening the next day the old man was dead.

When he and Anne-Marie came back to the empty flat after the funeral he did not know what to say to her; the silence was of a different quality from the usual silences between them. She began at once to pack away the old man's possessions, and, as if he had suddenly forgotten how Anne-Marie was, he tried to stop her, saying the conventional things: "Leave that now, you don't have to upset yourself." She was rummaging for a small box that would be just the right size and shape to hold her father's pocket watch and she put down her hands in a movement of finality and stared straight at him, then, without a word, went on with her intent orderliness trying first one box and then another.

Quietly, he began to do what he should have done from the first: take the covers off the cushions on the old man's chair and put them in the wash, stack his newspapers neatly, empty his tobacco pouch so that it could be laid away. He contented himself with heavy, timid sighs.

At last she said, "I'll go through his clothes tomorrow. There may be something that needs mending. He would have wanted them to go to the Railway Benefit."

She went out of the room to the bedroom. He sat down carefully and waited. He did not know whether he should read the newspaper. Was she crying again, in there? Should he go and say something, try to put his hand on that neatly waved head whose dusty-looking scrolls were preserved from one weekly visit to the hairdresser to the next by a contraption like a cobweb?

She appeared, turning her ring as she always did when she had just washed her hands. "There's that cold fish from the day before yesterday. Or a bit of sausage."

He said in the exaggerated voice of someone eager to be no trouble, "What does it matter. Anything."

"I can fry the sausage," she said.

"The fish's all right!"

While they ate she said, referring to the old man's clothes, "You could take them there on Friday."

"Friday?" He had the mildly dismayed dubiousness of someone who wondered how he would fit it in.

Again she put down her hands in that final gesture. "Why not?"

"All right. But I don't see the rush. If you've finished with them. Why should you drive yourself?"

She went on eating as if she had turned off communication with the flick of a switch. She stared straight ahead and was not disturbed by any movement of his that came before her line of vision. Now and then he ventured, in diminuendo cadence, "Ah! *Ja, ja, ja* . . ." but she gave no sign that she heard, and he had the feeling that she was thinking very hard, in an unstemmable stream of words, back through the past he had not known with her, in her own language, in forms so personal, regional, and idiomatic that he, with his imperfect, foreigner's grasp of it, would not have been able to understand a word even if she had been speaking aloud.

But in the morning—they both slept well—when he got up he knew that they were alone at last, the tension was gone, there was no one for her to protect him from any more, there was no old man with his hunter beside him sitting in the wheelchair. He shaved and she was in the kitchen busy with the breakfast and her sandwiches, and when he came out of the bathroom he was still in his slippers and he sat down to glance through the morning paper; no need to hurry this morning. He could take all day over it if he pleased. A trickle of warm pleasure, a new gland coming into secretion, started at the vision of the long quiet morning in the empty flat.

Anne-Marie came in with the coffee. She looked at her father's chair. But she would have slapped away a word like an unwelcome hand; he saw that she would not have him in on this sorrow of hers, he somehow did not have the right to lay claim to it in any way. You had no rights except those they told you. You had to report to the police every day; or you had to wait five years and then you could get citizenship papers.

"The laundry wasn't fetched."

He looked up with his great black eyes, shrugging as if to say, out of the question!

"You won't forget today?"

"Of course not."

When she had finished her coffee, put on her silk scarf,

brown hat and gloves, and taken her packet of sandwiches she turned at the door to say good-bye, and then seemed to fall into intent distraction as she saw him for the first time since her father had died. She forgot to say good-bye. She said, "Werner, what time are you going out this morning?"

A Company of Laughing Faces

When Kathy Hack was seventeen her mother took her to In-gaza Beach for the Christmas holidays. The Hacks lived in the citrus-farming district of the Eastern Transvaal, and Kathy was an only child; "Mr. Hack wouldn't let me risk my life again," her mother confided at once, when ladies remarked, as they always did, that it was a lonely life when there was only one. Mrs. Hack usually added that she and her daughter were like sisters anyway; and it was true that since Kathy had left school a year ago she had led her mother's life, going about with her to the meetings and afternoon teas that occupied the ladies of the community. The community was one of retired businessmen and mining officials from Johannesburg who had acquired fruit farms to give some semblance of productivity to their leisure. They wore a lot of white linen and created a country-club atmos-phere in the village where they came to shop. Mr. Hack had the chemist's shop there, but he too was in semi-retirement and he spent most of his afternoons on the golf course or in the club.

The village itself was like a holiday place, with its dazzling white buildings and one wide street smelling of flowers; tropical trees threw shade and petals, and bougainvillaea climbed over the hotel. It was not a rest that Mrs. Hack sought at the coast, but a measure of gaiety and young company for Kathy. Nat-urally, there were few people under forty-five in the village and most of them had grown-up children who were married or away working or studying in the cities. Mrs. Hack couldn't be ex-pected to part with Kathy—after all, she *is* the only one, she would explain—but, of course, she felt, the child must get out among youngsters once in a while. So she packed up and went on the two-day journey to the coast for Kathy's sake.

They travelled first class and Mrs. Hack had jokingly threat-
ened Mr. Van Meulen, the station master, with dire consequences if he didn't see to it that they had a carriage to themselves. Yet though she had insisted that she wanted to read her
book in peace and not be bothered with talking to some woman, the main-line train had hardly pulled out of Johannesburg
station before she and Kathy edged their way along the train
corridors to the dining car, and, over tea, Mrs. Hack at once got
into conversation with the woman at the next table. There they
sat for most of the afternoon; Kathy looking out of the window
through the mist of human warmth and teapot steam in which
she had drawn her name in with her forefinger and wiped a port-
hole with her fist, her mother talking gaily and comfortingly
behind her. ". . . yes, a wonderful place for youngsters, they
tell me. The kids really enjoy themselves there. . . . Well, of
course, everything they want, dancing every night. Plenty of
youngsters their own age, that's the thing. . . . *I* don't mind, I
mean, I'm quite content to chat for half an hour and go off to
my bed. . . ."

Kathy herself could not imagine what it would be like, this
launching into the life of people her own age that her mother
had in store for her; but her mother knew all about it and the
idea was lit up inside the girl like a room made ready, with
everything pulled straight and waiting. . . . Soon—very soon
now, when they got there, when it all began to happen—life
would set up in the room. She would know she was young.
(When she was a little girl, she had often asked, but what is it
like to *be* grown-up? She was too grown-up now to be able to
ask, but what do you mean by "being young," "oh, to be
young"—what is it *I* ought to feel?) Into the lit-up room would
come the young people of her own age who would convey the
secret quality of being that age; the dancing; the fun. She had
the vaguest idea of what this fun would be; she had danced, of
course, at the monthly dances at the club, her ear on a level
with the strange breathing noises of middle-aged partners who
were winded by whisky. And the fun, the fun? When she tried
to think of it she saw a blur, a company of laughing faces, the

faces among balloons in a Mardi Gras film, the crowd of bright-skinned, bright-eyed faces like glazed fruits, reaching for a bottle of Coca-Cola on a roadside hoarding.

The journey passed to the sound of her mother's voice. When she was not talking, she looked up from time to time from her knitting, and smiled at Kathy as if to remind her. But Kathy needed no reminder; she thought of the seven new dresses and the three new pairs of shorts in the trunk in the van.

When she rattled up the dusty carriage shutters in the morning and saw the sea, all the old wild joy of childhood gushed in on her for a moment—the sight came to her as the curl of the water along her ankles and the particular sensation, through her hands, of a wooden spade lifting a wedge of wet sand. But it was gone at once. It was the past. For the rest of the day, she watched the sea approach and depart, approach and depart as the train swung towards and away from the shore through green bush and sugar cane, and she was no more aware of it than her mother, who, without stirring, had given the token recognition that Kathy had heard from her year after year as a child: "Ah, I can smell the sea."

The hotel was full of mothers with their daughters. The young men, mostly students, had come in groups of two or three on their own. The mothers kept "well out of the way," as Mrs. Hack enthusiastically put it; kept, in fact, to their own comfortable adult preserve—the veranda and the card room—and their own adult timetable—an early, quiet breakfast before the young people, who had been out till all hours, came in to make the dining room restless; a walk or a chat, followed by a quick bathe and a quick retreat from the hot beach back to the cool of the hotel; a long sleep in the afternoon; bridge in the evening. Any young person who appeared among them longer than to snatch a kiss and fling a casual good-bye between one activity and the next was treated with tolerant smiles and jolly remarks that did not conceal a feeling that she really ought to run off—she was there to enjoy herself wasn't she? For the first few days Kathy withstood this attitude stolidly; she knew no one and it seemed natural that she should accompany her mother. But her mother made friends at once, and Kathy became a hanger-on, something her schoolgirl ethics had taught her to despise. She no longer followed her mother onto the veranda. "Well, where are you off to, darling?" "Up to change." She and her mother paused in the foyer; her mother was smiling, as if she caught a glimpse of the vista of the morning's youthful pleasures. "Well, don't be too late for lunch. All the best salads go first." "No, I won't." Kathy went evenly up the stairs, under her mother's eyes.

In her room, that she shared with her mother, she undressed slowly and put on the new bathing suit. And the new Italian straw hat. And the new sandals. And the new bright wrap, printed with sea horses. The disguise worked perfectly; she saw in the mirror a young woman like all the others: she felt the blessed thrill of belonging. This was the world for which she had been brought up, and now, sure enough, when the time had come, she looked the part. Yet it was a marvel to her, just as it must be to the novice when she puts her medieval hood over her shaved head and suddenly is a nun.

She went down to the beach and lay all morning close by, but not part of, the groups of boys and girls who crowded it for two hundred yards, lying in great ragged circles that were constantly broken up and re-formed by chasing and yelling, and the restless to-and-fro of those who were always getting themselves covered with sand in order to make going into the water worth while, or coming back out of the sea to fling a wet head down in someone's warm lap. Nobody spoke to her except two huge louts who tripped over her ankles and exclaimed a hoarse, "Gee, I'm sorry"; but she was not exactly lonely—she had the satisfaction of knowing that at least she was where she ought to be, down there on the beach with the young people.

Every day she wore another of the new dresses or the small tight shorts—properly, equipment rather than clothes—with which she had been provided. The weather was sufficiently steamy hot to be described by her mother, sitting deep in the shade of the veranda, as glorious. When, at certain moments, there was that pause that comes in the breathing of the sea, music from the beach tearoom wreathed up to the hotel, and at night, when the dance was in full swing down there, the volume of music and voices joined the volume of the sea's sound itself, so that, lying in bed in the dark, you could imagine yourself under the sea, with the waters sending swaying sound waves of sunken bells and the cries of drowned men ringing out from depth to depth long after they themselves have touched bottom in silence.

She exchanged smiles with other girls, on the stairs; she made a fourth, at tennis; but these encounters left her again, just exactly where they had taken her up—she scarcely remembered the mumbled exchange of names, and their owners disappeared back into the anonymous crowd of sprawled bare legs and sandals that filled the hotel. After three days, a young man asked her to go dancing with him at the Coconut Grove, a rickety bungalow on piles above the lagoon. There was to be a party of eight or more—she didn't know. The idea pleased her mother; it was just the sort of evening she liked to contemplate for Kathy. A jolly group of youngsters and no nonsense about going off in "couples."

The young man was in his father's wholesale tea business; "Are you at varsity?" he asked her, but seemed to have no interest in her life once that query was settled. The manner of dancing at the Coconut Grove was energetic and the thump of feet beat a continuous talc-like dust out of the wooden boards. It made the lights twinkle, as they do at twilight. Dutifully, every now and then the face of Kathy's escort, who was called Manny and was fair, with a spongy nose and small far-apart teeth in a wide grin, would appear close to her through the bright dust and he would dance with her. He danced with every girl in turn, picking them out and returning them to the pool again with obvious enjoyment and a happy absence of discrimination. In the intervals, Kathy was asked to dance by other boys in the party; sometimes a bold one from some other party would come up, run his eye over the girls, and choose one at random, just to demonstrate an easy confidence. Kathy felt helpless. Here and there there were girls who did not belong to the pool, boys who did not rove in predatory search simply because it was necessary to have a girl to dance with. A boy and a girl sat with hands loosely linked, and got up to dance time and again without losing this tenuous hold of each other. They talked, too. There was a lot of guffawing and some verbal sparring at the table where Kathy sat, but she found that she had scarcely spoken at all, the whole evening. When she got home and crept into bed in the dark, in order not to waken her mother, she was breathless from dancing all night, but she felt that she had been running, a long way, alone, with only the snatches of voices from memory in her ears.

She did everything everyone else did, now, waking up each day as if to a task. She had forgotten the anticipation of this holiday that she had had; that belonged to another life. It was gone, just as surely as what the sea used to be was gone. The sea was a shock of immersion in cold water, nothing more, in the hot sandy morning of sticky bodies, cigarette smoke, giggling, and ragging. Yet inside her was something distressing, akin to the thickness of not being able to taste when you have a cold. She longed to break through the muffle of automatism with which she carried through the motions of pleasure. There remained in her a desperate anxiety to succeed in being young, to grasp, not merely fraudulently to do, what was expected of her.

People came and went, in the life of the hotel, and their going was not noticed much. They were replaced by others much like them or who became like them, as those who enter into the performance of a rite inhabit a personality and a set of actions preserved in changeless continuity by the rite itself. She was lying on the beach one morning in a crowd when a young man dropped down beside her, turning his head quickly to see if he had puffed sand into her face, but not speaking to her. She had seen him once or twice before; he had been living at the hotel for two or three days. He was one of those young men of the type who are noticed; he no sooner settled down, lazily smoking, addressing some girl with exaggerated endearments and supreme indifference, than he would suddenly get up again and drop in on some other group. There he would be seen in the same sort of ease and intimacy; the first group would feel both slighted and yet admiring. He was not dependent upon anyone; he gave or withheld his presence as he pleased, and the mood of any gathering lifted a little when he was there, simply because his being there was always unexpected. He had brought to perfection the art, fashionable among the boys that year, of leading a girl to believe that he had singled her out for his attention, "fallen for her," and then, the second she acknowledged this, destroying her self-confidence by one look or sentence that made it seem that she had stupidly imagined the whole thing.

Kathy was not surprised that he did not speak to her; she knew only too well that she did not belong to that special order of girls and boys among whom life was really shared out, although outwardly the whole crowd might appear to participate. It was going to be a very hot day; already the sea was a deep, hard blue and the sky was taking on the gauzy look of a mirage. The young man—his back was half turned to her—had on a damp pair of bathing trunks and on a level with her eyes, as she lay, she could see a map-line of salt emerging white against the blue material as the moisture dried out of it. He got into some kind of argument, and his gestures released from his body the smell of oil. The argument died down and then, in relief at a new distraction, there was a general move up to the beach tearoom where the crowd went every day to drink variously coloured bubbly drinks and to dance, in their bathing suits, to the music of a gramophone. It was the usual straggling procession; "Aren't you fellows coming?"—the nasal, complaining voice of a girl. "Just a sec, what's happened to my glasses. . . ." "All right, don't *drag* me, man—" "Look what you've done!" "I don't want any more blisters, thank you very much, not after last night. . . ." Kathy lay watching them troop off, taking her time about following. Suddenly there was a space of sand in front of her, kicked up and tousled, but empty. She felt the sun, that had been kept off her right shoulder by the presence of the young man, strike her; he had got up to follow the others. She lay as if she had not heard when suddenly he was standing above her and had said, shortly, "Come for a walk." Her eyes moved anxiously. "Come for a walk," he said, taking out of his

mouth the empty pipe that he was sucking. She sat up; going
for a walk might have been something she had never done
before, was not sure if she could do.

"I know you like walking."

She remembered that when she and some others had limped
into the hotel from a hike the previous afternoon, he had been
standing at the reception desk, looking up something in a direc-
tory. "All right," she said, subdued, and got up.

They walked quite briskly along the beach together. It was
much cooler down at the water's edge. It was cooler away from
the crowded part of the beach, too; soon they had left it behind. Each time she opened her mouth to speak, a mouthful of
refreshing air came in. He did not bother with small talk—not
even to the extent of an exchange of names. (Perhaps, despite
his air of sophistication, he was not really old enough to have
acquired any small talk. Kathy had a little stock, like premature
grey hairs, that she had found quite useless at Ingaza Beach.)
He was one of those people whose conversation is an interior
monologue that now and then is made audible to others. There
was a ship stuck like a tag out at sea, cut in half by the horizon,
and he speculated about it, its size in relation to the distance,
interrupting himself with thrown-away remarks, sceptical of his
own speculation, that sometimes were left unfinished. He mentioned something an anonymous "they" had done "in the lab";
she said, taking the opportunity to take part in the conversation, "What do you do?"

"Going to be a chemist," he said.

She laughed with pleasure. "So's my father!"

He passed over the revelation and went on comparing the
performance of an MG sports on standard commercial petrol
with the performance of the same model on a special experimen-
tal mixture. "It's a lot of tripe, anyway," he said suddenly,
abandoning the plaything of the subject. "Crazy fellows tearing
up the place. What for?" As he walked he made a rhythmical
clicking sound with his tongue on the roof of his mouth, in
time to some tune that must have been going round in his
head. She chattered intermittently and politely, but the only
part of her consciousness that was acute was some small margi-

nal awareness that along this stretch of gleaming, sloppy sand he was walking without making any attempt to avoid treading on the dozens of small spiral-shell creatures who sucked themselves down into the ooze at the shadow of an approach.

They came to the headland of rock that ended the beach. The rocks were red and smooth, the backs of centuries-warm, benign beasts; then a gaping black seam, all crenellated with turban-shells as small and rough as crumbs, ran through a rocky platform that tilted into the gnashing, hissing sea. A small boy was fishing down there, and he turned and looked after them for a few moments, perhaps expecting them to come to see what he had caught. But when they got to the seam, Kathy's companion stopped, noticed her; something seemed to occur to him; there was the merest suggestion of a pause, a reflex of a smile softened the corner of his mouth. He picked her up in his arms, not without effort, and carried her across. As he set her on her feet she saw his unconcerned eyes, and they changed, in her gaze, to the patronizing, preoccupied expression of a grown-up who has swung a child in the air. The next time they came to a small obstacle, he stopped again, jerked his head in dry command, and picked her up again, though she could quite easily have stepped across the gap herself. This time they laughed, and she examined her arm when he had put her down. "It's awful, to be grabbed like that, without warning." She felt suddenly at ease, and wanted to linger at the rock pools, poking about in the tepid water for seaweed and the starfish that felt, as she ventured to tell him, exactly like a cat's tongue. "I wouldn't know," he said, not unkindly. "I haven't got a cat. Let's go." And they turned back towards the beach. But at anything that could possibly be interpreted as an obstacle, he swung her carelessly into his arms and carried her to safety. He did not laugh again, and so she did not either; it seemed to be some very serious game of chivalry. When they were down off the rocks, she ran into the water and butted into a wave and then came flying up to him with the usual shudders and squeals of complaint at the cold. He ran his palm down her bare back and said with distaste, "Ugh. What did you do that for."

And so they went back to the inhabited part of the beach and continued along the path up to the hotel, slowly returning to that state of anonymity, that proximity without contact, that belonged to the crowd. It was true, in fact, that she still did not know his name, and did not like to ask. Yet as they passed the beach tearoom, and heard the shuffle of bare sandy feet accompanying the wail and fall of a howling song, she had a sudden friendly vision of the dancers.

After lunch was the only time when the young people were in possession of the veranda. The grown-ups had gone up to sleep. There was an unwritten law against afternoon sleep for the young people; to admit a desire for sleep would have been to lose at once your fitness to be one of the young crowd: "Are you crazy?" The enervation of exposure to the long hot day went on without remission.

It was so hot, even in the shade of the veranda, that the heat seemed to increase gravity; legs spread, with more than their usual weight, on the grass chairs, feet rested heavily as the monolithic feet of certain sculptures. The young man sat beside Kathy, constantly relighting his pipe; she did not know whether he was bored with her or seeking out her company, but presently he spoke to her monosyllabically, and his laconicism was that of long familiarity. They dawdled down into the garden, where the heat was hardly any worse. There was bougainvillaea, as there was at home in the Eastern Transvaal—a huge, harsh shock of purple, papery flowers that had neither scent nor texture, only the stained-glass colour through which the light shone violently. Three boys passed with swinging rackets and screwed-up eyes, on their way to the tennis courts. Someone called, "Have you seen Micky and them?"

Then the veranda and garden were deserted. He lay with closed eyes on the prickly grass and stroked her hand—without being aware of it, she felt. She had never been caressed before, but she was not alarmed because it seemed to her such a simple gesture, like stroking a cat or a dog. She and her mother were great readers of novels and she knew, of course, that there were a large number of caresses—hair, and eyes and arms and even breasts—and an immense variety of feelings that would be attached to them. But this simple caress sympathized with her in the heat; she was so hot that she could not breathe with her lips closed and there was on her face a smile of actual suffering. The buzz of a fly round her head, the movement of a leggy red ant on the red earth beneath the grass made her aware that there were no voices, no people about; only the double presence of herself and the unknown person breathing beside her. He propped himself on his elbow and quickly put his half-open lips on her mouth. He gave her no time for surprise or shyness, but held her there, with his wet warm mouth; her instinct to resist the kiss with some part of herself—inhibition, inexperience— died away with the first ripple of its impulse, was smoothed and lost in the melting, boundaryless quality of physical being in the hot afternoon. The salt taste that was in the kiss—it was the sweat on his lip or on hers; his cheek, with its stipple of rough- ness beneath the surface, stuck to her cheek as the two surfaces of her own skin stuck together wherever they met. When he stood up, she rose obediently. The air seemed to swing together, between them. He put his arm across her shoulder—it was heavy and uncomfortable, and bent her head—and began to walk her along the path toward the side of the hotel.

"Come on," he said, barely aloud, as he took his arm away at the dark archway of an entrance. The sudden shade made her draw a deep breath. She stopped. "Where are you going?" He gave her a little urging push. "Inside," he said, looking at her. The abrupt change from light to dark affected her vision; she was seeing whorls and spots, her heart was plodding. Some- where there was a moment's stay of uneasiness; but a great unfolding impulse, the blind turn of a daisy toward the sun, made her go calmly with him along the corridor, under his influ- ence: her first whiff of the heady drug of another's will.

In a corridor of dark doors he looked quickly to left and right and then opened a door softly and motioned her in. He slipped in behind her and pushed home the old-fashioned bolt. Once it was done, she gave him a quick smile of adventure and com- plicity. The room was a bare little room, not like the one she shared with her mother. This was the old wing of the hotel, and it was certain that the push-up-and-down window did not have a view of the sea, although dingy striped curtains were drawn across it, anyway. The room smelled faintly of worn shoes, and the rather cold, stale, male smells of dead cigarette ends and ironed shirts; it was amazing that it could exist, so dim and forgotten, in the core of the hotel that took the brunt of a blazing sun. Yet she scarcely saw it; there was no chance to look round in the mood of curiosity that came upon her, like a movement down to earth. He stood close in front of her, their bare thighs touching beneath their shorts, and kissed her and kissed her. His mouth was different then, it was cool, and she could feel it, delightfully, separate from her own. She became aware of the most extraordinary sensation; her little breasts, that she had never thought of as having any sort of assertion of life of their own, were suddenly inhabited by two struggling trees of feeling, one thrusting up, uncurling, spreading, toward each nipple. And from his lips, it came, this sensation! From his lips! This person she had spoken to for the first time that morning. How pale and slow were the emotions engendered, over years of childhood, by other people, compared to this! You lost the sea, yes, but you found this. When he stopped kissing her she followed his mouth like a calf nuzzling for milk.

Suddenly he thrust his heavy knee between hers. It was a movement so aggressive that he might have hit her. She gave an exclamation of surprise and backed away, in his arms. It was the sort of exclamation that, in the context of situations she was familiar with, automatically brought a solicitous apology—an equally startled "I'm sorry! Did I hurt you!" But this time there was no apology. The man was fighting with her; *he did not care* that the big bone of his knee had bruised hers. They struggled clumsily, and she was pushed backwards and landed up sitting on the bed. He stood in front of her, flushed and burning-eyed, contained in an orbit of attraction strong as the colour of a flower, and he said in a matter-of-fact, reserved voice, "It's all right. I know what I'm doing. There'll be nothing for you to worry about." He went over to the chest of drawers, while she sat on the bed. Like a patient in a doctor's waiting room: the idea swept into her head. She got up and unbolted the door. "Oh no," she said, a whole horror of prosaicness enveloping her, "I'm going now." The back of the stranger's neck turned abruptly away from her. He faced her, smiling exasperatedly, with a sneer at himself. "I thought so. I thought that would happen." He came over and the kisses that she tried to avoid smeared her face. "What the hell did you come in here for then, hey? Why did you come?" In disgust, he let her go.

She ran out of the hotel and through the garden down to the beach. The glare from the sea hit her, left and right, on both sides of her face; her face that felt battered out of shape by the experience of her own passion. She could not go back to her room because of her mother; the idea of her mother made her furious. She was not thinking at all of what had happened, but was filled with the idea of *her mother*, lying there asleep in the room with a novel dropped open on the bed. She stumbled off over the heavy sand toward the rocks. Down there, there was nobody but the figure of a small boy, digging things out of the wet sand and putting them in a tin. She would have run from anyone, but he did not count; as she drew level with him, ten yards off, he screwed up one eye against the sun and gave her a crooked smile. He waved the tin. "I'm going to try them for bait," he said. "See these little things?" She nodded and walked on. Presently the child caught up with her, slackening his pace conversationally. But they walked on over the sand that the ebbing tide had laid smooth as a tennis court, and he did not speak. He thudded his heels into the firmness.

At last he said, "That was me, fishing on the rocks over there this morning."

She said with an effort, "Oh, was it? I didn't recognize you." Then, after a moment: "Did you catch anything?"

"Nothing much. It wasn't a good day." He picked a spiral shell out of his tin and the creature within put out a little undulating body like a flag. "I'm going to try these. No harm in trying."

He was about nine years old, thin and hard, his hair and face covered with a fine powder of salt—even his eyelashes held it. He was at exactly the stage of equidistant remoteness: he had forgotten his mother's lap, and had no inkling of the breaking voice and growing beard to come. She picked one of the spirals out of the tin, and the creature came out and furled and unfurled itself about her fingers. He picked one of the biggest. "I'll bet this one'd win if we raced them," he said. They went nearer the water and set the creatures down when the boy gave the word "Go!" When the creatures disappeared under the sand, they dug them out with their toes. Progressing in this fashion, they came to the rocks, and began wading about in the pools. He showed her a tiny hermit crab that had blue eyes; she thought it the most charming thing she had ever seen and poked about until she found one like it for herself. They laid out on the rock five different colours of starfish, and discussed possible methods of drying them; he wanted to take back some sort of collection for the natural-history class at his school. After a time, he picked up his tin and said, with a responsible sigh, "Well, I better get on with my fishing." From the point of a particularly high rock, he turned to wave at her.

She walked along the water's edge back to the hotel. In the room, her mother was spraying cologne down the front of her dress. "Darling, you'll get boiled alive, going to the beach at this hour." "No," said Kathy, "I'm used to it now." When her mother had left the room, Kathy went to the dressing table to brush her hair, and running her tongue over her dry lips, tasted not the salt of the sea, but of sweat; it came to her as a dull reminder. She went into the bathroom and washed her face and cleaned her teeth, and then quietly powdered her face again.

Christmas was distorted, as by a thick lens, by swollen, rippling heat. The colours of paper caps ran on sweating foreheads. The men ate flaming pudding in their shirtsleeves. Flies settled on the tinsel snow of the Christmas tree.

Dancing in the same room on Christmas Eve, Kathy and the young man ignored each other with newly acquired adult complicity. Night after night Kathy danced, and did not lack partners. Though it was not for Mrs. Hack to say it, the new dresses *were* a great success. There was no girl who looked nicer. "K. is having the time of her life," wrote Mrs. Hack to her husband.

"Very much in the swing. She's come out of herself completely."

Certainly Kathy was no longer waiting for a sign; she had discovered that this was what it was to be young, of course, just exactly this life in the crowd that she had been living all along, silly little ass that she was, without knowing it. There it was. And once you'd got into it, well, you just went on. You clapped and booed with the others at the Sunday night talent contests, you pretended to kick sand in the boys' faces when they whistled at your legs; squashed into an overloaded car, you yelled songs as you drove, and knew that you couldn't have any trouble with a chap (on whose knees you found yourself) getting too fresh, although he could hold your hand adoringly. The thickness of skin required for all this came just as the required sun-tan did; and everyone was teak-brown, sallow-brown, homogenized into a new leathery race by the rigorous daily exposure to the fierce sun. The only need she had, these days, it seemed, was to be where the gang was; then the question of what to do and how to feel solved itself. The crowd was flat or the crowd was gay; they wanted to organize a beauty contest or trail to the beach at midnight for a watermelon feast.

One afternoon someone got up a hike to a small resort a few miles up the coast. This was the sort of jaunt in which brothers and sisters who really were still too young to qualify for the crowd were allowed to join; there were even a few children who tagged along. The place itself was strange, with a half-hidden waterfall, like a rope, and great tiers of overhanging rock stretching out farther and farther, higher and higher, over a black lagoon; the sun never reached the water. On the other side, where the sea ran into the lagoon at high tide, there was open beach, and there the restless migration from Ingaza Beach settled. Even there, the sand was cool; Kathy felt it soothing to her feet as she struggled out of the shorts and shirt she had worn over her bathing suit while she walked. She swam steadily about, dipping to swim underwater when the surface began to explode all over the place with the impact of the bodies of the boys who soon clambered up the easier reaches of rock and dived from them. People swam close under the wide roof of rock and looked up; hanging plants grew there, and the whole undersurface was chalky, against its rust-streaked blackness, with the droppings of swallows that threaded in and out of the ledges like bats. Kathy called out to someone from there and her voice came ringing down at her: ". . . al-l-low!" Soon the swimmers were back on the sand, wet and restless, to eat chocolate and smoke. Cold drinks were brought down by an Indian waiter from the little hotel overlooking the beach; two girls buried a boy up to the neck in sand; somebody came out of the water with a bleeding toe, cut on a rock. People went off exploring, there was always a noisy crowd clowning in the water, and there were always a few others lying about talking on the sand. Kathy was in such a group when one of the young men came up with his hands on his hips, lips drawn back from his teeth thoughtfully, and asked, "Have you seen the Bute kid around here?" "What kid?" someone said. "Kid about ten, in green trunks. Libby Bute's kid brother." "Oh, I know the one you mean. I don't know—all the little boys were playing around on the rocks over there, just now." The young man scanned the beach, nodding. "Nobody knows where he's got to."

"The kids were all together over there, only a minute ago."

"I know. But he can't be found. Kids say they don't know where he is. He might have gone fishing. But Libby says he would have told her. He was supposed to tell her if he went off on his own."

Kathy was making holes in the sand with her forefinger. "Is that the little boy who goes fishing up on the rocks at the end of our beach?"

"Mm. Libby's kid brother."

Kathy got up and looked round at the people, the lagoon, as if she were trying to reinterpret what she had seen before. "I didn't know he was here. I don't remember seeing him. With those kids who were fooling around with the birds' nests?"

"That's right. He was there." The young man made a little movement with his shoulders and wandered off to approach some people farther along. Kathy and her companions went on to talk of something else. But suddenly there was a stir on the

beach; a growing stir. People were getting up; others were coming out of the water. The young man hurried past again; "He's
not found," they caught from him in passing. People began
moving about from one knot to another, gathering suppositions,
hoping for news they'd missed. Centre of an awkward, solicitous, bossy circle was Libby Bute herself, a dark girl with long
hands and a bad skin, wavering uncertainly between annoyance
and fear. "I suppose the little tyke's gone off to fish somewhere,
without a word. I don't know. Doesn't mean a thing that he
didn't have his fishing stuff with him, he's always got a bit of
string and a couple of pins." Nobody said anything. "He'll turn
up," she said; and then looked round at them all.

An hour later, when the sun was already beginning to drop
from its afternoon zenith, he was not found. Everyone was
searching for him with a strange concentration, as if, in the
mind of each one, an answer, the remembrance of where he
was, lay undisturbed, if only one could get at it. Before there
was time for dread, like doubt, like dew, to form coldly, Kathy
Hack came face to face with him. She was crawling along the
first ledge of rock because she had an idea he might have got it
into his head to climb into what appeared to be a sort of cave
behind the waterfall, and be stuck there, unable to get out and
unable to make himself heard. She glanced down into the
water, and saw a glimmer of light below the surface. She leant
over between her haunches and he was looking at her, not more
than a foot below the water, where, shallow over his face, it
showed golden above its peat-coloured depths. The water was
very deep there, but he had not gone far. He lay held up by the
just-submerged rock that had struck the back of his head as he
had fallen backwards into the lagoon. What she felt was not
shock, but recognition. It was as if he had had a finger to his
lips, holding the two of them there, so that she might not give
him away. The water moved but did not move him; only his
little bit of short hair was faintly obedient, leaning the way of
the current, as the green beard of the rock did. He was as
absorbed as he must have been in whatever it was he was doing
when he fell. She looked at him, looked at him, for a minute,
and then she clambered back to the shore and went on with the

search. In a little while, someone else found him, and Libby Bute lay screaming on the beach, saliva and sand clinging round her mouth.

Two days later, when it was all over, and more than nine pounds had been collected among the hotel guests for a wreath, and the body was on the train to Johannesburg, Kathy said to her mother, "I'd like to go home." Their holiday had another week to run. "Oh I know," said Mrs. Hack with quick sympathy. "I feel the same myself. I can't get that poor little soul out of my mind. But life has to go on, darling, one can't take the whole world's troubles on one's shoulders. Life brings you enough troubles of your own, believe me." "It's not that at all," said Kathy. "I don't like this place."

Mrs. Hack was just feeling herself nicely settled, and would have liked another week. But she felt that there was the proof of some sort of undeniable superiority in her daughter's great sensitivity; a superiority they ought not to forgo. She told the hotel proprietor and the other mothers that she had to leave; that was all there was to it: Kathy was far too much upset by the death of the little stranger to be able simply to go ahead with the same zest for holiday pleasures that she had enjoyed up till now. Many young people could do it, of course; but not Kathy. She wasn't made that way, and what was she, her mother, to do about it?

In the train going home they did not have a carriage to themselves, and very soon Mrs. Hack was explaining to their lady travelling companion—in a low voice, between almost closed teeth, in order not to upset Kathy—how the marvellous holiday had been ruined by this awful thing that had happened.

The girl heard, but felt no impulse to tell her mother—knew, in fact, that she would never have the need to tell anyone the knowledge that had held her secure since the moment she looked down into the lagoon: the sight, there, was the one real happening of the holiday, the one truth and the one beauty.

Through Time and Distance

They had been on the road together seven or eight years, Mondays to Fridays. They did the Free State one week, the northern and eastern Transvaal the next, Natal and Zululand a third. Now and then they did Bechuanaland and Southern Rhodesia and were gone for a month. They sat side by side, for thousands of miles and thousands of hours, the commercial traveller, Hirsch, and his boy. The boy was a youngster when Hirsch took him on, with one pair of grey flannels, a clean shirt, and a nervous sniff; he said he'd been a lorry driver, and at least he didn't stink—"When you're shut up with them in a car all day, believe me, you want to find a native who doesn't stink." Now the boy wore, like Hirsch, the line of American-cut suits that Hirsch carried, and fancy socks, suede shoes, and an antimagnetic watch with a strap of thick gilt links, all bought wholesale. He had an ear of white handkerchief always showing in his breast pocket, though he still economically blew his nose in his fingers when they made a stop out in the veld.

He drove, and Hirsch sat beside him, peeling back the pages of paperbacks, jerking slowly in and out of sleep, or scribbling in his order books. They did not speak. When the car flourished to a stop outside the veranda of some country store, Hirsch got out without haste and went in ahead—he hated to "make an impression like a hawker," coming into a store with his goods behind him. When he had exchanged greetings with the storekeeper and leaned on the counter chatting for a minute or two, as if he had nothing to do but enjoy the dimness of the interior, he would stir with a good-humoured sigh. "I'd better show you what I've got. It's a shame to drag such lovely stuff about in this

51

dust. Philip!"—his face loomed in the doorway a moment—"get a move on there."

So long as it was not raining, Philip kept one elbow on the rolled-down window, the long forearm reaching up to where his slender hand, shaded like the coat of some rare animal from tea-rose pink on the palm to dark matt brown on the back, appeared to support the car's gleaming roof like a caryatid. The hand would withdraw, he would swing out of the car onto his feet, he would carry into the store the cardboard boxes, suit-cases, and, if the store carried what Hirsch called "high-class goods" as well, the special stand of men's suits hanging on a rail that was made to fit into the back of the car. Then he would saunter out into the street again, giving his tall shoulders a cat's pleasurable movement under fur—a movement that conveyed to him the excellent drape of his jacket. He would take ciga-rettes out of his pocket and lean, smoking, against the car's warm flank.

Sometimes he held court; like Hirsch, he had become well known on the regular routes. The country people were not exactly shy of him and his kind, but his clothes and his air of city know-how imposed a certain admiring constraint on them, even if, as in the case of some of the older men and women, they disapproved of the city and the aping of the white man's ways. He was not above playing a game of *morabaraba*, an ancient African kind of draughts, with the blacks from the grain-and-feed store in a dorp on the Free State run. Hirsch was always a long time in the general store next door, and, mean-while, Philip pulled up the perfect creases of his trousers and squatted over the lines of the board drawn with a stone in the dust, ready to show them that you couldn't beat a chap who had got his training in the big lunch-hour games that are played every day outside the wholesale houses in Johannesburg. At one or two garages, where the petrol attendants in foam-rubber baseball caps given by Shell had picked up a lick of passing sophistication, he sometimes got a poker game. The first time his boss, Hirsch, discovered him at this (Philip had overes-timated the time Hirsch would spend over the quick hand of Klabberyas he was obliged to take, in the way of business, with a local storekeeper), Hirsch's anger at being kept waiting vanished in a kind of amused and grudging pride. "You're a big fella, now, eh, Philip? I've made a man of you. When you came to me you were a real pickanin. Now you've been around so much, you're taking the boys' money off them on the road. Did you win?"

"Ah, no, sir," Philip suddenly lied, with a grin.

"Ah-h-h, what's the matter with you? You didn't win?" For a moment Hirsch looked almost as if he were about to give him a few tips. After that, he always passed his worn packs of cards on to his boy. And Philip learned, as time went by, to say, "I don't like the sound of the engine, boss. There's something loose there. I'm going to get underneath and have a look while I'm down at the garage taking petrol."

It was true that Hirsch had taught his boy everything the boy knew, although the years of silence between them in the car had never been broken by conversation or an exchange of ideas. Hirsch was one of those pale, plump, freckled Jews, with pale blue eyes, a thick snub nose, and the remains of curly blond hair that had begun to fall out before he was twenty. A number of his best stories depended for their denouement on the fact that somebody or other had not realized that he was a Jew. His pride in this belief that nobody would take him for one was not conventionally anti-Semitic, but based on the reasoning that it was a matter of pride, on the part of the Jewish people, that they could count him among them while he was fitted by nature with the distinguishing characteristics of a more privileged race. Another of his advantages was that he spoke Afrikaans as fluently and idiomatically as any Afrikaner. This, as his boy had heard him explain time and again to English-speaking people, was essential, because, low and ignorant as these back-veld Afrikaners were—hardly better than the natives, most of them —they knew that they had their government up there in power now, and they wouldn't buy a sixpenny line from you if you spoke the language of the *rooineks*—the red-neck English.

With the Jewish shopkeepers, he showed that he was quite at home, because, as Philip, unpacking the sample range, had overheard him admit a thousand times, he was Jewish born and bred—why, his mother's brother was a rabbi—even though he knew he didn't look it for a minute. Many of these shops were husband-and-wife affairs, and Hirsch knew how to make himself pleasant to the wives as well. In his chaff with them, the phrases "the old country" and "my father, God rest his soul" were recurrent. There was also an earnest conversation that began: "If you want to meet a character, I wish you could see my mother. What a spirit. She's seventy-five, she's got sugar, and she's just been operated for cataract, but I'm telling you, there's more go in her than . . ."

Every now and then there would be a store with a daughter as well: not very young, not very beautiful, a worry to the mother who stood with her hands folded under her apron, hoping the girl would slim down and make the best of herself, and to the father, who wasn't getting any younger and would like to see her settled. Hirsch had an opening for this subject too, tested and tried. "Not much life for a girl in a place like this, eh? It's a pity. But some of the town girls are such rubbish, perhaps it's better to marry some nice girl from the country. Such rubbish—the Jewish girls too; oh, yes, they're just as bad as the rest these days. I wouldn't mind settling down with a decent girl who hasn't run around so much. If she's not so smart, if she doesn't get herself up like a film star, well, isn't it better?"

Philip thought that his boss was married—in some places, at any rate, he talked about "the wife"—but perhaps it was only that he had once been married, and, anyway, what was the difference when you were on the road? The fat, ugly white girl at the store went and hid herself among the biscuit tins; the mother, half daring to hope, became vivacious by proxy; and the father suddenly began to talk to the traveller intimately about business affairs.

Philip found he could make the same kind of stir among country blacks. Hirsch had a permit to enter certain African reserves in his rounds, and there, in the humble little shops owned by Africans—shanties, with the inevitable man at work on a treadle sewing machine outside—he used his boy to do

business with them in their own lingo. The boy wasn't half bad
at it, either. He caught on so quick, he was often the one to
suggest that a line that was unpopular in the white dorps could
be got rid of in the reserves. He would palm off the stuff like a
real showman. "They can be glad to get anything, boss," he
said with a grin. "They can't take a bus to town and look in the
shops." In spite of his city clothes and his signet ring and all,
the boy was exactly as simple as they were, underneath, and he
got on with them like a house on fire. Many's the time some old
woman or little kid came running up to the car when it was all
packed to go on again and gave him a few eggs or a couple of
roasted mealies in a bit of newspaper.

Early on in his job driving for Hirsch, Philip had run into a
calf; it did not stir on the deserted red-earth road between walls
of mealie fields that creaked in a breeze. "Go on," said his boss,
with the authority of one who knows what he is doing, who has
learned in a hard school. "Go on, it's dead, there's nothing to
do." The young man hesitated, appalled by the soft thump of
the impact with which he had given his first death-dealing blow.
"Go on. There could have been a terrible accident. We could
have turned over. These farmers should be prosecuted, the way
they don't look after the cattle."

Philip reversed quickly, avoided the body in a wide curve, and
drove on. That was what made life on the road; whatever it was,
soft touch or hard going, lie or truth, it was left behind. By the
time you came by again in a month or two months, things had
changed, forgotten and forgiven, and whatever you got yourself
into this time, you had always the secret assurance that there
would be another breathing space before you could be got at
again.

Philip had married after he had been travelling with Hirsch
for a couple of years; the girl had had a baby by him earlier, but
they had waited, as Africans sometimes do, until he could get a
house for her before they actually got married. They had two
more children, and he kept them pretty well—he wasn't too
badly paid, and of course he could get things wholesale, like the
stove for the house. But up Piet Retief way, on one of the
routes they took every month, there was a girl he had been

sleeping with regularly for years. She swept up the hair cuttings in the local barbershop, where Hirsch sometimes went for a trim if he hadn't had a chance over the weekend, in Johannesburg. That was how Philip had met her; he was waiting in the car for Hirsch one day, and the girl came out to sweep the step at the shop's entrance. "Hi, *wena sisi*. I wish you would come and sweep my house for me," he called out drowsily.

For a long time now she had worn a signet ring, nine carats, engraved with his first name and hers; Hirsch did not carry anything in the jewellery line, but of course Philip, in the fraternity of the road, knew the boys of other travellers who did. She was a plump, hysterical little thing, with very large eyes that could accommodate unshed tears for minutes on end, and— something unusual for black women—a faint moustache outlining her top lip. She would have been a shrew to live with, but it was pleasant to see how she awaited him every month with coy, bridling passion. When she pressed him to settle the date when they might marry, he filched some minor item from the extensive women's range that Hirsch carried, and that kept her quiet until next time. Philip did not consider this as stealing, but as part of the running expenses of the road to which he was entitled, and he was trustworthy with his boss's money or goods in all other circumstances. In fact, if he had known it and if Hirsch had known it, his filching fell below the margin for dishonesty that Hirsch, in his reckoning of the running expenses of the road, allowed: "They all steal, what's the good of worrying about it? You change one, you get a worse thief, that's all." It was one of Hirsch's maxims in the philosophy of the road.

The morning they left on the Bechuanaland run, Hirsch looked up from the newspaper and said to his boy, "You've got your passbook, eh?" There was the slightest emphasis on the "You've," an emphasis confident rather than questioning. Hirsch was well aware that, although the blurred front-page picture before him showed black faces open-mouthed, black hands flung up triumphant around a bonfire of passbooks, Philip was not the type to look for trouble. "Yes, sir, I've got it," said

Philip, overtaking, as the traffic lights changed, a row of cars driven by white men; he had driven so much and so well that there was a certain beauty in his performance—he might have been skiing, or jumping hurdles.

Hirsch went back to the paper; there was nothing in it but reports of this anti-pass campaign that the natives had started up. He read them all with a deep distrust of the amorphous threat that he thought of as "trouble," taking on any particular form. Trouble was always there, hanging over every human head, of course; it was only when it drew near, "came down," that it took on a specific guise: illness, a drop in business, the blacks wanting to live like white men. Anyway, he himself had nothing to worry about: his boy knew his job, and he knew he must have his pass on him in case, in a routine demand in the streets of any of the villages they passed through, a policeman should ask him to show it.

Philip was not worried, either. When the men in the location came to the door to urge him to destroy his pass, he was away on the road, and only his wife was at home to assure them that he had done so; when some policeman in a dorp stopped him to see it, there it was, in the inner pocket of the rayon lining of his jacket. And one day, when this campaign or another was successful, he would never need to carry it again.

At every call they made on that trip, people were eager for news of what was happening in Johannesburg. Old barefoot men in the dignity of battered hats came from the yards behind the stores, trembling with dread and wild hope. Was it true that so many people were burning their passes that the police couldn't arrest them all? Was it true that in such-and-such a location people had gone to the police station and left passes in a pile in front of the door? Was it the wild young men who called themselves Africanists who were doing this? Or did Congress want it, did the old Chief, Luthuli, call for it too? "We are going to free you all of the pass," Philip found himself declaiming. Children, hanging about, gave the Congress raised-thumb salute. "The white man won't bend our backs like yours, old man." They could see for themselves how much he had already taken from the white man, wearing the same clothes as the white man, driving the white man's big car—an emissary from the knowledgeable, political world of the city, where black men were learning to be masters. Even Hirsch's cry, "Philip, get a move on there!" came as an insignificant interruption, a relic of the present almost become the past.

Over the border, in the British Protectorate, Bechuanaland, the interest was just as high. Philip found it remarkably easy to talk to the little groups of men who approached him in the luxurious dust that surrounded village buildings, the kitchen boys who gathered in country hotel yards where cats fought beside glittering mounds of empty beer bottles. "We are going to see that this is the end of the pass. The struggle for freedom . . . the white man won't stand on our backs. . . ."

It was a long, hot trip. Hirsch, pale and exhausted, dozed and twitched in his sleep between one dorp and the next. For the last few months he had been putting pills instead of sugar into his tea, and he no longer drank the endless bottles of lemonade and ginger beer that he had sent the boy to buy at every stop for as long as he could remember. There was a strange, sweetish smell that seemed to follow Hirsch around these days; it settled in the car on that long trip and was there even when Hirsch wasn't; but Philip, who, like most travellers' boys, slept in the car at night, soon got used to it.

They went as far as Francistown, where, all day, while they were in and out of the long line of stores facing the railway station, a truckload of Herero women from farther north in the Kalahari Desert sat beside the road in their Victorian dress, turbaned, unsmiling, stiff and voluminous, like a row of tea cosies. The travelling salesmen did not go on to Rhodesia. From Francistown they turned back for Johannesburg, with a stop overnight at Palapye Road, so that they could make a detour to Serowe, an African town of round mud houses, dark euphorbia hedges, and tinkling goat bells, where the deposed Chief and his English wife lived on a hill in a large house with many bathrooms, but there was no hotel. The hotel in Palapye Road was a fly-screened box on the railway station, and Hirsch spent a bad night amid the huffing and blowing of trains taking water and the bursts of stamping—a gigantic Spanish dance—of shunting trains.

They left for home early on Friday morning. By half past five in the afternoon they were flying along toward the outskirts of Johannesburg, with the weary heat of the day blowing out of the windows in whiffs of high land and the sweat suddenly deliciously cool on their hands and foreheads. The row of suits on the rack behind them slid obediently down and up again with each rise and dip accomplished in the turn of the road. The usual landmarks, all in their places, passed unlooked at: straggling, small-enterprise factories, a brickfield, a chicken farm, the rose nursery with the toy Dutch windmill, various gatherings of low, patchy huts and sagging houses—small locations where the blacks who worked round about lived. At one point, the road closely skirted one of these places; the children would wave and shout from where they played in the dirt. Today, quite suddenly, a shower of stones came from them. For a moment Hirsch truly thought that he had become aware of a sudden summer hailstorm; he was always so totally enclosed by the car it would not have been unusual for him not to have noticed a storm rising. He put his hand on the handle that raised the window; instantly, a sharp grey chip pitted the fold of flesh between thumb and first finger.

"Drive on," he yelled, putting the blood to his mouth. "Drive on!" But his boy, Philip, had at the same moment seen what they had blundered into. Fifty yards ahead a labouring green bus, its windows, under flapping canvas, crammed with black heads, had lurched to a stop. It appeared to burst as people jumped out at door and windows; from the houses, a jagged rush of more people met them and spread around the bus over the road.

Philip stopped the car so fiercely that Hirsch was nearly pitched through the windscreen. With a roar the car reversed, swinging off the road sideways onto the veld, and then swung wildly around onto the road again, facing where it had come from. The steering-wheel spun in the ferocious, urgent skill of the pink and brown hands. Hirsch understood and anxiously trusted; at the feel of the car righting itself, a grin broke through in his boy's face.

But as Philip's suede shoe was coming down on the accelerator, a black hand in a greasy, buttonless coat sleeve seized his arm through the window, and the car rocked with the weight of the bodies that flung and clung against it. When the engine stalled, there was quiet; the hand let go of Philip's arm. The men and women around the car were murmuring to themselves, pausing for breath; their power and indecision gave Hirsch the strongest feeling he had ever had in his life, a sheer, pure cleavage of terror that, as he fell apart, exposed—tiny kernel, his only defence, his only hope, his only truth—the will to live. "You talk to them," he whispered, rapping it out, confidential, desperately confident. "You tell them—one of their own people, what can they want with you? Make it right. Let them take the stuff. Anything, for God's sake. You understand me? Speak to them."

"They can't want nothing with this car," Philip was saying loudly and in a superior tone. "This car is not the government."

But a woman's shrill demand came again and again, and apparently it was to have them out. "Get out, come on, get out," came threateningly, in English, at Hirsch's window, and at his boy's side, a heated, fast-breathing exchange in their own language.

Philip's voice was injured, protesting, and angry. "What do you want to stop us for? We're going home from a week selling on the road. Any harm in that? I work for him, and I'm driving back to Jo'burg. Come on now, clear off. I'm a Congress man myself—" A thin woman broke the hearing with a derisive sound like a shake of castanets at the back of her tongue. "Congress! Everybody can say. Why you're working?" And a man in a sweat shirt, with a knitted woollen cap on his head, shouted, "Stay-at-home. Nobody but traitors work today. What are you driving the white man for?"

"I've just told you, man, I've been away a week in Bechuanaland. I must get home somehow, mustn't I? Finish this, man, let us get on, I tell you."

They made Hirsch and his boy get out of the car, but Hirsch, watching and listening to the explosive vehemence between his boy and the crowd, clung to the edge of a desperate, icy confidence: the boy was explaining to them—one of their own people. They did not actually hold Hirsch, but they stood around him, men whose nostrils moved in and out as they breathed; big-breasted warriors from the washtub who looked at him, spoke together, and spat; even children, who filled up the spaces between the legs so that the stirring human press that surrounded him was solid and all alive. "Tell them, can't you?" he kept appealing, encouragingly.

"Where's your pass?"

"His pass, his pass!" The women began to yell.

"Where's your pass?" the man who had caught Philip through the car window screamed in his face. And he yelled back, too quickly, "I've burned it! It's burned! I've finished with the pass!"

The women began to pull at his clothes. The men might have let him go, but the women set upon his fine city clothes as if he were an effigy. They tore and poked and snatched, and there—perhaps they had not really been looking for it or expected it—at once fell the passbook. One of them ran off with it through the crowd, yelling and holding it high and hitting herself on the breast with it. People began to fight over it, like a souvenir. "Burn! Burn!" "Kill him!" Somebody gave Philip a felling blow aimed for the back of his neck, but whoever it was was too short to reach the target and the blow caught him on the shoulder blade instead. "O my God, tell them, tell them, your own people!" Hirsch was shouting angrily. With a perfect, hypnotizing swiftness—the moment of survival, when the buck outleaps the arc of its own strength past the lion's jaws—his boy was in the car, and with a shuddering rush of power, shaking the men off as they came, crushing someone's foot as the tires scudded madly, drove on.

"Come back!" Hirsch's voice, although he could not hear it, swelled so thick in his throat it almost choked him. "Come back, I tell you!" Beside him and around him, the crowd ran. Their mouths were wide, and he did not know for whom they were clamouring—himself or the boy.

The Worst Thing of All

When Sarah Mann came out on a visit after twelve years it was pretty inevitable that they should meet her somewhere. Simone knew all about it, of course; the morose beauty of Denys when the affair broke up was the first thing that had drawn her attention when she saw him at the summer school twelve years ago. People gossiped; and then he himself had responded to her attraction to him as an opportunity to offload, to talk out his pain. For years Simone had been able to recreate for herself, extraordinarily vividly, in the middle of one of the comfortable and placid domestic tasks of their married life, the moment in broad daylight when he had delivered himself of it: "A month ago today I tried to kill myself."

She could feel again the starting surge (just like the surge of milk to her breasts when one of the babies cried) of need for him, while embarrassment for suffering that she could not claim to know had tied her tongue.

Then he had said, "I woke up in a kind of nursing home. There were bars on the window. But I was allowed to go home and when I walked out and saw the trees in the morning and walked over the wet grass . . ."

When they began to make love she embraced him and he embraced life, and the bruises that yearning and desire for Sarah Mann had knuckled round his eyes disappeared. Denys had recognized only suffering and joy before; he had never allowed for the existence of well-being. As he moved into this previously unaccounted state he was able to talk to Simone about Sarah Mann as about a remarkable experience survived, with only the involuntary shudder and twitch with which, like a dreaming dog, he relived it. Simone got to know his whole

63

history with Sarah so well that sometimes she could correct him: "But wasn't that later, the time when she said she wanted to live alone, and started to fix up the shack on Southey's farm?" Although she had never met Sarah, she would recognize Sarah's taste or "touch" simultaneously with him; they would exchange wry smiles over objects or situations that were reminiscent of Sarah.

Sarah Mann was a theatrical producer. It was the best kind of fame, hers; the kind they respected. She had been a tremendous success overseas, not in the ordinary commercial theatre, nor only in obscure, arty theatre clubs, but as an innovator who saw the theatre first of all as an arena for ideas in action and who could produce them with the flourish of a circus. Her productions still began their run in the Tom & Dick Theatre which was her company's home, but they soon moved to the West End —always, at her insistence, remaining under the management of the Tom & Dick, so that no big commercial management could dictate any changes. Similarly, in New York, if she went there it was always to produce on Broadway a play that one would have said was categorically off-Broadway. She had been guest producer at the Theatre Workshop; first producer to stage the work of Olaf Barnes, the savage young satirist; chosen by Laurence Olivier to direct two plays in his latest season; responsible for introducing, in collaboration with Barrault, a festival of international new plays; and the only Westerner (it was said) who had ever worked a season with the Berliner Ensemble. Since she had left Johannesburg quite suddenly on a cheap unscheduled flight twelve years before (an old duffel coat against the winter cold of Europe, little luggage, and less money, the way he and she had been going to leave together), she had done all this.

All this, Denys had always held, was plainly there in her then, years ago, when he and she were running their People's Theatre, and God, how she was making him suffer—which also meant how happy he had been, though he could not say it; from the beginning he had talked to Simone of his happiness with Sarah by describing his misery. Sarah and he wrote plays and mimes and put them on in garages, trade-union offices, African school halls and—once—even a clinic. Sarah was an orphan from some village in the Cape, sent to the university in Johannesburg by an uncle. There had never been any way of placing her, no family, no background; only the crowd of men students who, at the time he met her, constantly sat about in her room in the building above the Greek tearoom. Later, when he was sleeping with her in her narrow bed until five every morning and then going home to creep into his own before his mother came to call him to breakfast, he asked Sarah whether she let those boys make love to her, and she said cheerfully, "A few. Oh well." She meant that *they* mattered, she and Denys, and the poetry that flowed out of him in those days like semen. His background was a respectable one (lace doilies and ambition, but few books and no ideas) and the pair of them were let loose together among the extraordinary possibilities of life as it could be read about in the writings of poets, philosophers, politicians, and playwrights, argued, expressed rhythmically in bed, swallowed in the form of beer, and celebrated by the fact that they were going to share what they discovered for themselves, by transmuting it into art.

Later she lived in two rooms in the back yard of a house in a run-down area where there was no caretaker to kick up a fuss about their black friends or the noise of rehearsals that went on until three in the morning. He had fixed it up for her, with Basuto blankets hanging a splendid sunset on the walls, and lamps made of the woven straw beer strainers that Africans use. That room, closing out the ugly yard, where the patterns of light thrown through the straw drew a diamond net across her face, sunlight and leaves across her shape . . . that room. He moved in there with her, but it remained her room. One person's bed where two people slept; and when he wanted to buy a big bed she said, oh, this one's fine—but he knew (afterwards, anyway) it was because all the time, in spite of everything, she thought of herself as a single entity, separate, self-defined. He had wanted to marry her too; couldn't resist it, in the end. She had not given any pompous reasons why they shouldn't marry—but she always said: when we've finished this next play; or, just before we go off to Europe—yes, the day before, and then we'll have one name to travel under, shall we?

Then it all piled up, raced toppling towards the end. The Italian introduced her to Southey and Southey offered her the shack on the farm. And Denys said to her—oh, mad, mad with pain—I suppose you want to make love to Southey? And saw that *then*, perhaps only *then*, she did, she would. And she fixed up the damned shack near the river, and she disappeared there for days and weeks on end, and she was sleeping with Southey, not because she had to, not because she was ever under obligation to anyone, but because she felt like it, in a terrible, absent-minded sexual way, really only interested in the little cardboard sets she whistled over all day out there. And then she came back and he didn't do a damned thing about it, couldn't give her up, just as she, in her way, it seemed, couldn't give him up (only she looked at it differently, she didn't set herself any finalities, any decisions of this kind) until that night she told him that she was going away, and he really went mad, and wept in front of her, and wanted to kill Southey and wouldn't believe the worst thing of all, the truth that she was going alone.

There was a picture of her coming down the gangway from the plane. She looked up out of the newspaper with the quick smile of someone who has been watching her step and suddenly realizes that she has arrived. Simone, who had just picked up the paper from where the delivery man stuck it, once-folded, between the slats of the garden gate, met the picture as if she and this woman had come face to face. Composure dropped like a flap instantly into place. Eyes fixed at a polite social level, Simone might have been in a welcoming party, watching with the required attention, concealing possible boredom, while the celebrity accepted flowers and speeches.

They were not invited to the cocktail party given for Sarah by the Actors' Association, or the luncheon given by the mayor, where the dessert was apparently an ice-cream stage, with a Sarah Mann effigy, made of marzipan, taking a bow on it. . . .

This city-father socializing was hardly their line. Denys gave a spluttering laugh when he read about the ice-cream cake. "Be the keys of the city next," said Simone languidly.

"She'd've preferred the back doors, once," he said. The sharp, cosy exchange brought an excited smile to his face, at once satyr-like and derisive. He nicked the end off a cigar with his strong white teeth shining with saliva; one of the long black cheroots that he had taken to and that Simone thought suited, by dash and contrast, his protracted boyishness. Her father was chairman of one of the biggest tobacco companies in the country ("Purveyors of the real opium of the people," she liked to say) and Denys had turned out to be a surprising success in the business; though she would never have expected it to work and had wanted to go on living on the earnings of the night-school teaching and theatrical odd jobs he had been living by when she got to know him.

Finally they met Sarah Mann in someone's house after a charity show. It was the first night of an all-African revue staged by a white committee, and they were there because this *was* their line—progressive, cultural, flouting the colour bar yet not political. They were merely ordinary members of the audience on this occasion, though Denys had sometimes been on the organizing committee for similar ventures, and Simone, between babies, had sold tickets or fed hot dogs to casts in rehearsal. Sarah was not in the audience—they could not possibly have missed her—and so they unthinkingly accepted the usual sort of invitation called over the backs of people drifting through the foyer: "Come for a drink after the show?" As they crossed the road to the car, a friend came tilting on high heels to catch up. "Simone! You going to the cast party?" "Where's Roddie?" "He's had to go and pick someone up. Sarah Mann's coming. She couldn't see the show tonight, but she's promised to come to the party."

"What do you think, Denys? Are you tired?" Simone neatly seized the moment of silence before it could fall. They were looking at each other closely in the dark, though neither could see the face of the other distinctly. "Well, how do you feel—do you want to skip it, or—?" "Oh *come!*" The friend chattered her heels on the pavement in emphasis. "Let the nanny sit up late for once. Can I hop in with you?"

What possessed them both as they drove chatting to the party was the extraordinary fact that this woman, who was part of the normal social context of their life together, apparently did not know. Was it possible that she simply had no idea that the famous woman and the pale profile in the driver's seat were intimately connected forever, sealed up together in the past; was she not aware that when she talked of Sarah Mann (and how idiotically she nattered, "They say this . . . I believe that . . ." telling them snippets of things of which they knew the whole) as someone set apart by genius and fame from the three of them in the car and all the guests who would be at the party—was she not aware that Simone's husband, the man sitting there in the driver's seat, was set apart up there with her? Simone was monosyllabic with irritation. When they reached the house where the party was in progress, she was careful to lose their passenger among the crush and coats in the hall, so that she and Denys could make their entrance together and alone.

Sarah was already there. By a miracle there was to be no wait, keeping one's eyes away from the door, no moment when one would look up and find her at the distance at which she could no longer be ignored. They were pushed, drifted almost straight across the room to the group in which she was standing, making a point with a fillip of the hand to one man in particular, but keeping up smiling, throw-away remarks to the other people with the ease of someone used to such a position. The group casually shifted apart for them as they were shepherded: You know the Cadmans, Jean and Leon Best, Bud Riley . . . you know Simone and Denys, of course . . . and this is Ann Zwane, Wilson Mtetwa . . . and . . . and . . . And all the time, from the moment she had seen them, Sarah Mann kept her eyes, fearless, gentle, and warm, on Denys. When the introduction came he cut in quickly in a low, dramatic voice, "We know each other," but Sarah Mann didn't bother about the introduction, she was smiling at him with her lips pressed together and her eyes brimming with light. He said, "Hullo," still very low. But she ignored this too and put out both hands, palms up, so that after a moment of confusion and reluctance which she must have noticed but that did not shake her confidence, he had to give her his numb hands. "Denys."

And now he laughed and said, "Good Lord!" Simone saw him fall at once into the mood Sarah set, though the next moment he withdrew himself. "This is my wife, Simone." She turned to Simone with the face of frank and interested pleasure of someone who meets a great many people. He watched Sarah with slight belligerence; the prerogative of intimacy to see how she would behave. But she was saying to Simone, "We really don't know each other? Or didn't you live in Johannesburg when I was here? But you were still a schoolgirl—" And she laughed to admit that the real reason was her "advanced" age. Simone, for her part, was too sophisticated to want to take the compliment; she was older than Sarah, two years and a month, she knew, to the day. "Not a schoolgirl, I assure you. I was at the Sorbonne for a bit, and then in Siena . . . and so on. I was only here for holidays."

"Oh, all the things we wanted to do! I'd never been out of this country until I left twelve years ago, you know."

"I know," Simone said.

"I've picked up Italian not badly, and a bit of German, but often when I work out of England I provide a lot of amusement when I'm trying to explain something."

"You could read French all right, though," Denys's voice came between them, quite an intrusion. For a flash she looked as if she couldn't remember what he was referring to, but she said, "Oh that's all right. I can manage in France, I mean. . ."

Good Lord, manage! She had worked with Barrault! She didn't mention these names, he noticed: didn't want, before him, to be seeming to let it be evident that these were the people she mixed with, ordinarily, now.

She and Simone were talking about Siena. She said, "What do you do?" Simone said with the ironic self-satisfaction of the woman who has chosen without regret, "Look after babies and mend my sons' bicycle punctures." The women laughed. "It's a full-time occupation!" Sarah did not persist, and so it was not necessary for Simone to mention the study of medieval music, the courses on Romanesque art and Byzantine painting that amass in the painstaking rich girl's pursuit of art in academic places.

"—Sons?" Sarah said to Denys.

"Yes" he said, "I've got five sons."

Other people were pressing in; everyone expected to meet her. "Sarah darling . . . there's someone here who's just dying . . . Alan D'Anceville, here she is." Before she had to turn away, brilliant, she said to Denys, "I didn't know where I'd see you."

Simone and Denys went over to the bar and had a drink. There was a big jug of martinis and he said, "Let's have this," and poured them each what amounted to a double because the glasses were large ones. There was a saucer full of olives stuck with toothpicks and he picked one up and said, "Want?" and put two in her glass and she said, "Really!" but laughed and ate them. Then he put another one into her drink, and they moved away, he holding her elbow. He didn't often drink and sometimes when he decided to, the very idea, the glass in his hand, seemed to intoxicate him at once. Already his lips were shining and his head was thrown back. They moved through the people with an air of animation. There was a bit of space near the open French doors and they could lean against the windowsill alongside, he with one leg hitched up boyishly. "Good God!" he said, grinning. "That salon manner, the press conference charm—I mean. . . Good God!"

Simone pursed her mouth indulgently in reproach. "Mm . . . m, she was quite natural."

He was shaking his head in the assurance that he knew better. "And her hair! You should've seen her hair. She had wonderful hair."

"But what's wrong with it? A bit girlish-looking for her now, that's all." Suddenly Simone realized that she had actually seen her, at last: when the moment came this was just a woman, unknown though imagined a thousand times. The hair was not worn as it was in the press pictures but as it was in the old photographs Denys had taken of her that kept turning up although he had made a bonfire when they moved into their first house. She had a beautifully shaped mouth but her teeth were not good—she must smoke too much. Skin neglected, with the bluish pocks where there had been blemishes showing under careless powdering. Only the eyes—lighter than he had always said: really brilliant, with untidy thick eyelashes and unplucked eyebrows. You could notice her eyes even from where they were standing now.

"It was like a live thing on its own, she never used to bother with it—"

"Your hair fades as you get older," said Simone, speaking for her sex. Her hair had never been anything but discreet tinted blond and she made no secret of it.

"Good God. . . ." he said, gloatingly disgusted, as if he expected the laws of nature to be suspended where his interests were concerned. He threw the last of his drink down his throat with a convulsion of the Adam's apple. He had managed to seat himself on the sill and now he leaned towards his wife and grinned closely up into her face the way he sometimes came over and grinned at her in bed when he was going to climb in and lie on top of her. He looked his best, flushed and young. "Well, what d'you think?"

She smiled to show there was no question about it—just as she did in bed. "She's a very attractive sort of person."

"Oh yes. She knows how to bring it off." But his smile was dreamy, amused, and behind his eyes, open to hers, he was touching upon many things.

"God, she's changed!" he murmured triumphantly.

She looked like a rather haggard girl, really; not older. Simone thought: a girl who doesn't eat properly and never gets enough sleep. The truth is that *both* of us look ten years older than he.

Denys and Simone felt responsive to the talk and laughter in the room and moved in deliberately on one of the groups around them. They were far from Sarah Mann until the party thinned out. Then she was in the middle of talk that seemed to have caught her interest vividly and she caught sight of Denys and called over, ". . . you will know? Denys! He'll be the person to know." Somebody said, "You'll never get them, I assure you." "What do you think, Denys?" Sarah asked professionally. "Can it be done here?"

"What be done?" he said in the same brisk tone.

"I want to do *Mutter Courage* with an African cast."

The faces around her were excitedly aware only of her. But because of her, they waited for Denys to speak. He took his time, since they were waiting. "It must be African?"

They all laughed, the black men among them and Sarah too. That was just the point: could one find the right actors among Africans? Sarah said, "It's the only way I can get round Equity, for one thing." She could say this sort of thing; everyone knew that, on the contrary, she was one of the most important signatories to the English actors' and producers' restrictions on playing before or producing for white segregated audiences.

"I should think you'd have some difficulty," he said with a little snort. "Some difficulty. If you don't mind my saying so . . ." He raised a hand to a tall, handsome black man whom he knew well, and who said consideringly, "Of course, good actors don't grow on trees. I don't know if . . ." But everyone broke in again, in particular the white enthusiasts who had sponsored African theatre. What a chance, to get Sarah Mann to produce for them! And she had even told the newspapers that she had "simply come home for a bit" and was not going to do any work whatsoever! What a chance, to have a producer of her calibre, and for nothing! They began to discuss names and possibilities; it was unthinkable that this opportunity should be missed. Most of the names were not known to her— she came up with a few herself: "Jimmy Lediga? And what was his name—Dan? No, Bud—Bud Busewayo?" But no one had heard of them; they were the people she had worked with in the People's Theatre, with the homemade sets and the homemade plays. "What's happened to them?" Her question came to rest on Denys. He was smiling wryly, away from her. He didn't answer. They had gone away, or forgotten the struggling ambition to stand up there and speak the English of the stage. That was twelve years ago.

A little later, when the discussion had divided into smaller harangues, she turned to him. "Well, but who've you got now?"

"Oh, I don't do anything any more" he said, as one speaks of some amusement one no longer has time for.

But it seemed she couldn't imagine him doing anything else. She said vaguely, "But you must know who the good people are. All the work that's been done—there must be good people coming up." She mentioned a play with an African cast that had done well a year ago. She had not seen it, of course, but apparently she had been told about it. "What d'you think of the woman who played the bus driver's wife?"

"What, she's twenty years old!"

"Ah well, if that's the—"

"But wait a minute; hey—what about that woman from Cape Town you got up for the Steinbeck that time?" With the air of putting his mind to it if he must, Denys interrupted a man near him. And while he questioned him, Sarah Mann followed attentively, and Simone, her wrap over her arm, stood patient, indulgently bored, waiting for her husband to be able go home.

He left the group abruptly and steered her by the arm to the car, but in his face in the moment when he opened the door for her and the light went on automatically, she saw elation too strong for speech or sign.

They did not discuss the evening, between themselves, as much as they had expected to while it was in progress. In the end, it seems that time is an absorbent that takes in everything, runs violet and grey together, and renders the caustic passion harmless in the bland solution of social routine. Denys's whole life had been shaped by his association with that girl, that woman—by the association and by its termination—but now that life was like the shape of a tree, which is the only sign of the storm that has blown it that way. They could meet Sarah Mann; for Simone it was possible, and for Denys, this was what it had come to.

A week went by and one evening when Denys came home

from town Simone had a message for him. Chris Ford, one of the African theatre club people, wanted to speak to him. "Sarah Mann has asked them to get your advice," said Simone, quoting Ford.

"Oh yes?" He made a jaunty, deprecating face. "Is that so?"

They both smiled. "And what's it about, I may say?"

"Didn't tell me," she said with mock respect.

"I told her I don't play around with 'the theatre' any more."

"Well, he said please to ring him. So you'd better."

When he came back from the telephone he said sullenly, "Committee for the presentation of *Mother Courage*, to be produced by Sarah Mann. Will I be on it. She told them they should ask my advice about getting people to audition, so now they want me on their committee." He smiled and gave one of his snorts.

She stood there following his words with faint unconscious inclinations of the head. She thought a moment and said with cheerful interest, "When's it going to be put on?"

"April. They hope. We're having a meeting next week."

Now she nodded.

"When next week? Not Thursday or Friday?"

"Thursday."

"My father's coming to dinner. I'll have to put him off." On the telephone, she said, "Denys's tied up with the arrangements for the Sarah Mann play—she's doing a play for the Africans, you know, it's really a tremendous thing. . . ."

Sarah came herself to the first meeting. There were only half a dozen people and Denys was as close to her across the table as he had been at the many tables in all the many times they had eaten together. As she spoke there was the hairline of a gold filling not quite concealed between two of her teeth—good God! But her hands were the same, the thin hands with the nails cut off like a boy's, and not always too clean, either. She wore a dark dress and an extraordinary necklace—nuts, he thought, but as it moved on her collarbones it turned out to be faces, or rather minute heads, carved out of wood. They were strung on what looked like a bit of plastic fishing line— handmade, the whole thing was. Although he couldn't make out the detail, the fact that the effect had none of the sameness of a string of beads made him realize that each face must be unlike any other.

Who had made *that* for her?

The choice of a set designer was being discussed, but out of an old right he was silently challenging her, confronting her with how only too well he knew her way of doing things in *this* particular field, never mind "the theatre," where the whole world knew her abilities, now. And she was aware of the old challenge. Was she? "What I do not want is something that will be meaningful here, but elsewhere, in theatres of different proportions . . ." As her body strained as she made her point to Chris Ford and Humphrey Bellair he read for himself in the tension that set the slight rise of her breasts at an angle under the dress, the same old flouting evasiveness. She referred to him repeatedly on purely professional questions; it was clear that she trusted him to know what she herself would have known about local conditions had she not been absent for twelve years. He answered bluntly, impersonally, and fully. The irony of it brought an inward laughter that was the closest he came to the pain he had had from her, the—but it stopped there, stopped short of that ravage of feeling that he had lived without, ever since. ". . . the props of the human condition," she was saying to the attentive committee. "What are they, exactly? A cooking pot? Machine gun? A wheel? *That's* what the designer must tell me." The great theatrical lady, but I know the bitch. Ay? My lovely bitch.

"A set that is no place but a place in the world," he said, on her ground. But she only said, to all of them, as if in relief at their cooperation, "*Exactly!*"

After the meeting, when they moved into the Fords' living room for coffee, they continued to talk shop. Chris leant deferentially over old Betsy Portas, offering the sugar: "What gimmick are you thinking up this time, Betsy? It'd better be good." Mrs. Betsy Portas was "a marvellous old girl"; born into one rich family and widowed in another, her name and her age made it impossible for any merchant or magnate to refuse her charitable or philanthropic dunning. She had got bored with organizing white charity balls, and for the last year or two had given her very special talents to the young people who launched African artists. Leaving their hands clean, as it were, she made African shows fashionable, and so made them pay. She was in charge of selling programme advertising space at vast price, and she always thought up some money-making plan for the front of the house on her gala first night. "What about a champagne bar in the foyer? With free orchids for the women and cigars for the men? I know someone I can get the orchids out of, it's only the cigars."

"Well, you don't have to look far." Chris indicated Denys.

"I suppose it could be managed," said Denys, with the smile of one for whom influence makes nothing of a difficulty. Simone had been keeping Eve Ford company while the meeting was on, and now she brought him a cup of coffee as Sarah said, laughing, "Why, have you got a hot line to Castro or something?"

"Something like that."

"I shall want—let's see—five hundred good cigars," old Betsy announced.

"Of course they'll be good cigars." He pretended to be flirtatiously indignant with her.

"But where will you get cigars from, for heaven's sake?" Sarah asked.

Chris laughed. "He's only Wells-Danzig."

"Well, not quite," murmured Simone dryly.

"The tobacco people? What've they got to do with you?" Sarah said to Denys.

He said, "I'm a director." But she was not held off by the hauteur. In amazement she said, bewildered, "You're not!" Then she quickly turned delighted to the room. "Well how splendid to have a committee that can even find five hundred cigars! Aren't I lucky?" And as they laughed, ready to do anything for her: "I do feel reassured!"

Auditions for the Sarah Mann production began and Denys did some of the preliminary weeding out. At the final auditions he sat silent, at the back of the theatre; she had to come to him. "Do you think that's the best we can do?" Good God, how well he knew that look, obstinate, yet eager, deeply caught up already in the stream of being that would become the play, her hair gone limp as string and her hands, if you could touch them, warm and dry—dog's nose, as they used to say to each other.

"The big chap is hopeless."

But she had seen something in the big chap, something that she would go after and bring out. "Not hopeless. Not right, but . . ."

"A monolith."

The heads on the necklace were turned wrong side out, faces against her neck. Barrault, Olivier, the Berliner Ensemble, but she still listened to him. "I know," she admitted.

He could walk out without saying good night and after that first "Hullo" at the party he never gave her a conventional polite greeting again. The curt professionalism was a private language, but politeness—ordinary common politeness—*that* was surely impossible between them. Yet some things that would have seemed to be impossible—in a different way—were not, at least for her. One evening at Betsy's after a meeting she said, "What happened to Bizniz?"

That car, bought for thirty pounds, that had carried their props and where they'd made love when there was nowhere else! The skirt she was wearing now, in this room full of admiring people, could cover her sitting astride his lap in the little dark old car with him hidden inside her and no one could see.

He had been saying, "You'd better take my car to Pretoria tomorrow"—Barto, the young stage designer, wanted to show her some of his work there—"but it's a brand-new Mercedes, Barto, goes like hell, so watch it."

"Oh it's all right, I've got a car," she said.

"Not that thing outside?" Denys remembered a rusty, fenderless baby Fiat that he knew didn't belong to any of the others.

"Barto's friend who runs the coffee bar—he's lending it to me for as long as I like."

"You'll never get her to Pretoria in that thing," he said to Barto. "Better take the Mercedes, for goodness' sake. So long as you don't let it run away with you. Perhaps I'd better send it with a driver." And it was then she said, "What happened to Bizniz?"

Quite by the way. Oh yes!

He said distantly, with offhand mockery towards an old inanimate friend, "Long ago out of business. Long ago." He gave her the profile of a private grin that, had he looked at her, would have gone home straight to the recesses of her body and being, that were not secret, to him.

"Has she ever asked you what you do?" Simone was lying back in bed with a book face down on her chest over one of the hand-stitched satin nightgowns that her mother kept her supplied with. She was often in bed when he came back from meetings or rehearsals; the baby woke her early in the mornings.

He was in his underpants. "She knows what I do."

"Yes, I know. About the cigars that first time. You told her you were a director. In my father's firm—she will have gathered that." She made a lipless mouth for a moment, drawing the skin in over her teeth so that it whitened.

He went about the room carrying still the vivid air of someone who has been among people of purpose.

"But she's never asked what you *do*? I mean one would think, after twelve years, and she sees you nearly every day now, one would ask. . . . Aren't you supposed to earn a living? You should have just stayed *left behind*. . . . By her."

He turned to Simone's presence with a broad smile. "Look, I promise you, I hardly exchange a personal word with her. I've never been alone with her for five minutes." And he laughed generously.

But Simone showed none of the grateful warmth of a jealous woman. "The trusted stagehand who knows her ways and his place."

He didn't bother to listen; he knew what to do with her. "Shift over," he said, smiling, with tender authority. Pyjama jacket unbuttoned, hair wet-ended from the bathroom, he jostled himself down beside Simone. "She's running about with Barto and all his geniuses and shebeen laureates. Can you imag-

ine it. They were going to Pretoria tomorrow in some old jalopy she's found herself, but I offered him the Mercedes—"
"And was she impressed?" said Simone.

Their daily lives were increasingly bound up with the production of *Mother Courage*. Simone was roped in by Betsy Portas for her women's subcommittee. Chris Ford and the other members of the main committee had fallen into the practice of assuming that Denys was the one through whom to approach Sarah Mann when there were any changes, objections, or difficulties to be discussed; he was the one who would be likely to know how these things would affect what she had in mind. One way and another, they did see her almost every day. She was in their house when it happened to be the place where meetings were held. Once or twice she had had to telephone Denys about some matter, so that someone would say, just as if it were anyone else ringing up, "It's Sarah Mann on the line." What had lain behind their life, remote and omnipresent, the jagged peak of eternal snows covered in cloud, was down there among them; and it was possible to deal with it in the ordinary way of that life, quietly, extraordinarily, as gods or devils, taking on human form, make it possible for people to deal with them without noticing their impossible divinity or dreadfulness.

Quite apart from anything else, it was difficult to believe, on the face of it, that she was the famous person with an international reputation and all that goes with it, while the members of the committee were the amateurs of a cultural backwater, unknown and inconsiderable. They drove their big cars while she used her little borrowed tin can; she had taken a flat, but it was modest, even ugly, in comparison with their elegant contemporary houses with their swimming pools, hi-fi, Thai silk curtains, and abstract paintings. She must have made a great deal of money, but there were few signs of it; a crate of books, sent out by air, that lay about backstage and was never opened, the once-beautiful coat, used for a knee-rug in the draughty theatre, that had a Balmain label hanging by a thread. She never wore any jewellery except that thing with the faces around her neck. And her manner, too; *they* were the ones who used the language of the *avant garde*, learned from the appropriate reviews. She spoke of her problems with the play in the everyday words that, among them, would have been taken as a sign of naïveté and ignorance.

Simone had the feeling that Sarah was not quite sure who she, Simone, was. Sometimes she even called her Eve (Chris's wife's name) without noticing her mistake. She had for them all—all the women on the subcommittee—the same expression of frank and interested pleasure (she's so *natural*, they said) that she had shown towards Simone the night that Denys had introduced Simone to her. "This is my wife, Simone." If she had been anybody, it would not have been necessary for Denys to introduce her with the prefix; "This is Simone"—that would have been enough. There it was. And what a difference between the very names—Sarah, ancient, speaking from the sources of law and poetry, noble through common use; and *Simone!* How pretentious, how bourgeois, what a give-away, the fancy French name—it could be chosen only by parents like her own, Simone knew. Just as if her good, generous, ambitious father had stuck a label on her with his bank balance written on it.

The kind of generic anonymity bestowed upon Simone by Sarah Mann enabled Simone to observe her, as it were, unseen. And through her, Denys. The demands made upon his time and energy by the organizing committee seemed to renew both. He displayed a dynamic unfamiliar—to Simone at least—in him. Was it something that existed only for *her?* His dealings with her were businesslike and he took care to let her know that he had come a long way from the poor Bohemian boy who was her lover. Simone saw the scrupulous and unequivocal attention with which Sarah discussed matters of production with him; but she found herself becoming agitated at the polite, pleasant attention of indifference with which Sarah heard him through when he casually thrust under her nose his affluence and secure position in the ordinary world. Simone became so morbidly alert to this that she felt herself begin to anticipate his words before he had actually begun to say them, and several times she was unable to control a bristling impulse to interrupt on some pretext, so that they would not be said and Sarah Mann would not listen with that pleasant smile. He quickly suspected these interruptions, and teased his wife. "I was merely reassuring her that if we should need more money I can speak to the chairmen of various boards I'm on."

He had protested that he had never been alone with her for five minutes. Had she been alone with him? That moment, perhaps, when he said, "I'm a director," and she said, "You're not!" Almost alone. Simone had seen her face.

It was true, too, that he hardly exchanged a personal word with her. But his vitality and purposefulness—tearing about in the Mercedes in which he looked like an adventurous boy, slumped with the impressive moodiness of responsibility in the dark auditorium during rehearsals, running an exasperated hand through his bright hair, as if through the pedestrian discussion, at a meeting—all this potency of personality was roused by the secret, intimate grin that Simone saw on his face when he was where Sarah was. Not talking to her, or looking at her; a grin so secret, so finally intimate that it felt without touching, possessed blindly, without looking. His vigour was all blood; nothing but the blood that made his face glow handsome, his ears warm and alive as an animal's, while he smiled. That smile. Who could know it better than Simone herself? Sarah Mann, she supposed; but she didn't see it, wasn't aware of it. He's come to both of us with that ruttish smile.

Denys did not take much notice of what he thought of as Simone's mood: not so much cold towards him as calculating and flat. It was surely in the very foundations of their particular relationship that this particular woman should cause her pain. He was not cruel; but this was a jealousy she must have accepted long ago, when she met him. He would deal with her. In the meantime, they were both so frantically busy with the play. There was hardly any chance for *them* to exchange a personal word, which was just as well. The working arrangements of marriage—care of the children, contingencies of the household —provided him with a neutral ground of professionalism with her, too. The weeks raced towards opening night. And then it was there: Betsy Portas's champagne and cigars in the twittering foyer; backstage, Sarah's omnipotent concentration about to make from pasteboard, light, the sweat of stagehands and the men and women trapped behind their greasepaint, like a world out of cooling matter, explosive gases, and cosmic dark, the play. The curtain went up and this world was flung into the well-dressed laps. It overcame the perfume and the scent of good cigars; the light from it that fell upon their upturned faces discovered them unconsoled by the champagne, afraid of war, death, and each other. In the intermissions, powdering their noses and drinking more champagne, they had no necessity to admit it, and when the curtain came down at the end, now that the whole business was over it had become a play and a tremendous success. They clapped while the curtain rose on the actors again and again, and there was a standing ovation for Sarah Mann.

The affectionate elation that breaks out among the cast and all others concerned with the successful first night of a play made the party afterwards gay and emotional. Mother Courage —the thin little coloured woman from Cape Town whom Denys had remembered just in time—appeared in a matron's dress of blue lace, with pearls. The cast presented Sarah with a fine kaross made of jackal skins. (They had wanted to give her one of those dressing-cases with empty bottles and jars held by ruched silk bands, but Denys, when consulted, had known the sort of thing that she would like.) When the casual guests and older people had gone the real drinking and dancing began, safe from the eyes of Betsy Portas, who was always a little worried in case the dear boys and girls went a bit too far with their racial mixing and risked spoiling the sale of tickets. Denys had a lot to drink, and in the feeling between cast and committee that they had got to know each other better than anyone else they'd ever known in their lives, found it difficult to keep any sort of distance from Sarah. There had been a bit of a fight between two chaps, quickly stopped. Chris Ford, just as if Eve weren't there, kept coming up to Denys and asking with drunken secretiveness in a voice loud enough not to be missed, why Dora Makaba was so offhand with him tonight. "I don't know what the score is. . . ." In the general atmosphere of licence Denys went up and said suddenly to Sarah, "That thing around your neck. What's it all about, ay? Who is this sculptor or whatever he is?" He stood there before her with a glass of gin in his hand, scornful, knowing, exerting his rights. She was beautiful. She was the only one who had ever been beautiful like that. Lines round her mouth, grey hairs, and the lot. She had on a long dark dress, split to her knee at the side, but round her neck was that damned thing, as usual. Oh he knew how she cherished certain things, carried them around with her always, never spoke about them and so filled them with meaning that was only for her.

She laughed and her hand flew up to her neck. But when she felt the thing there her fingers merely stirred along it, gentle and slow. "It's nice, isn't it . . . I like it. . . ." She spoke as one does of something one has picked up in passing, off the counter of a department store.

"Come on. What's it all about?" That man who had sat and carved them for her with the restraint and careful patience that scaled down all his creation into something too close to the pulse in her neck to be seen in the ordinary approach of one being to another. All the power of his vision of life packed down into these heads—maddeningly too small to be read, not an adornment; someone of whom she could ask, or by whom was offered, this. Good God, who did she think she was? He suddenly remembered, not with his mind but the skin of his hand, thrusting that hand up her skirt to sudden scalding wet warmth against the wall behind the rough scaffolding of some backstage. It was as if he had done it again now, making with the thrust of that hand everyone else in the room disappear. He said roughly, "Well? Come on." But she laughed, in the admiring admittance of someone whose taste is praised. "It *is* rather nice, isn't it. . . . A friend of mine makes them."

Simone had a good time at the party. She had never been popular with African men before because of her rather matronly air beside her husband, but at this party all customary combinations were shaken up and the various elements scattered in some extraordinary new affinities. She saw Denys's excited bravado approach, tête-à-tête with Sarah, part of the general mood that thought no more of her own dancing on and on, never missing a step, close to a tall black man who talked away incessantly in her ear but whose name she never caught. Like everyone else, she and Denys found each other in time to go home. He said in the car, turning attention to her pleasantly, "You came out of your shell all right, my girl. Who was that chap who was dancing with you all the time?" "I've no idea." He laughed indulgently. Then said, "Sarah seemed to find so much she had to talk to me about—I don't know." He shrugged. "It seems the show could never have gone on without me. . . . And what-not."

Simone was smiling now, it was an hour of the night when they never talked, they were driving through empty streets. She smiled as she looked over his profile beside her. "But that's not what you've had in mind, have you?"

"Had in mind?"

"You don't want her grateful thanks."

Half offended, half debonair, he said, "I don't give a damn either way."

Simone said with intense interest, "No, you don't care a damn about her thanks any more than you care a damn about her consulting you and deferring to your opinion. You're only thinking all the time about the things you've done with her. The love-making. All the rest comes right off the top of your head."

He laughed, but she laughed with him, and making an attempt to keep his laughter on a level of detached amusement above hers—whatever it was—he even threw back his head in a mime's gesture.

"Every time you walked into a room your hand was up her skirt."

In the cover of the dark of the car, the dark inside his body, his blood seemed to convulse, drawing in from the extremities. The coarse shaft stuck the centre of him: all that was left of what had once been the strong and delicate complex of his being. When he could, he said, in the tone of someone who is amused and pretends to be shocked, "Simone, gin so late at night doesn't agree with you!"

But when they were in bed and he wanted to make everything all right by making love to her, she turned away in tears because she no longer wanted him any more, either.

The Pet

Gradwell worked for some people called Morgan. The house in Johannesburg was a small house with a large garden, three cypresses, and a splendid view. The plates were always hot and the ice was plentiful; the sheets smelled of sun and the fires burned brilliantly at any time of year that Erica Morgan felt like having one lit. The Morgans had no children and were happier and more prosperous than many of their friends who did; which somehow did not seem fair. Still, there it was; the Morgans went to Europe every two years, bought books and records and even an occasional picture, and lived with their dogs in their delightful little house attended by excellent servants.

Gradwell vacuum-cleaned the carpets, polished the silver and Reg Morgan's shoes, and changed into a white drill suit twice a day to serve lunch and dinner. He was a Nyasa with a face so black that the blackness was an inverted dazzle—you couldn't see what he was thinking. He was deft and quiet about the dining room, and on those nights on which the Morgans went out, he sat up with the dogs to take care of the house. Erica Morgan (she sometimes had educated Africans to lunch) told him that he could sit in the living room and listen to the radio if he liked, but he never did. He sat in the kitchen at the table and wrote to his wife. The two dogs, pretty Scottish terriers with tartan collars, snored at his feet. In the four or five years that he had been writing letters to his wife to this accompaniment, he had never mentioned it to her; he wondered as little at the fact that it was his duty to sit up with the dogs as he did at the incomprehensible ritual of the order of dishes that he served so efficiently at the Morgans' dining table.

He did not know his wife very well. He had married her four years before, when he went home to Nyasaland on leave for six months. He had not been back since, not only because of the money—the train fare for a journey of nearly three thousand miles ate up a disproportionate amount of his wages—but because he was working in Johannesburg illegally, anyway, an immigrant without a permit, and he was afraid that if he went out of the place he would not be able to get back in again. It was impossible to stay at home in Nyasaland, of course; how could he work for two pounds a month there, when in Johannesburg he could earn ten? He sent money home to his wife every month, or rather to his uncle, to keep for his wife, and he had bought himself a waterproof watch as well as a set of the sort of well-cut clothing a man wears in a city.

Not that he went into the city itself very often. As he had no papers, it was risky for him to hang about the streets; he was safer at home, in Dauchope Road, in the anonymous apron of domestic service. He had long ago stopped going out even to the suburban post office or the shops—he always asked Mrs. Morgan to buy the stamps and envelopes that he needed, and the tobacco with which, with paper from the pantry, he rolled his own cigarettes. On his days off, he went to sit in the rooms of other exiles like himself; men from his own village who worked in the suburbs, foreigners who kept a wordless familiarity beneath their conformity of Stetson or starched uniform. At first he sought them out because he was lost—in all the world, only the Nyasaland village was recognizable to him—but later, as the years went by, he went to them out of habit, as there are always, even in the most cosmopolitan of cities, little groups of men who have forgotten the old country, but continue to meet because of it.

When he had first come back to Johannesburg after he was married he had been moody for a while. He, who was, as Mrs. Morgan said, the "nicest, most docile person in the world," had quarrelled with the cook, and had taken offence at the first word of reproach from Mrs. Morgan. He had even taken the risk of going out to get drunk at a shebeen one night, but all the luxurious, painful pleasure of a debauch was lost because he could not sit in the sun and recover, next day, as they did at home in Nyasaland, but had to be in attendance at a luncheon party about which Mrs. Morgan had been giving special instructions all week. "I'm sorry, Gradwell," she had said, firmly, humourously, "but you must go through with it today. These guests are people we stayed with at the Cape last year, and lunch has got to be decently served. Here, take this, and you'll cope—anyway, if you feel awful, it'll teach you not to get into the habit of drinking, which is just as well." And she gave him two Alka-Seltzers in a glass of water. It was true, of course, that if he began to drink, he would be much more likely to be picked up by the police—the Morgans, too, ran a risk with him; while he would be packed off back to Nyasaland or drafted to farm labour if he were found out, they would be fined for employing an illegal immigrant from another territory. "It's a sort of little conspiracy we're in together," Mrs. Morgan would explain to friends who complimented her on Gradwell's efficiency.

But soon the awareness of the eighteen-year-old girl, his wife, wore away, faded off his mind and his skin; he had come back again, to Johannesburg, to Dauchope Road, to sleep alone in the European bed and the decent European outbuildings that the Morgans provided. He went with prostitutes, but his deeper feelings hibernated; he never thought to acclimatize them; this was not home, for them. There was a child, born to the girl in Nyasaland some months after he had gone. He felt responsible, jaunty, and somehow accepted into the world of men, when the letter came telling of the boy's birth. Mrs. Morgan sent the child toys at Christmas and wondered that he did not at least have a photograph of the boy; but he explained that there would be no one in the village with a camera. Two years later there was a letter from his uncle, saying that the child had died. He did not know what to feel; he had never seen it. For his wife—well, next time he went back he would make another child, what else could he do? He had a post-office savings book, now (Mrs. Morgan deposited his money for him), and he drew out some money and bought his wife a dress.

He was even quieter than usual as he went about his work.

The Morgans thought he was depressed, and made signs of understanding to each other, behind his back, but the truth was that he was listening; to himself. Listening; for something to sound, some note from—there was a place there, on his breast-bone. But nothing came. He simply went on, waiting at table, polishing the silver, even cleaning up after the new dog—there was a new dog in the house, a bulldog puppy—without disgust. In the afternoons, he sat in the yard outside his room in the sun, wiped a piece of bread round his dinner-plate, and was content; there was no use denying it.

"Next year, when we go to Europe, we must take a chance and you must go home to Nyasaland while we're away. We'll have to try and work something, some sort of document that will pass," said Mrs. Morgan.

At this time, Mrs. Morgan was much preoccupied with the bulldog. It was her dog—she had admired bulldogs as a child, in a fascinated, horrified sort of way—but Reg Morgan had consented to buy it chiefly because there had been such an outbreak of burglaries in Johannesburg that he felt they ought to have a really good watchdog around the place. The Scotties were alert little chaps, but one couldn't expect anyone to be deterred from entering the garden by the sight of them.

When the bulldog came, he was a squat, shambling puppy, terrified by his own ability to knock things flying. He seemed to feel the world of inanimate objects cower before him, and his power appalled him. He messed all over the house and ate with uncontrollable gluttony, often disgorging his food again as fast as it went down. Mrs. Morgan adored him; at last, her childlessness took revenge on her, and she cradled a beast. She loved and petted and spoiled the Scotties, but for the bulldog she had hopes—the test of the real maternal passion. "Wait till I train him," she would say. "To us, he'll be the nicest, the most docile thing in the world, a handsome, dignified, well-behaved, *clean* bully-boy. And to those wicked burglars—murder!"

The dog grew up. He slept about the house all day, but the muscles of a pugilist formed on his thick shoulders and his barrel-bellied body; his huge, hard head with its giant nutcracker jaw under the flapping, dribbling chops could push you downstairs if he wanted to pass you on the top step. Gradwell and the other Morgan servants hated him from the moment they set eyes on him; had hated him even before then, the bulldog—symbol of all the white man's savage glee in turning the black man from his door. He felt their hatred and showed the obscure shame of a beast, flattening his little hippopotamus-ears on his ugly head as he went past them, crouched low to the ground.

But there was nothing else that he understood, it seemed. Erica Morgan did succeed in teaching him to be clean, though he left his snail-trail of saliva wherever his snout brushed by— but all her sensible patience and quiet, controlled commands could not teach him the simplest obedience, and as for being a watchdog, he slept through all warnings of intruders given by the Scotties, and allowed strangers to walk past him up to the front door without so much as a bark. It had proved impossible to anthropomorphize him into a handsome, dignified, well-behaved bully-boy; and somewhere along the unsuccessful process, he had lost the instincts of a dog, into the bargain. Erica Morgan was disappointed in her pet. The final touch came when she found a lovely mate for him, a beautiful brindle bully-girl for her bully-boy. The bitch was brought to the house in Dauchope Road, because the Morgans thought he was too "highly strung" to be sent to the kennels. But though the bull-dog and the bitch were given carefully supervised privacy and were shut up in the garden shed together for three days, the poor bulldog would not mate. He ran away and sat, with his fat, miserable back hunched against the door of Gradwell's room— Gradwell, who, when he put the dog's food down before him, did it with repugnance.

"It's no good, Gradwell" Erica Morgan said on the third day, with irritation and exasperation, clipping the lead to the bitch's collar. "I'll take her back to the kennel. Really, I *am* fed up. If at least we'd had a pup from him . . ." She felt she could say anything to Gradwell; he was rather a favourite of hers among her servants. They were, as she put it to herself, two human beings, never mind the colour or the master-servant thing.

Gradwell opened the garage doors and the gates and closed

them again behind her as she drove away with the bitch. It was just before three o'clock in the afternoon; he went into the kitchen and fetched his lunch, which was in the oven, keeping warm. The other servants were already in their rooms, and he sat down on a barrel in the yard outside his room, making a threatening movement of his foot towards the bulldog as he did so. But the beast, unaware, as usual, of what he had done wrong, but always conscious of wrong-doing, of failure, only shivered with appeal along his thick back, and pressed against the closed door of the room.

The man sat there eating bread in the dry Transvaal winter sun that has as much bite as the morning frost, a man who had no child, who loved no woman, who scarcely ever went outside the gate of Erica Morgan's yard. At last, something moved, there at his breastbone; but dully, a depression. He broke off a piece of bread and threw it, saying in his own language to the dog, "Here!" And startled, changing swiftly from the expectation of a blow, the dog snapped the morsel into its great mouth.

One Whole Year, and Even More

I was waiting for Iscott in the foyer of the Savoy yesterday when the two of them started nattering next to me.

"This one's a Swede—we wouldn't take an Italian again; no thank you!" ". . . We always have Finns. I mean she's perfectly trustworthy and sensible, but she hasn't picked up much of the language yet, and once the children come in from school they are inclined to lead her rather a dance. . . ." The two silly bitches were turned out into the street by the revolving door, their huge fur hats displayed jerkily like the busbies of toy soldiers.

The one we had was a German.

People in England do talk about their *au pair* girls like this. Everyone seems to have their favourite brand, the most reliable, the most equable—you'd think they were discussing beer or cigarettes. Once they've had a "bad experience" with an Italian, Italians are out. Once they've had a good Spaniard, Spaniards are in. Some even swear by outlandish tastes—a preference for something like Finns. The girls want to come to England to learn English, and if, like us, you live in a part of London they favour (not too far from the West End, not too far from the language schools and foreign students' clubs) you can take your pick. They're not servants, of course. Then what are they? "Help in the house," Sheila said. "Someone to take a bit of the drudgery off one's shoulders without loss of self-respect on either side."

Sheila is a South African and before she married me and came to live in England she was brought up in a house with real servants, but she says that once she was grown up, because they were black she was ashamed to treat them as servants. When she got a list of girls from the *au pair* agency that time, she said to me, "The trouble is, all the ones that sound best for us seem to be Germans."

"So what?"

"Well, I don't know." As so often happens between two people who are thoroughly mixed up with each other, Sheila feels far more strongly than I do myself about my family history in the hands of the Germans. I was born in Germany and left the country with my father, who's an Englishman, when I was five years old. My mother was German and Jewish; I can just remember her, and I've never been able to connect her with the gas ovens that I've seen in documentary films and atrocity books, and in which it is a fact that she was destroyed.

"What's the difference?"

But the more I showed her it didn't affect me the more she stiffened on my behalf. "I don't see why we should go out of our way to have a German in the house."

"Don't see why we should go out of our way to avoid one, if the most suitable girl happens to be German."

"I'll ask them one more time if they haven't got anything else." Sheila was in the middle of doing something, I remember she had a baby's bottle or some bit of shrunken clothing in one hand, and the list from the agency in the other, and she squatted down a minute beside my drawing board, taking time out for a smoke, like a workman on the job. I left the detailed drawings of the public conveniences or whatever great piece of architecture it was that I was engaged on for Iscott at the moment, and twirled my stool so that I could swing my legs up onto the windowsill the way I like to. And so we stayed until yells from the kitchen—the foreman's whistle—got her scrambling back on to her feet and me back to the drawing board again. I realize now it's extraordinary how much alike we've come to look at moments like these. We both wear the same cheap and convenient clothes, blue jeans, and pullovers that fit either of us indiscriminately. We both have short hair in need of cutting—Sheila just hasn't time to do her hair the way she used to. With each child, her little breasts have got smaller; her hips have got so lean, we look like a couple of boys around the house.

Even when Renate—that's the German girl—came, Sheila continued to feel for a while some affront to me in having her there. I heard her on the phone, for instance, purposely bringing up the fact of the girl's nationality, brazen before the anticipation of criticism. And sometimes when the girl, exasperated by the effort to express herself in English, would turn to me with a burst of fluency in German, Sheila would make a face to me behind her back. I exhibit exactly the same kind of anxiety towards Sheila over Negroes as she does towards me over Germans. Knowing how much, as a privileged white, she loathed the colour bar where she comes from, I bristle when I sense colour feeling in people, in her presence, and I always thank Christ she can't see the anti-black graffiti in the men's all over London these days. Like the Brecht song, I look out for her, and she looks out for me; and that's the institution of marriage, that's what it's come to, the crazy, delightful need we had— well!

I suppose the girl turned out better than we expected—she did at the beginning, anyway. She got the kids up in the mornings and by the time I came down into the kitchen she was already there, standing at the sink washing up last night's dinner dishes with the two little girls eating at table, and the baby drumming and smearing and spilling in his high chair. Sheila said that the girl was reluctant about the housework she had to do, but she was fine with the children—and no one could blame her; Sheila hates housework too. The girl would go on with whatever she was doing for a few seconds, when you came in, before she showed she was aware of your presence and greeted you. She would stand there in her tight green pants and black sweater, rubber gloves on her hands, lifting a dripping wrist now and then to push the hanging hair out of her face. As if some invisible photographer were there to instruct her, she "held it" for just that moment in which you knew she knew you were there; then: "Good morning, Mr. Stephens"—her hoarse little voice would discover you while she shook back a lank and by now soapy strand of hair. Sheila called it a voice of "sweet suffering" but I argued that it was a "brave" one. After we had laughed about it, Sheila would say, "Poor Renate! It must be ghastly to be plonked into a houseful of strangers."

Sometimes Renate would "hold it" before the baby's high chair. You'd find her turned away from the dirty dishes, dripping rubber gloves clasped worshipfully on the wooden flap before the baby, neck held forward, long as a Sienese madonna's, hair falling intimately between the baby's face and hers— "Here's Renate," she would say, over and over, soft, long-drawnout, wheedling and comforting—"Here's Renate, Renate."

Sheila was embarrassed at first, she said privately that the baby hated people to thrust their faces at him. But the baby reacted just like an old man who thinks he's past it and finds a girl ogling him. He would look at Renate open-faced, astonished; then he'd lift his lip, show his teeth, wrinkle his nose delightedly; break into a low and excited laugh and bring his forehead cosily against hers. She would draw away with head-tilted reluctance, her under jaw thrust up yearningly, blinking slowly at him; and then turn to us suddenly with a smile. It was the smile of the girl who will always have men. I don't mean the really stunning or beautiful smile, but the one that anyone instantly recognizes.

She went conscientiously to her classes every afternoon and worked hard at learning English. Sheila told me that she never took the children to the park without her English grammar in the pocket of her duffel coat. We told her to help herself to our books and to listen to records whenever she wanted to. One afternoon during those first weeks she came into the living room, which is also where I work, at home, and stood before the rows and piles of books wedged up and down the wall; I knew that feeling of resentment before a mass of books in a foreign language. "Please, you tell me a book, Mr. Stephens." I didn't want to tax her knowledge of English but to give her something that would hold her interest easily while introducing her to decent writing. She watched while I hesitated over several spines. I gave her a witty novel set in the London she must be getting to know—the London of coffee bars, Kensington, and King's Road. "*Vielen Dank*," she said, and took it, but when, next evening as we were on our way out and she was baby-sitting in the living room, I saw her reading and was about to ask how she was getting on with it, I suddenly noticed, crushed, that the book in her hands was *Ulysses*. We made no suggestions about records, but whatever she thought of our stack, she seemed to settle for Brahms' Number 1 Piano Concerto and an American Negro singer, Mahalia Jackson—we often heard one or the other when we opened the front door at night.

Sheila had turned what used to be a dining room, in the basement next to the kitchen, into a room for the girl, and so she could come and go as she pleased through the kitchen entrance. In no time at all she appeared to have made friends and to have a life that took her out whenever she was free, transformed, by preparations in that basement room, from a Cinderella in rubber gloves to a fair copy of a fashion model— much more difficult than changing into a dowdy princess. Sheila admired her. "You should have seen Renate today—she bought herself two yards of green tweed at Pontings' sale and she's made a kind of waistless dress that looks marvellous on her figure. For fifteen bob!" She added, "You can't believe it's the same grubby little slut around the house."

Sheila used to ask her, when she'd been out, whether she had enjoyed herself.

The girl seemed to come with an effort from some comparison before which the evening in question had no reality, while the kind, platitudinous inquiry hung. Then, prefaced with a sigh: "Pretty good, Mrs. Stephens. My girl-friend made me go with her to a party, after we saw the film. Some people . . . I don't know—they were nice, yes."

One day she said, "Mrs. Stephens, the name Canahan—what would be the name Canahan—Scotch?"

"Irish, more likely, I should think."

"Are Irish dark people?"

Sheila was curious. "Why? Yes, they can be dark. Celtic people, you know."

"I met a man, he makes a great fuss, he wants me to go out. Dinner, I don't know what . . ." Renate lifted and dropped her shoulders at the importunity of men. "He is so dark, though. In London you never know. I hope it's not a nigger or so."

Even Sheila laughed. "You ought to know a West Indian by now when you see one."

But this distaste of the girl for colour made our life with her unexpectedly simpler. Everyone had warned us against the mistake of feeling obliged to have the *au pair* girl included in our relationships with friends—yet we had both felt that when friends come to dinner, or when we had the occasional party, we couldn't let her sit listening to the voices, from her room. It so happened that just after she came to us, we had a drinks party for a friend of mine with whom I used to work when I was with a firm in America. Apart from Iscott and a few other architects, it was our usual crowd, with among its regulars the black South African exiles who were Sheila's friends from home. Renate had some success early in the evening, laughing throatily where she stood pinned against the wall by the attention of Pam Iscott's ass of a brother, but once the party thinned out and a few chaps got a bit high and matey, she disappeared to her room. We noticed this because old Dizzy Mgadi kept wandering round accusing people—"Hey! Where's that chick with the long hair! I'mn'a sing for her, man."

After that there was no awkwardness at all; Renate had her own friends, and although she helped Sheila prepare for ours, she took it as her right rather than a banishment that she did not appear among our guests when they were actually in the house. Our tastes, she seemed to imply, were not hers. The rather exaggerated respect with which she employed our names so frequently when addressing us (Sheila was only five years older than she was)—was it merely the unintentional formality of a stranger using a foreign language, or was it sarcastic? You couldn't tell. Certainly, we didn't get to know what her tastes in company were. She never took advantage of Sheila's suggestion that she should ask a boy-friend to keep her company some evenings when she had to sit up for the children.

"Mrs. Main says she entertains in her room, though," Sheila remarked.

"And what does the old girl mean by that?" Mrs. Main is the daily woman who comes in to clean for the two BBC queers who rent our second story.

"Well, when Mrs. Main uses a phrase like 'entertains in her room'—"

"Yes, I know, I can hear the leer in the old cow's voice. What business's it of hers—and how does she know, anyway? Good God, she only gets here about eight in the morning."

But we both knew how Mrs. Main knew: in the way that a hard-worked plain woman of forty-five who looks fifty-five and whose life is bounded by Grandma's bad turn and an inability to "do anything" with little Johnny, knows that a young girl, and a foreigner, at that, is stealing love and pleasure.

That summer was the first real summer we'd had in England for years. Nobody's forgotten it. You could feel the sun, day after day, drawing deeper and deeper on the old, cold damp in the bricks and bones of our houses and leaving them dry and sweet. Pipe-fug and cabbage-steam burned out; black beetles and gobs of winter phlegm disappeared, evaporated in the sun. God, we couldn't get enough of it. My father and his wife live in the country near Lavenham, and we used to go down there every weekend we could manage; but it's quite an undertaking to move three small children and all their equipment on Friday, only to repeat the operation in reverse on Sunday night, and we decided it would be a good idea to rent a cottage where Sheila could camp with the children for longer peroids. We couldn't afford it, really, but my father found a friend who let us have almost for nothing a converted boathouse in a village on the Suffolk coast. It was exactly what one needed for that summer, and was worth the longish drive to get there. I would take the whole crew down one weekend, drive myself back to London on Sunday night, and return to spend the following weekend with them and bring them home. Sheila said that it was the first time since she'd been living in England that it was warm enough to bathe and lie about on a beach; she was proud and excited, as if she could at last prove that there was nothing she missed by leaving her home in South Africa.

I worked a lot in the house, while they were away and it was quiet and more or less empty; our bachelors were upstairs, of course, and Mrs. Main clanging and Hoovering overhead during the day. Renate sometimes went with Sheila (Sheila needed her, to give herself a break from babies) but we didn't like to take her away from her classes too often, and, besides, although I can cook and look after myself all right, the house had to be cleaned up in between times. Renate had a lot of free time when only I was at home. She had got herself a splendid tan on her visits to the cottage and she took great care to keep it going, basting herself with oil and lying out in our little oblong of back garden in her bikini. This place, usually a soggy well between two narrow houses back to back, was one of the miracles brought about by the sun. Instead of the gritty green sponge oozing beneath the pressure of your shoes, there was warm thick grass like fur to the soles of your feet. The chestnut tree threw a black hole of shade, smelling of dust, into the brilliant cube of sunlight against which the rosy walls warmed their backs. There were no rows of wet sooty napkins strung clinging together criss-cross on lines; it was a garden, smelt like a garden, looked like a garden, and there was even a girl in it, belly up in the sun.

I was working in the kitchen one afternoon (I'd been entirely alone the previous week—Renate had been down at Udgewick with Sheila—and it was easier to work where I could grab a snack or a cold beer when I wanted it) when Renate came in from the garden, holding her toes stiffly up from the floor as people do when they are barefoot, and dragging the rug she'd been lying on. "It's awful," she confided. "You know, I can't stay in the garden? That man in the other house looks at me with glasses. What do you call them?" With her free hand she mimed a telescope or binoculars. I laughed. "Well, I suppose it's an unusual sight in a London garden." "Ach, men, why do they make a nuisance of themselves." She bridled sulkily, slanting a look towards the door as if the offender were standing there.

"Don't worry, Renate, even with binoculars he can't see any more of you than your bikini shows, and you've **been** wearing it quite happily on the beach at Udgewick, haven't you?"

She did not answer but stood there breathing crossly, the strong muscle of her diaphragm sucking in a dent above her belly-button. One doesn't realize how much the body, never mind the face, can express of a person's reactions and thoughts; if she'd been dressed I shouldn't have seen this dent, exactly like the one that appears above the baby's pot-belly when he stiffens before tears, and shouldn't have felt suddenly that what I had said was patronizing and tactless.

"Would you mind, Mr. Stephens, if I lie down here?"

"Of course not." And I went on drawing while she spread her rug on the floor in the sun that was pouring through the open windows, and arranged herself on her stomach. Later she got up and made some coffee for me, and drinking it, we had a little chat, mostly about Udgewick, which she adored, before she went off to get dressed and go to her class.

I found her sunbathing on the kitchen floor several afternoons after that. She lay propped on her elbows reading German picture magazines and did not bother me with chatter. At some point she would get up, put the water on for coffee, lie down again until the kettle whistled. Towards the end of the week I said, as I happened to look down and see her turn over, sigh, and settle on her back, facing me, "Man with his binoculars still around?"

She did something she had never, so far as I remember, done before; she reacted spontaneously, without calculation for effect. She giggled, and lifted her arm floppily and let the back of her curled hand fall covering her smile.

Then we both laughed, and I said briskly, "What about coffee now?" Groaning, very slowly, stretching and sighing, she got up and set about making it. While the water was boiling she went out of the room, and appeared again in a big gown like a bathtowel, carrying our portable record-player with a small pile of records on top. "Here you are," she said, setting down the burden efficiently on the cupboard, close to an electric plug point. "You always like to work with music upstairs, eh? Now I bring it for you here."

I had thought of it myself but had been too lazy to do

anything about it. She had brought the records I play over and over again, but she had slipped Mahalia Jackson in along with them, too. I put on some music now while she made the coffee, and we sat listening as we drank it. The white towelling gown showed only her brown bare feet and hands, and her oily brown face in which the teeth were as white as the gown; an effect of which she was clearly aware. I wanted to say to her, "I wonder if your friend with the binoculars would bother now," but I didn't. That evening I saw her going out, obviously dressed up to meet the boy-friend. She really looked like something that had just stepped off the plane from St. Tropez; no one would have believed that it was only our back garden.

Sheila came back to London but after ten days the change in the children was dismaying, and she said to me, shamefaced, "Would you think it crazy if I went to Udgewick again on Friday?" The baby had kept us awake between three and five night after night, and the two little girls' nagging was obviously their way of showing how confined they felt, after the freedom of the fields and the beach. "For heaven's sake—who knows when we'll ever get a summer like this again?"

She took Renate with her and when I went down the following weekend they were all looking marvellous. The two nights I was there, there wasn't a sound from the boy before half past seven in the morning, and the girls had the charm of children who have found completely satisfactory outlets for their fierce energy. Renate was teaching them to swim. Sheila said how much nicer the girl was, down at Udgewick; much more natural— "None of that posing, and looking out of the corner of one eye to catch the effect. How's she when she's with you in London, now—not sour about doing things, I hope, is she?" I told Sheila how, on the contrary, the girl was very amiable. Did what she had to do in the house and didn't pester me with chatter. "Of course, she hasn't much to do, and that suits her." And I told Sheila how she spent hours maintaining her tan, and had had to come indoors to escape someone spying on her through binoculars. "Ah yes, that's an old story, with Renate," said Sheila, smiling to see that I had been taken in as she had.

"At first it was Basil from upstairs looking at her on the landing when she came to the bathroom. She told me she always hung her dressing gown over the keyhole." We both giggled; thinking of the man rather than the girl. "I told her that Basil was madly in love with Rodney and that if he did forget himself long enough to look at a woman, a skinny one like me would be more to his taste than a pear-bottomed beauty like her." I grinned at Sheila. "How'd she take that?" "Oh poor Renate! Said there were plenty of *them* in Germany, too; she can't seem to make up her mind—she feels herself somehow the prey of men, and yet she's affronted at the idea that there are some who prefer another quarry."

Renate came back with me to London on Sunday night. It was such a lovely evening and Sheila and I were feeling so fond of each other that I didn't leave till later than usual. With the girl beside me I drove through the beautiful Constable country in the darkening desertion of a country night, and just before closing time we stopped at the pub where I usually break the journey. It was true that quite a few people did look at her as we sat drinking our beer; specially the wife of the pub-keeper. Renate had on tight cotton trousers that got caught between the two halves of her backside when she walked and that sitting in the car had creased in front from the point of her pelvis up each thigh. She leant on the bar sleepily, her hair hanging tangled over her fists, and smiled with a croaky little clearing of her throat, now and then. It was true, too (seeing them together on the beach that afternoon), that although she and Sheila used the same chemical oil to make themselves brown, the girl's tan was alive, like the colour of a plant in full sap, while Sheila's was a dark, leathery polish on her wrists and cheekbones and the curved blade of each calf.

Renate had given up talking to me in German as soon as her English became more fluent than my German, but in the pub that night, for some reason she suddenly began to talk to me in German. It was not much; just a remark or two, at intervals, and a snatch of conversation, but it produced the effect of a couple who want to communicate without having others understand what they say. The atmosphere of the pub, very friendly and general when we came in, turned aside from us as from the presence of intimacy. I was embarrassed, because it seemed so absurd; all she said was some remark about the dog, and then a harmless anecdote about the fisherman's pub at Udgewick. As we got into the car again, I said, "Why are you talking German tonight?" and she said, in English now, "German? I didn't realize. If I'm tired sometimes, I suppose, I . . ." And I felt again, as it is so easy to do with these foreign girls, that I'd stupidly hurt her feelings.

But half an hour later, when her head sagged against my shoulder as if in sleep, I had the strong feeling that she was *not* asleep, and was ready to doubt her again. What was she up to? Well, not much mystery about that—what could she be up to; but then, she might really be asleep. . . . The car was going down the middle of empty streets through the ugly endless town of Essex; the only wakeful creature passing before closed doors and shop windows full of dummies, I was carried in silent procession like a conqueror from whom the whole population has shut itself away. At last, there was a cat under a streetlight. The girl breathed with deep, suspicious evenness. Her hair, not far from my left ear, was a different colour from what it had been when she arrived in England; I noticed that now it was bleached silvery-blond in streaks, and—looking down on it from close quarters like this—was seen to be made much fairer altogether. It was thick straight hair and very pretty, in this tabby-cat version. The cat in the road was a black one. Perhaps the dark hair she had had when she came was not real, either; I idly remembered the fine, reddish springs of hair stuck against the bath lately—with Sheila away, it wasn't cleaned as scrupulously as it might have been. The girl against my side felt so warm she might really be asleep now, and yet I still felt sure she wasn't. The warmth of another human being is a strange sort of communication that you can't attain in any other way. You can know a person extremely well—I'm not talking of a girl like the one who was leaning against me that night, but someone with whom you have had real understanding and sympathy for a long time—and still if the occasion arises when you are brought into close physical contact with him or her you become aware of an ever-present being whom you did not know at all. With a girl like this—her youngness, her consciously paraded innocent femaleness made palpable and personal in weight and contact —certain thoughts were inevitable. I wondered if I would have taken the weight so impersonally if I hadn't happened to have made love with Sheila the previous night, and then again that afternoon when everyone in the cottage was supposed to be having a Sunday nap. It's easy not to use people, even women, when both desire and human isolation have been put safely into the hands of another. Certainly if I hadn't just spent the weekend with Sheila, my body at least, if not the more selective manifestations of myself, would have responded. I had nothing to congratulate myself on. I drove, taking the pressure of the girl as if I had been her own grandfather, but weight under these circumstances grows more and more unbearable and at last I pulled my shoulder and arm firmly away and reached for the packet of cigarettes on the ledge below the windscreen. Then I was quite sure, from the way she "woke up," that she had not been asleep at all. "Ach, that's fantastic . . . I'm so sorry . . . !"

"You weigh a ton, Renate, I can tell you that."

But she took it well. It was always by taking things well that she also took the advantage from you. "Oh, I've got fat, lazing away at Udgewick. I think more than five pounds."

"Well, stay awake now, will you? We'll be home in about an hour."

"I sing to keep awake. That's okay?" She threw back her tousled hair, gave a long yawn that cut off like an impatient snarl, and hugging her arms across her body began to sing German songs she must have learnt at school.

I suppose I may remember them, must have heard them around me in the streets and so on; I was only just of school-going age when I left, and so I never went to school there. But the association of these songs with the Horst Wessel crowd, the marching youths and militant mobs, seems reinforced, for me, by something ungraspable that comes from Germany itself, from memory itself. When I hear these songs it is not quite as Sheila or others hear them. And that night, as Renate sang, again I recognized something; it's not more than that. I looked at Renate's profile, she who had learnt the songs after Hitler was dead. My mother must have learnt them too, before Hitler was heard of. They are old, patriotic, sentimental, heart-thumping, drum-thumping martial songs that seem to fit any regime the Germans are capable of. If I turn on the radio and hear those songs I at once turn it off, but I let Renate go on singing because, driving along fast at night alone with the songs I had the feeling that I might be able to grasp what it was that I always only vaguely recognize; there was curiosity as well as curiousness in the feeling. Sometimes she paused between one verse and the next, making a false start, or running over words she was not sure of. I said, "I suppose you must've had a grim time as a little kid, just after the war. It was Cologne you lived in, wasn't it?"

"Oh, my family went away. A relation had a big house—in the mountains. He was working with the Americans afterwards, so we were all right, we were with him all the time. It was a big house and everything." She seemed put off, unable to remember what she had been singing. She was silent for a minute—a minute is a long time when you are being borne along in a car without distraction—and then she began again, a different song: "*Es war ein-mal ein treuer Husar . . . der liebt sein Mädchen ein ganzes Jahr . . . Ein ganzes Jahr, und noch viel mehr, die Liebe nahm kein Ende mehr. . . . Die Lie-be nahm kein Ende mehr. . . .*" Now I had the feeling that *she* was echoing something privately recognized, something that had nothing to do with a sing-song in a car, and that she had not learnt at school. The genre of the song predated her in a different way from the jolly marching songs; love-sickness, for her, would find expression in the repertoire of rock singers. I heard in her voice the Cologne waitress or factory girl who must have been her mother, impatiently waiting about on rainy streetcorners for the Nazi soldier or SS man who was her lover.

"In Bavaria? Your uncle worked with the Occupation Forces?"

"Well, he was all over the place."

No uncle. Probably no Bavarian mountains, either. Only

flattened Cologne, the rats in the rubble, the children scaveng-
ing for frozen potatoes, that I had seen, as I had seen the
pictures of the gas ovens where my mother was burnt, in magazines and newsreels.

"*Ein ganzes Jahr, und noch viel mehr . . . Die Liebe nahm
kein Ende mehr . . .*" she sang.

But Mahalia Jackson was what she really liked, in the daylight, in London, in our kitchen. She played it when I was
there, now, too. She was always about when I was working; I
didn't move upstairs to the living room, either. The rug under
the windows took on the permanency of a piece of furniture,
with magazines, books, ashtrays, apples, and dirty coffee cups
consolidating its existence. Often I squatted down on it in the
sun while we drank our coffee. We even took to eating our
lunch cheese and fruit there, instead of at the kitchen table.
Renate wore her bikini or wrapped herself in the big towelling
gown, which was no longer so white. Sheila had once said,
admiring Renate dressed up to go out, you would never think
she could be "the same grubby slut" you saw around the house;
which just goes to show how little women really know about
attractiveness, although they're always practising attraction.
Renate's marvellous sluttishness was just what was wonderful
about her, and what made her different from all the smart little
London girls she got herself up to resemble when she went out.
She was *real*—not in the down-to-earth way that my darling
Sheila, procreator and friend, is real—but in the way that the
abstraction "life" suddenly becomes real when you're out on a
river and the smell of the water and the glare of the light given
off it come in your face, all at once. There Renate was, with a
biscuit crumb caught in her navel, the long tips of her carefully
grown and painted nails scratching with monkey absentness in
her untidy hair while she read—occasionally silently mouthing a
difficult word—far more voluptuous, in a way she herself would
never understand, than the voluptuous image of herself that she
tried to sustain. I looked at her and wondered if she complained
about me—"looking at her," "after" her—as she complained to
me about other men. I noticed that she kept the door from the

kitchen into the garden locked, now, and I knew why: she didn't want Mrs. Main to come walking into the kitchen and find her lying on her rug in the bikini; find us together; from the garden you couldn't see anything in the room below windowsill level. It was as if the intimacy that she had so absurdly shammed by talking to me in her hoarse voice in German in the pub that night couldn't be shaken off.

Often she came and looked over my shoulder at my drawings. One morning she said, "It's nice."

"You mean the working drawings of a cantilever roof for a garage in Middlesex?"

"I mean it's nice being able to work at home, like you." She had on the towelling gown and it smelled, so near me, of the slightly rancid sun-tan oil; she saved her perfume for when she went out. "It's nice if you're married, I mean, and you can be at home together."

"Yes, but it doesn't work that way, does it? There are babies and the house is full."

She moved round and stood at the side of the drawing board, the hard edge visibly cutting into her stomach while she squinted at the plan. "Yes, I know. Of course I don't think I'll get married, not soon."

She accepted freedom with a show of nonchalance. I wanted to take it from her, to thrust my hand between the towelling revers crossed over her breasts, down between, where the crucifix and some other little amulet hung.

"It's funny, I suppose I feel at home with you because you're really German too."

I said in stiff reservation, "My mother was German." I wondered if Sheila had ever told her the rest; I could not, I could not give it to her. My hand remained on the board, trembling.

Two weeks passed like this and then the weather changed and I went to fetch Sheila home. When we got back to London the rug had gone, and the gramophone; only my drawing board remained in the kitchen. But with the children running about and cooking going on, there was no room, and I took the board upstairs to the living room. "How dreary it feels in here!" Sheila said, opening the windows. It was true that without the passage of human use, the waves of people's voices touching furniture and books and walls, a room can go dead in two weeks. The fog began, we lit the gas fire for the first time, the boy wet the carpet—soon the room was informed with life again. Winter came and the rain, and from where I worked I looked down on rows of sodden napkins hiding the back garden.

At the beginning of December, Renate was taken ill at the breakfast table. She was giving the baby his porridge when she suddenly doubled up with cramp in her stomach. She had been out the evening before, and Sheila, suspecting snack bars and tearoom pies, immediately said, "What did you eat?" Renate said, no, nothing—and then remembered that, for a joke, really, she had tried some cockles, off a street barrow. The pain came back and she had to lie down. Her face was cheese-pale and damp. Sheila said, "Any kind of shellfish poisoning's no joke. We'd better get the doctor." She telephoned and caught him before he went on his morning round, so that he arrived before I had gone off to the office. He's a friend of ours and when I heard him coming upstairs after examining the girl, I came out of our bedroom to see him off. Instead, he turned into the living room, signalling me in after him with a jerk of the head. "She's having a miscarriage," he said.

"*What?*"

He smiled. "Fish poisoning. It happens every day."

"But, good God, we never noticed anything? How is it possible?"

He was still smiling patiently. "Well, I don't suppose she's more than four months. She may have looked a little thicker round the middle, that's all."

"Oh Christ."

"It happens all the time with these girls. Hundreds of them. Can you get her to the hospital quickly? I'll arrange everything there, for you. I'm sorry, I can't wait now."

As we walked to the front door he asked, "D'you know the boy-friend?"

"She never brought anyone here."

He put on his checked schoolboy scarf and raincoat. "Probably a Pakistani. With German girls, it's nearly always Pakistanis."

"Oh no," I said, "not this one. Certainly not a Pakistani."

Sheila was with Renate, and when I went down and knocked at the bedroom door, they were packing a suitcase. Renate sat on the bed with her duffel coat on already, and while I stood waiting to take the case she got up slowly and went over to the dressing table and combed her hair. She drew it back very tight and secured it with the sort of metal clips that Sheila uses for the little girls; it was a kind of ritual putting aside of vanity. Remnants of last night's make-up were dark round her eyes. Her forehead shone high and greasy. She had the faraway, listening expression of someone awaiting the return of pain. When it came, her slightly open mouth closed on it. Only practical remarks were exchanged between the three of us, and when I met Sheila's eyes her eyebrows lifted faintly for a moment in helpless communication. She fussed around the car before we left, filled with anguish, I could see, at the idea of this girl going, alone, as a stranger, through an ordeal that she herself had known with the support of love and the familiar. She kept telling me the best way to get to the hospital without being too much delayed by traffic. "Yes, yes, all right. I know how to look after her, don't worry. I've got you to the hospital safely three times, don't forget." Again, it was the wrong thing to have said; I saw the tendons in Sheila's neck tauten as she tried to shake her head vehemently at me without moving it, as we drove away.

Renate, beside me, said, "I'm sorry. And you have to go to town today." She was referring to the fact that I was wearing my decent suit, that I had emerged, as a man can, from the domestic messiness in which we all lived, ready to disappear into the orderly ease of consultations and expense-account lunches. It didn't occur very often, with me; but that happened to be one of the days when Iscott had decided we ought to play the big boys and give a prospective client the full "leading architect" treatment: which, so far as Iscott is concerned, means lunch at the Savoy. "It's okay. Only at lunchtime."

We drove in silence for a block and then I said, "Is there

anyone you'd like me to get in touch with—to let know that
you're in hospital?"

"No, no one."

We had both spoken without glancing at each other.

"Are you quite sure? Isn't there someone you ought to tell,
Renate?"

"No."

"Isn't that rather foolish?"

"I don't think so."

It couldn't have been a Pakistani, with Renate, but did it
matter who else it could have been? An Italian, an Englishman,
a Welshman, an Irishman with a name she thought was Scots?
What did another label matter in a situation that was already a
label, attached to hundreds of girls like her? Four months. It
must have been going on when she was spending her time between Udgewick with Sheila, and London; sometime when she
was alone with me, those two weeks. It probably happened
then. Extraordinary to think that she was going out and sleeping with somebody, then. It couldn't possibly have been a Pakistani, with Renate, but it could have been me. It might have
been me. If she hadn't been a German, it might have been me.
It would have been me. Nothing stood between me and Renate's body but a simple prejudice, the smoke from the pyre of
my mother's innocent body reeking round a body that was no
doubt equally innocent. I could congratulate myself on that if I
wanted to.

"Well, if you don't even want to tell us who it was, that's
your affair, I suppose."

For the second time since she'd been living with us she answered without projecting any picture of herself, without playing a role of any kind. "It was me, myself, wasn't it?" she said,
turning with a dull smile.

As we reached the hospital she said, "I should take my examination on Friday, too." Her English course at the foreign students' institute was just about completed.

"Oh well, perhaps you can sit for it later." I supposed that
she'd be going home, back to Germany, now, anyway. It occurred to me that I had no idea what it was that she hoped to do

with her English "proficiency" certificate; what these girls did, when they got back home. "Will it matter, if you don't get the certificate? I mean, you've learnt the language, certificate or not."

"No, no I must have it, otherwise I won't qualify."

"For what?"

"Someone promised for me a job with Lufthansa. An air hostess. You must have the English certificate."

An air hostess. Oh yes, I'd heard—now I remembered—all these girls long to be air hostesses; just as I'd since heard that when they got "in trouble" it was always Pakistanis.

We went into the hospital. I sat with her until they wheeled her away to the operating theatre. There was nobody else to come.

It was after that that we had our bad time with her. She used to get the blues, the crying fits that Sheila says are inevitable for a woman who has lost a baby. I protested that she could hardly be said to have "lost" something she had never seen, hadn't wanted, and whose existence she had never even admitted. But Sheila was indignant, the female championing her kind against the male, whose kind I, of course, shared with whoever the man was who had given Renate a child. "It's not a matter of reason, darling. It's simply what happens." "You can't tell me she doesn't consider herself damn lucky she got rid of it so easily." "Well yes, of course, I mean she came here to learn English, she wanted to go back home to Germany with—" "And become an air hostess. Yes, I know. Well, now she's free again to go back and be one." "But all this doesn't matter—she's *still* a woman who's lost a child. In her body and in her being, whatever she felt about it."

Well, this aspect of the girl's femaleness was as remote from me as the other aspect, when we had been together alone in the house those weeks, had been close to me. But I put up with her, or rather put up with Sheila's putting up with her, and behaved as I was told we should. Renate got much thinner but remained very attractive. She had sat for and passed her exam but there seemed to be no sign of her going home; when I asked about this, Sheila said that Renate had begged to stay on a while. "The poor thing feels so muddled up and disturbed, she says she can't face her family so soon." We arranged with the *au pair* agency to extend her permit. She and Sheila seemed quite intimate now. "I'm trying to help her as much as I can," Sheila said; but she couldn't disguise that the effort got on her nerves. Renate was now as expansive about herself as she had once been reserved. Sheila said that she followed her around, talking until Sheila could have screamed. She had even confided in Sheila some explanation about the pregnancy—it had been some very important man with whom she had been secretly having an affair in the summer, a man whose identity she couldn't possibly have confessed because his career and reputation were too important to be risked by such a happening; she didn't even want him to know that it had occurred. "Poor thing," said Sheila, when she had finished telling me this, putting her hand on my shoulder to stop me saying what both of us were thinking: that not a word of it was true. I said, "It doesn't matter a damn, anyway, at this stage."

"No, of course not. But she's going about with someone again."

"Oh, she is? I see that she's done something else with her hair."

"Yes . . . and I haven't the faintest idea who the chap is. She tells me all sorts of stories, about an Oxford don who plays the piano in a Soho club, and what-not. And somebody else from the Third Programme whose brother is a Member of Parliament."

"Good God, Sheila, you're not her mother. She came here to help you look after the kids, not to be looked after by you. Why doesn't she go home to Germany? We're going to have the same business all over again in the next few months!"

"But we can't throw her out? We can't push her away in the shaky state she's in, knowing what happened to her? We don't even know if she's got a real home to go back to in Germany. Do we?"

Sheila felt in the pocket of my shirt for my cigarettes and took one. She sat down, and drawing the smoke back into her lungs with wide nostrils, said, "I don't know, is she much cleverer, deeper, and more sensitive than she looks? And do you get the impression, at moments, that she's pathetically inadequate and naïve—stupid, even—only because she can't break through the strangeness of being an exile, because she's shut up in her other tongue and other life? I just don't know. You see, even if the important man never did exist—the reason why she won't bring one of her young men to sit with her at night when she's with the babies is not shyness, but some kind of scorn for us—the implication that her 'friends' are too lofty, too sophisticated to be asked to share baby-sitting like any other student. *That* sort of sham—is it real, or does she know only too well it's nonsense, and use it only to put us off her track, since we'll never understand whatever it is she really is, anyway?"

"A potential air hostess."

Sheila reproved with a short bark of a laugh. "That's all very well."

But at last, one day about six months ago, Renate did go home to Germany. Sheila came to me and said, "I've talked to Renate about going back. It was all quite amicable; I just told her that she had a jolly good working knowledge of English now, and that she ought to be putting it to better use than talking baby-talk to Charlesie." I laughed out loud and put my arm round her. "Clever girl. Good for you. But what bit you, all of a sudden?" "Well, I've been feeling I simply couldn't stick it any longer. And she's fine again now; she has to go home sometime."

Renate left at the end of the month. She was busily engaged at the sewing machine in the kitchen for the last two weeks; Sheila said she had bought up some remnants and was making herself a new wardrobe to take along. One evening in the last week she appeared at the living-room door with an armful of books. "Oh, Mr. Stephens, I must return to you your books." I had no idea she had such a sizable chunk of our library in her room; there was a splotch of nail varnish, hard and bright as sealing wax, on the cover of one book, and something that looked like a coffee stain on another. As I pushed them in where I could find spaces on the shelves I noticed curiously what her choice had been—as a magpie, picking on a "right" sounding title or author, or as a reader?—Auden, A. J. P. Taylor, Kingsley Amis, Faulkner—and *Ulysses* was still among them. She kept emerging from her basement room with things that she had to return; a weekend case, a box of paper clips, even a programme of some forgotten concert. Despite this leisurely clearing-up her room was apparently still in a terrible mess on the day before she was due to leave. Sheila had promised one of her African student friends that he could move in for a month and she was rather annoyed that Renate should take so casually the normal obligation to leave the place habitable. "It's a pigsty," Sheila told me in an indignant whisper; Renate was in the hall outside, looking for her raincoat among the pile collected there.

Renate promised cheerfully that she would shampoo the rug and clean out the room while we were out that last evening. But when we came home after midnight she was sitting in the living room, Mahalia Jackson singing, and Charlesie, who was eighteen months then, and quite a lump, in her arms. She smiled at us over him. Her hair, dark again now, touched his, which was the same colour. The warmth of sleep had risen to his cheeks and cherry nose; the same colour showed in her cheeks. She mouthed, "Sh-hh-h . . ." and got up slowly under his weight and put him in his mother's arms.

Sheila whispered, "But why isn't he in bed?"

"I've been holding him two hours. He couldn't go to sleep."

When Sheila had put the child into his cot, she came back for an explanation. "He was so unhappy, poor Charlesie," Renate was saying to me, flushed and laughing, wiggling her bare feet and stretching her legs in the old tight green pants. "I don't know, if he had a stomach-ache or what . . . ? I was not able to do a thing, to finish my packing, nothing. I held him in my arms two hours. . . ."

As we closed our bedroom door, Sheila burst out, "But why

couldn't she have put him down once he *was* asleep, for heaven's sake! What did she have to hold him for, all the time! Now she'll never clean the room, of course."

I came home from town at lunchtime next day and said, "Renate get away all right?" but I didn't need to ask; the moment I walked into the house I could feel that she was gone.

A Chip of Glass Ruby

When the duplicating machine was brought into the house, Bamjee said, "Isn't it enough that you've got the Indians' troubles on your back?" Mrs. Bamjee said, with a smile that showed the gap of a missing tooth but was confident all the same, "What's the difference, Yusuf? We've all got the same troubles."

"Don't tell me that. We don't have to carry passes; let the natives protest against passes on their own, there are millions of them. Let them go ahead with it."

The nine Bamjee and Pahad children were present at this exchange as they were always; in the small house that held them all there was no room for privacy for the discussion of matters they were too young to hear, and so they had never been too young to hear anything. Only their sister and half-sister, Girlie, was missing; she was the eldest, and married. The children looked expectantly, unalarmed and interested, at Bamjee, who had neither left the dining room nor settled down again to the task of rolling his own cigarettes, which had been interrupted by the arrival of the duplicator. He looked at the thing that had come hidden in a wash-basket and conveyed in a black man's taxi, and the children turned on it too, their black eyes surrounded by thick lashes like those still, open flowers with hairy tentacles that close on whatever touches them.

"A fine thing to have on the dining-room table," was all he said at last. They smelled the machine among them; a smell of cold black grease. He went out, heavily on tiptoe, in his troubled way.

"It's going to go nicely on the sideboard!" Mrs. Bamjee was busy making a place by removing the two pink glass vases filled

117

with plastic carnations and the hand-painted velvet runner with the picture of the Taj Mahal.

After supper she began to run off leaflets on the machine. The family lived in the dining room—the three other rooms in the house were full of beds—and they were all there. The older children shared a bottle of ink while they did their homework, and the two little ones pushed a couple of empty milk bottles in and out the chair legs. The three-year-old fell asleep and was carted away by one of the girls. They all drifted off to bed eventually; Bamjee himself went before the older children—he was a fruit and vegetable hawker and was up at half past four every morning to get to the market by five. "Not long now," said Mrs. Bamjee. The older children looked up and smiled at him. He turned his back on her. She still wore the traditional clothing of a Moslem woman, and her body, which was scraggy and unimportant as a dress on a peg when it was not host to a child, was wrapped in the trailing rags of a cheap sari, and her thin black plait was greased. When she was a girl, in the Transvaal town where they lived still, her mother fixed a chip of glass ruby in her nostril; but she had abandoned that adornment as too old-style, even for her, long ago.

She was up until long after midnight, turning out leaflets. She did it as if she might have been pounding chillies.

Bamjee did not have to ask what the leaflets were. He had read the papers. All the past week Africans had been destroying their passes and then presenting themselves for arrest. Their leaders were jailed on charges of incitement, campaign offices were raided—someone must be helping the few minor leaders who were left to keep the campaign going without offices or equipment. What was it the leaflets would say—"Don't go to work tomorrow," "Day of Protest," "Burn Your Pass for Freedom"? He didn't want to see.

He was used to coming home and finding his wife sitting at the dining-room table deep in discussion with strangers or people whose names were familiar by repute. Some were prominent Indians, like the lawyer, Dr. Abdul Mohammed Khan, or the big businessman, Mr. Moonsamy Patel, and he was flattered, in a suspicious way, to meet them in his house. As he came home from work next day he met Dr. Khan coming out of the house, and Dr. Khan—a highly educated man—said to him, "A wonderful woman." But Bamjee had never caught his wife out in any presumption; she behaved properly, as any Moslem woman should, and once her business with such gentlemen was over would never, for instance, have sat down to eat with them. He found her now back in the kitchen, setting about the preparation of dinner and carrying on a conversation on several different wave lengths with the children. "It's really a shame if you're tired of lentils, Jimmy, because that's what you're getting— Amina, hurry up, get a pot of water going—don't worry, I'll mend that in a minute, just bring the yellow cotton, and there's a needle in the cigarette box on the sideboard."

"Was that Dr. Khan leaving?" said Bamjee.

"Yes, there's going to be a stay-at-home on Monday. Desai's ill, and he's got to get the word around by himself. Bob Jali was up all last night printing leaflets, but he's gone to have a tooth out." She had always treated Bamjee as if it were only a mannerism that made him appear uninterested in politics, the way some woman will persist in interpreting her husband's bad temper as an endearing gruffness hiding boundless goodwill, and she talked to him of these things just as she passed on to him neighbours' or family gossip.

"What for do you want to get mixed up with these killings and stonings and I don't know what? Congress should keep out of it. Isn't it enough with the Group Areas?"

She laughed. "Now, Yusuf, you know you don't believe that. Look how you said the same thing when the Group Areas started in Natal. You said we should begin to worry when we get moved out of our own houses here in the Transvaal. And then your own mother lost her house in Noorddorp, and there you are; you saw that nobody's safe. Oh, Girlie was here this afternoon, she says Ismail's brother's engaged—that's nice, isn't it? His mother will be pleased; she was worried."

"Why was she worried?" asked Jimmy, who was fifteen, and old enough to patronize his mother.

"Well, she wanted to see him settled. There's a party on

Sunday week at Ismail's place—you'd better give me your suit to give to the cleaners tomorrow, Yusuf."

One of the girls presented herself at once. "I'll have nothing to wear, Ma."

Mrs. Bamjee scratched her sallow face. "Perhaps Girlie will lend you her pink, eh? Run over to Girlie's place now and say I say will she lend it to you."

The sound of commonplaces often does service as security, and Bamjee, going to sit in the armchair with the shiny armrests that was wedged between the dining-room table and the sideboard, lapsed into an unthinking doze that, like all times of dreamlike ordinariness during those weeks, was filled with uneasy jerks and starts back into reality. The next morning, as soon as he got to market, he heard that Dr. Khan had been arrested. But that night Mrs. Bamjee sat up making a new dress for her daughter; the sight disarmed Bamjee, reassured him again, against his will, so that the resentment he had been making ready all day faded into a morose and accusing silence. Heaven knew, of course, who came and went in the house during the day. Twice in that week of riots, raids, and arrests, he found black women in the house when he came home; plain ordinary native women in doeks, drinking tea. This was not a thing other Indian women would have in their homes, he thought bitterly; but then his wife was not like other people, in a way he could not put his finger on, except to say what it was not: not scandalous, not punishable, not rebellious. It was, like the attraction that had led him to marry her, Pahad's widow with five children, something he could not see clearly.

When the Special Branch knocked steadily on the door in the small hours of Thursday morning, he did not wake up, for his return to consciousness was always set in his mind to half past four, and that was more than an hour away. Mrs. Bamjee got up herself, struggled into Jimmy's raincoat, which was hanging over a chair, and went to the front door. The clock on the wall—a wedding present when she married Pahad—showed three o'clock when she snapped on the light, and she knew at

once who it was on the other side of the door. Although she was
not surprised, her hands shook like a very old person's as she
undid the locks and the complicated catch on the wire burglar-
proofing. And then she opened the door and they were there—
two coloured policemen in plain clothes. "Zanip Bamjee?"
"Yes."

As they talked, Bamjee woke up in the sudden terror of
having overslept. Then he became conscious of men's voices.
He heaved himself out of bed in the dark and went to the
window, which, like the front door, was covered with a heavy
mesh of thick wire against intruders from the dingy lane it
looked upon. Bewildered, he appeared in the dining room,
where the policemen were searching through a soapbox of papers beside the duplicating machine. "Yusuf, it's for me," Mrs.
Bamjee said.

At once, the snap of a trap, realization came. He stood there
in an old shirt before the two policemen, and the woman was
going off to prison because of the natives. "There you are!" he
shouted, standing away from her. "That's what you've got for
it. Didn't I tell you? Didn't I? That's the end of it now. That's
the finish. That's what it's come to." She listened with her head
at the slightest tilt to one side, as if to ward off a blow, or in
compassion.

Jimmy, Pahad's son, appeared at the door with a suitcase; two
or three of the girls were behind him. "Here, Ma, you take my
green jersey." "I've found your clean blouse." Bamjee had to
keep moving out of their way as they helped their mother to
make ready. It was like the preparation for one of the family
festivals his wife made such a fuss over; wherever he put himself, they bumped into him. Even the two policemen mumbled,
"Excuse me," and pushed past into the rest of the house to
continue their search. They took with them a tome that Nehru
had written in prison; it had been bought from a persevering
travelling salesman and kept, for years, on the mantelpiece.
"Oh, don't take that, please," Mrs. Bamjee said suddenly, clinging to the arm of the man who had picked it up.

The man held it away from her.

"What does it matter, Ma?"

It was true that no one in the house had ever read it; but she said, "It's for my children."

"Ma, leave it." Jimmy, who was squat and plump, looked like a merchant advising a client against a roll of silk she had set her heart on. She went into the bedroom and got dressed. When she came out in her old yellow sari with a brown coat over it, the faces of the children were behind her like faces on the platform at a railway station. They kissed her good-bye. The policemen did not hurry her, but she seemed to be in a hurry just the same.

"What am I going to do?" Bamjee accused them all.

The policemen looked away patiently.

"It'll be all right. Girlie will help. The big children can manage. And Yusuf—" The children crowded in around her; two of the younger ones had awakened and appeared, asking shrill questions.

"Come on," said the policemen.

"I want to speak to my husband." She broke away and came back to him, and the movement of her sari hid them from the rest of the room for a moment. His face hardened in suspicious anticipation against the request to give some message to the next fool who would take up her pamphleteering until he, too, was arrested. "On Sunday," she said. "Take them on Sunday." He did not know what she was talking about. "The engagement party," she whispered, low and urgent. "They shouldn't miss it. Ismail will be offended."

They listened to the car drive away. Jimmy bolted and barred the front door, and then at once opened it again; he put on the raincoat that his mother had taken off. "Going to tell Girlie," he said. The children went back to bed. Their father did not say a word to any of them; their talk, the crying of the younger ones and the argumentative voices of the older, went on in the bedrooms. He found himself alone; he felt the night all around him. And then he happened to meet the clock face and saw with a terrible sense of unfamiliarity that this was not the secret night but an hour he should have recognized: the time he always got up. He pulled on his trousers and his dirty white hawker's coat and wound his grey muffler up to the stubble on his chin and went to work.

The duplicating machine was gone from the sideboard. The policemen had taken it with them, along with the pamphlets and the conference reports and the stack of old newspapers that had collected on top of the wardrobe in the bedroom—not the thick dailies of the white men, but the thin, impermanent-looking papers that spoke up, sometimes interrupted by suppression or lack of money, for the rest. It was all gone. When he had married her and moved in with her and her five children, into what had been the Pahad and became the Bamjee house, he had not recognized the humble, harmless, and apparently useless routine tasks—the minutes of meetings being written up on the dining-room table at night, the government blue books that were read while the latest baby was suckled, the employment of the fingers of the older children in the fashioning of crinkle-paper Congress rosettes—as activity intended to move mountains. For years and years he had not noticed it, and now it was gone.

The house was quiet. The children kept to their lairs, crowded on the beds with the doors shut. He sat and looked at the sideboard, where the plastic carnations and the mat with the picture of the Taj Mahal were in place. For the first few weeks he never spoke of her. There was the feeling, in the house, that he had wept and raged at her, that boulders of reproach had thundered down upon her absence, and yet he had said not one word. He had not been to inquire where she was; Jimmy and Girlie had gone to Mohammed Ebrahim, the lawyer, and when he found out that their mother had been taken—when she was arrested, at least—to a prison in the next town, they had stood about outside the big prison door for hours while they waited to be told where she had been moved from there. At last they had discovered that she was fifty miles away, in Pretoria. Jimmy asked Bamjee for five shillings to help Girlie pay the train fare to Pretoria, once she had been interviewed by the police and had been given a permit to visit her mother; he put three two-shilling pieces on the table for Jimmy to pick up, and the boy, looking at him keenly, did not know whether the extra shilling meant anything, or whether it was merely that Bamjee had no change.

It was only when relations and neighbours came to the house that Bamjee would suddenly begin to talk. He had never been so expansive in his life as he was in the company of these visitors, many of them come on a polite call rather in the nature of a visit of condolence. "Ah, yes, yes, you can see how I am— you see what has been done to me. Nine children, and I am on the cart all day. I get home at seven or eight. What are you to do? What can people like us do?"

"Poor Mrs. Bamjee. Such a kind lady."

"Well, you see for yourself. They walk in here in the middle of the night and leave a houseful of children. I'm out on the cart all day, I've got a living to earn." Standing about in his shirt sleeves, he became quite animated; he would call for the girls to bring fruit drinks for the visitors. When they were gone, it was as if he, who was orthodox if not devout and never drank liquor, had been drunk and abruptly sobered up; he looked dazed and could not have gone over in his mind what he had been saying. And as he cooled, the lump of resentment and wrongedness stopped his throat again.

Bamjee found one of the little boys the centre of a self-important group of championing brothers and sisters in the dining room one evening. "They've been cruel to Ahmed."

"What has he done?" said the father.

"Nothing! Nothing!" The little girl stood twisting her handkerchief excitedly.

An older one, thin as her mother, took over, silencing the others with a gesture of her skinny hand. "They did it at school today. They made an example of him."

"What is an example?" said Bamjee impatiently.

"The teacher made him come up and stand in front of the whole class, and he told them, 'You see this boy? His mother's in jail because she likes the natives so much. She wants the Indians to be the same as natives.'"

"It's terrible," he said. His hands fell to his sides. "Did she ever think of this?"

"That's why Ma's *there*," said Jimmy, putting aside his comic and emptying out his schoolbooks upon the table. "That's all the kids need to know. Ma's there because things like this happen. Petersen's a coloured teacher, and it's his black blood that's brought him trouble all his life, I suppose. He hates anyone who says everybody's the same, because that takes away from him his bit of whiteness that's all he's got. What d'you expect? It's nothing to make too much fuss about."

"Of course, you are fifteen and you know everything," Bamjee mumbled at him.

"I don't say that. But I know Ma, anyway." The boy laughed.

There was a hunger strike among the political prisoners, and Bamjee could not bring himself to ask Girlie if her mother was starving herself too. He would not ask; and yet he saw in the young woman's face the gradual weakening of her mother. When the strike had gone on for nearly a week one of the elder children burst into tears at the table and could not eat. Bamjee pushed his own plate away in rage.

Sometimes he spoke out loud to himself while he was driving the vegetable lorry. "What for?" Again and again: "What for?" She was not a modern woman who cut her hair and wore short skirts. He had married a good plain Moslem woman who bore children and stamped her own chillies. He had a sudden vision of her at the duplicating machine, that night just before she was taken away, and he felt himself maddened, baffled, and hopeless. He had become the ghost of a victim, hanging about the scene of a crime whose motive he could not understand and had not had time to learn.

The hunger strike at the prison went into the second week. Alone in the rattling cab of his lorry, he said things that he heard as if spoken by someone else, and his heart burned in fierce agreement with them. "For a crowd of natives who'll smash our shops and kill us in our houses when their time comes." "She will starve herself to death there." "She will die there." "Devils who will burn and kill us." He fell into bed each night like a stone, and dragged himself up in the mornings as a beast of burden is beaten to its feet.

One of these mornings, Girlie appeared very early, while he was wolfing bread and strong tea—alternate sensations of dry solidity and stinging heat—at the kitchen table. Her real name was Fatima, of course, but she had adopted the silly modern name along with the clothes of the young factory girls among whom she worked. She was expecting her first baby in a week or two, and her small face, her cut and curled hair, and the sooty arches drawn over her eyebrows did not seem to belong to her thrust-out body under a clean smock. She wore mauve lipstick and was smiling her cocky little white girl's smile, foolish and bold, not like an Indian girl's at all.

"What's the matter?" he said.

She smiled again. "Don't you know? I told Bobby he must get me up in time this morning. I wanted to be sure I wouldn't miss you today."

"I don't know what you're talking about."

She came over and put her arm up around his unwilling neck and kissed the grey bristles at the side of his mouth. "Many happy returns! Don't you know it's your birthday?"

"No," he said. "I didn't know, didn't think—" He broke the pause by swiftly picking up the bread and giving his attention desperately to eating and drinking. His mouth was busy, but his eyes looked at her, intensely black. She said nothing, but stood there with him. She would not speak, and at last he said, swallowing a piece of bread that tore at his throat as it went down, "I don't remember these things."

The girl nodded, the Woolworth baubles in her ears swinging. "That's the first thing she told me when I saw her yesterday—don't forget it's Bajie's birthday tomorrow."

He shrugged over it. "It means a lot to children. But that's how she is. Whether it's one of the old cousins or the neighbour's grandmother, she always knows when the birthday is. What importance is my birthday, while she's sitting there in a prison? I don't understand how she can do the things she does when her mind is always full of woman's nonsense at the same time—that's what I don't understand with her."

"Oh, but don't you see?" the girl said. "It's because she doesn't want anybody to be left out. It's because she always remembers; remembers everything—people without somewhere to live, hungry kids, boys who can't get educated—remembers all the time. That's how Ma is."

"Nobody else is like that." It was half a complaint.

"No, nobody else," said his stepdaughter.

She sat herself down at the table, resting her belly. He put his head in his hands. "I'm getting old"—but he was overcome by something much more curious, by an answer. He knew why he had desired her, the ugly widow with five children; he knew what way it was in which she was not like the others; it was there, like the fact of the belly that lay between him and her daughter.

The African Magician

Ships always assemble the same cast, and this one was no exception. The passengers were not, of course, the ones you would meet on any of those liners described as floating hotels that take tourists to and fro between places where they never stay long enough to see the bad season come. But, as if supplied by some theatrical agency unmindful of a change of style in the roles available in the world, these passengers setting off up the Congo River instead of across an ocean were those you might have met at any time as long as the colonial era lasted, travelling between the country in Europe where they were born, and the country across the sea where its flag also flew. There was the old hand who inevitably trapped my husband by the hour; released at last, he would come to me deeply under the man's deadly fascination. ". . . twenty-two years . . . prospecting for minerals for the government . . . torpedoed going back to Belgium in the war . . . Free French . . . two and a half years in a Russian prison camp . . . he still carries his card signed by de Gaulle . . ."

"Oh I know, I know, I don't want to see it."

But when the old hand interrupted his evening stroll round the deck to sit down where we sat, outside our cabin, no measure of aloofness, head bent to book, would prevent him from cornering my eye at some point and growling with a pally wink, "Two more year and I sit and drink beer and look at the girls in Brussels. Best beer, best girls in the world." When he saw us, leaning together over the rail but lost from each other and ourselves in the sight of the towering, indifferent fecundity of the wilderness that the river cleaved from height to depth, he would pause, hang about, and then thrust the observation between our heads—"Lot of bloomin' nothing, eh? Country full of nothing. Bush, bush, trees, trees. Put you two metres in there and you won't come out never." His mind ran down towards some constant, smug yet uncertain vision of his retirement, that must have been with him all the twenty-two years. "Bush, nothing."

There were sanitary officers, a police officer, a motor mechanic, agricultural officers, and research workers, returning with their wives and children from home leave in Belgium. The women looked as if they had been carved out of lard, and were in the various stages of reproduction—about to give birth, or looking after small fat children who might have been believed to be in danger of melting. There was a priest who sat among the women in the row of deck-chairs all day, reading paperbacks; he was a big elderly man with a forward-thrust, intelligent jaw, and when he stood up slowly and leant upon the rail, his hard belly lifting his cassock gave him the sudden appearance of an odd affinity with the women around him. There was a newly married couple, of course—that look of a pair tied up for a three-legged race who haven't mastered the gait yet. The husband was ordinary enough but the girl was unexpected, among the browsing herd setting to over the first meal aboard. She was very tall, the same size as her husband, and her long thin naked legs in shorts showed the tense tendon, fleshless, on each inner thigh as she walked. On the extreme thinness and elongation of the rest of her—half pathetic, half elegant—was balanced a very wide square jaw. In profile the face was pretty; full on, the extraordinary width of her blemished forehead, her thick black eyebrows above grey eyes, her very big straight mouth with pale lips, was a distortion of unusual beauty. Her style could have been Vogue model, or beatnik. In fact she was a Belgian country girl who had hit naturally, by an accident of physique and a natural sluttishness, upon what I knew only as a statement of artifice of one kind or another.

The white boat, broad and tiered top-heavy upon the water like a Mississippi paddle steamer, had powerful Diesel engines beating in her flat floor, and we pushed two barges covered with cars, jeeps, and tanks of beer, and another passenger boat, painted drab but soon fluttering with the flags of the third class's washing. There was a lot of life going on down there at the other boat; you could look down the length of the two barges from the deck in front of our cabin and see it— barbering, cooking, a continual swarming and clambering from deck to deck that often overflowed onto the barges. Jars of palm wine passed between our galley and crew's quarters, and their galley. A tin basin full of manioc spinach appeared at intervals moving along in the air from the bowels of the boat beneath our feet; then we saw the straight, easygoing body of the black beauty on whose turban it was balanced. She went down the street of the barges with the languor characteristic of attractive kitchen maids, winding easily between the tethered cars, stopping to disparage a basket of dried fish that had just been dumped aboard from a visiting canoe, or to parry some flattering and insulting suggestion from a member of the crew lounging off duty, and finally disappeared into the boat at the other end.

The police officer's wife noticed a scribble chalked on the barge below us. "My God, take a look at that, will you!" It did not consist, as messages publicly addressed to no one in particular usually do, of curses or declarations of love, but hailed, in misspelt French and the uneven script of some loiterer in Léopoldville harbour, the coming of the country's independence of white man's rule, that was only two months away. "They are mad, truly. They think they can run a country." She was a gay one, strongly made-up, with a small waist and wide jelly-hips in bright skirts, and she had the kind of roving alertness that put her on chatting terms with the whole boat within twenty-four hours. In case I had missed the point, she turned to me and said in English, "They are just like monkeys, you know. We've taught them a few tricks. Really, they are monkeys out from *there*." And she gestured at the forest that we were passing before night and day, while we looked and while we slept.

Our passengers were all white, not because of a colour bar, but because even those few black people who could afford the first class thought it a waste of money. Yet except for the Belgian captain, who never came down among us from his quarters

on the top deck, the entire crew was black, and we were kept
fed and clean by a small band of Congolese men. They managed this with an almost mysterious ease. There were only three
stewards and a barman visible, and often, five minutes before
the bell rang for a meal, I would see them sitting on their
haunches on the barge below us, barefoot and in dirty shorts,
murmuring their perpetual tide of gossip. But however
promptly you presented yourself at table, they were there before
you, in mildewed white cotton suits and forage caps decorated
with the shipping company's badge. Only their bare feet provided a link with the idlers of a few minutes before. The idlers
never looked up and did not notice a greeting from the decks
above them; but the stewards were grinning and persuasive,
pressing food on you, running to get your wine with a happy,
speedy slither that implied a joking reference to your thirst.
When we stopped at river stations and the great refrigerated
hold was opened, we recognized the same three, grunting as
they tossed the weight of half a frozen ox from hand to hand;
once I remarked to George, who waited on us and even took it
upon himself to wake us in time for breakfast, pounding on our
cabin door and calling "Chop! Chop!"—"You were working
hard this afternoon, eh?"

But he looked at me blankly. "Madam?"

"Yes, unloading. I saw you unloading meat."

"It wasn't me," he said.

"Not you, in the green shirt?"

He shook his head vehemently. It appeared as if I had in-
sulted him by the suggestion. And yet it was he, all right, his
gruff laugh and small moustache and splayed toes. "No, no, not
me." Wasn't it a known fact that to white people all black faces
look alike? How could I argue with him?

In the evenings the priest put on grey flannel trousers and
smoked a big cigar; you would have said then that he was a big
businessman, successful and yet retaining some residue of sensitivity in the form of sadness—my husband found out that he
was in fact the financial administrator of a remote and very
large complex of mission schools. I was often aware of him,
without actually seeing him, when I was in our cabin at night:

he liked to stand alone on the deserted bend of the deck, outside. The honeymoon couple (as we thought of the newly married pair, although their honeymoon was over and he was taking her to the inland administrative post where he worked) formed the habit of coming there too, during the hot hours when everyone was resting after lunch. He, with his fair curly hair and rather snouty, good-looking face, would stand looking out at the leap and glitter of the water, but she could see nothing but him, he was blown up to fill the screen of her vision, and in this exaggerated projection, every detail, every hair and pore held her attention like the features of a landscape. Fascinated, she concentrated on squeezing blackheads from his chin. I used to come noisily out of the cabin, hoping to drive this idyll away. But they were not aware of me; she was not aware of the presence of another woman, like herself, recognizing the ugliness of some intimacies when seen, as they never should be, as a spectator. "Why must they choose our deck?" I was indignant.

My husband was amused. "Come on, what's the matter with love?" He lay on his bed grinning, picking at a tooth with a match.

"That's not love. I wouldn't mind nearly so much if I found them copulating on the deck."

"Oh wouldn't you? That's because you never have."

The thing was that I could not help expecting something of that face—the girl's face. As I have said, it was not a fraud in the ways that it might have been—a matter of fashion in faces or ideas. She had come by it honestly, so to speak, and I could not believe that it was not the outward sign of some remarkable quality, not, perhaps, an obvious one, like a talent, but some bony honesty of mind or freshness of spirit. It disappointed me to see that face, surfeit as a baby's bleary with milk with the simplest relationship with a commonplace man. I was reluctant to admit that her intensity at table was merely a ruthless desire to get the choice bits of every dish shovelled onto his plate. I felt irritated when I came upon her, sitting placidly cobbling the torn ribbon of a vulgar frilly petticoat made of rainbow-coloured net: it was simply a face, that was all, clapped on the same old bundle of well-conformed instincts and the same few feelings. Yet every time I saw it I could not suppress a twinge of hopeful disbelief; this was part of the mild preoccupation with a collection of lives you will never touch on again, that, because it is entirely gratuitous, makes a voyage so restful.

Our first stop was in the middle of the night, and next morning we woke up to find the ivory sellers aboard. They came from the forest and the expressions on their faces were made difficult to read by distracting patterns of tattooing, but they wore white cotton vests from a trading store. Out of cardboard school cases they spread ivory toothpicks, paper-knives, and bracelets on the narrow deck, and squatted among them. Nearly all the Belgians had seen this tourist bric-a-brac many times before, but they gathered round, asking prices challengingly, and then putting the stuff down and walking away. A few women, sheepish about it, bought bracelets, and shook them on their wrists as if deciding they were not so bad, after all. One of the agricultural officers, whose child, learning to walk, hampered his father's left leg like a manacle, said, "Have you locked your door? You want to, while these fellows are about. They'll take anything."

The vender outside our cabin hadn't taken anything, but I don't think he had sold anything, either. Just before lunchtime he packed his cardboard case again and went off down to the public thoroughfare of the barges, where a pirogue was tied, trailing alongside in the water like a narrow floating leaf. He did not seem downcast; but then, as I have remarked, it was difficult to tell, with those rows of nicks running in curved lines across his forehead, and the sharp cuts tightening the skin under the eyes.

People brought all sorts of things aboard to sell, and they were all sorts of people, too, for we were following the river a thousand miles through the homes of many tribes. Sometimes old hags with breasts like bellpulls and children with dusty bellies sprang up on the dark river-bank and yelled " '*depen-DANCE!*" The young men and girls of the same village would swim out ahead of our convoy, and drift past us with darting, uplifted eyes, begging for jam tins from the galley. Those men who managed to scramble aboard, to our eyes dressed in their sleek wet blackness, hid their penises between their closed thighs with exactly that instinct that must have come to Adam when he was cast out of the Garden. The gesture put them, although they lived alone in the forest among the wild creatures, apart from the animal life they shared, just as it had done to him, for himself and them, forever.

The pirogues came with live turtles, and with fish, with cloudy beer and wine made from bananas, palm nuts, or sorghum, and with the smoked meat of hippopotamus and crocodile. The venders did a good trade with our crew and the passengers down at the third-class boat; the laughter, the exclamations, and the argument of bargaining were with us all day, heard but not understood, like voices in the next room. At stopping places, the people who were nourished on these ingredients of a witches' brew poured ashore across the single plank flung down for them, very human in contour, the flesh of the children sweet, the men and women strong and sometimes handsome. We, thank God, were fed on veal and ham and Brussels sprouts, brought frozen from Europe.

When our convoy put off some contribution to the shore instead of taking on some of its fruits, the contribution was usually something outlandish and bulky. A product of heavy industry, some chunk of machinery or road-making tractor, set down in a country that has not been industrialized, looks as strange as a space-ship from Mars might, set down in a city. A strip of landing-stage with a tin shed, a hut or two, not quite native and not quite a white man's house, a row of empty oil drums, and a crane, standing like some monster water-bird on three legs above the water: the crane came into action with the rattle of chains playing out, and there, hanging in the air ready to land where its like had never been seen, where, in fact, there was nothing that could prepare one for the look of it, were the immense steel angles of something gleaming with grey paint and intricate with dials where red arrows quivered. Cars and jeeps went ashore this way, too, dangling, but they seemed more agile, adaptable, and accepted, and no sooner were they ashore than some missionary or trader jumped in, and they went scrambling away up the bank and disappeared.

We stopped, one day, long enough for us to be able to go ashore and wander round a bit; it was quite a place—white provincial offices in a garden with marigolds on a newly cleared space of raw red earth, a glass and steel hospital in the latest contemporary architecture, an avenue of old palms along the waterfront leading to a weathered red brick cathedral. And when the taxi we had hired drove a mile out along the single road that led away into the forest, all this was hidden by the forest as if already it were one of those ancient lost cities that are sometimes found in a rich humus grave, dead under the rotting green, teeming culture of life. Another day, we stopped only long enough for us to go ashore but stay within sight of the boat. There was nothing much to see; it was Sunday, and a few Portuguese traders and their fat wives in flowered dresses were sitting on the veranda of a house, drinking lemonade; opposite, a tin store sold sewing machines and cigarettes. A crumbling white fort, streaked with livid moss and being pushed apart by the swelling roots of trees like the muscles of Samson, remained from the days eighty years ago when the Arab slave-traders built it. The native village that they had raided and burned, incidentally providing a convenient place for the fort, had left no trace except, perhaps, the beginning of the line of continuity that leads men always to build where others, enemies or vanished, have lived before them.

Someone came aboard at this brief stopping-place, just as, at the stop in the ivory country behind us, the ivory venders had.

At dinner that evening we found slips of paper with a typewritten announcement on our tables. There was to be an entertainment, at 8 p.m., in the bar. Gentlemen, 80 francs, Ladies, 70 francs. There was a stir of amusement in the dining room. I thought, for a moment, of a Donkey Derby or Bingo game. My husband said, "A choir, I'll bet. Girls singing mission-school hymns. They must have been practising down at the other boat."

"What's this?" I asked George.

"You will like it," he said.

"But what is it, a show or what?"

"Very good," he said. "You will see. A man who does things you have never seen. Very clever." When we had finished eating the sweet course he came skidding back to hit at our swiftly cleared table with a napkin, scattering crumbs. "You are coming in the bar?"—he made sure. It was a kindly but firm command. We began to have that obscure anxiousness to see the thing a success that descends upon one at school concerts and amateur theatricals. Oh yes, we were coming, all right. We usually took coffee on deck, but this time we carried our cups straight into the lounge, where the bar occupied one wall and the fans in the low panelled ceiling did not dispel the trapped heat of the day, but blew down upon the leather chairs a perpetual emanation of radio music coming from loudspeakers set in grilles overhead. We were almost the first there; we thought we might as well take good seats at one of the tables right in front of the space that had been cleared before the bar. The senior administrator and his daughter, who sat in the bar every night playing tric-trac, got up and went out. There were perhaps fourteen or fifteen of us, including the honeymoon couple, who had looked in several times, grinning vaguely, and at last had decided to come. "What a lot of mean bastards, eh?" said my husband admiringly. It did seem a surprising restraint that could resist an unspecified local entertainment offered in the middle of a green nowhere. The barman, a handsome young Bacongo from Léopoldville, leaned an elbow on the counter and stared at us. George came in from the dining room and bent his head to talk closely to him; he remained, hunched against the counter, smiling at the room with the reassuring, confident smile that the compère sends out into the proscenium whether it is addressed to faces set close as a growth of pinhead mould, or a blankness of empty seats.

At last, the entertainment began. It was, of course, a magician, as we had understood from George it must be. The man walked in suddenly from the deck—perhaps he had been waiting there behind the stacked deck-chairs for the right moment. He wore a white shirt and grey trousers and carried an attaché case. He had an assistant with him, a very black, dreamy squat chap, most likely picked up as a volunteer from among the passengers down at the third-class boat. He spent most of the performance sitting astride a chair with his chin on his arms on the high back.

There was a hesitant spatter of clapping as the magician came in, but he did not acknowledge it and it quickly died out. He went to business at once; out of the attaché case, that was rather untidily filled, came bits of white paper, scissors, a bunch of paper flowers, and strings of crumpled flags. His first trick was a card trick, an old one that most of us had seen many times before, and one or two of us could have done himself. There were a few giggles and only one person attempted to clap; but the magician had already gone on to his next illusion, which involved the string of pennants and a hat. Then there was the egg that emerged from his ear. Then the fifty-franc note that was torn up before our eyes and made whole again, not exactly before them, but almost.

Between each item of his performance there was an interval when he turned his back protectively to us and made some preparation hidden beneath a length of black cloth. Once he spoke to the barman, and was given a glass. He did not seem to be aware of the significance of applause when he got it, and he went through his revelations without a word of patter, not even the universally understood exclamations, like *Abracadabra!*, or *Hey presto!* gestures without which it is impossible to imagine a magician bringing anything off. He did not smile and we saw his small filed white teeth in his smooth black face only when his upper lip lifted in concentration; his eyes, though they met ours openly, were inner-focused. He went through what was clearly his limited repertoire, learned God knows where or from whom (perhaps even by some extraordinary correspondence course?), without mishap, but only just. When he crunched up the glass and ate it, for instance, he did not wear the look of eye-rolling agony that is this trick's professional accompaniment, and makes even the most sceptical audience hold its breath in sympathy—he looked fearful and anxious, his face twitching like the face of someone crawling through a barbed-wire fence. After half an hour he turned away at the conclusion of a trick and began folding up the string of flags, and we assumed that there would now be an interval before the second part of the performance. But at once the assistant got up from his chair and came round the room with a plate, preceded by George, who handed out all over again the slips of paper that we had found on our tables at dinner: *An entertainment, 8 p.m., in the bar. Gentlemen, 80 francs, Ladies, 70 francs.* The performance was over. The audience, who had felt flat anyway, felt done down. One of the Belgian ladies demurred, smiling, "Seventy francs for this!"

Tomorrow morning, at ten o'clock, George announced proudly to each table, there would be a repeat performance, same prices for adults, 30 francs for children. We could all see the magician again then.

"It's too much, too expensive." One of the Belgians spoke up for us all. "You can't charge eighty francs for only half an hour. Is this all he knows?"

There were murmurs of half-interested assent; some people were inclined to go off to bed, anyway. The objection was explained to George, and his organizer's pride died slowly, wonderingly, out of his manner. Suddenly he waggled a reassuring palm of the hand; it would be all right, he would make it all right, and his idiotic assurance, based on what, we could not imagine—eventual return of our money? another performance, free?—was so sweeping that everybody handed over their 70 and 80 francs doggedly, as a condition he expected us to fulfil.

Then he went to the magician and began to talk to him in a low, fast, serious voice, not without a tinge of scorn and exasperation, whether directed towards the magician or towards us we did not know, because none of us understood the language being spoken. The barman leaned over to hear and the assistant stood stolidly in the little huddle.

Only two members of the audience had gone to bed, after all; the rest of us sat there, amused, but with a certain thread of tension livening us up. It was clear that most of the people did not like to be done down, it was a matter they prided themselves on—not to be done down, even by blacks, whom they didn't expect to have the same standards about these things and whom they thought of as thievish anyway. Our attitude—that of my husband and myself—was secretly different, though the difference could not show outwardly. Tempted though we were to treat the whole evening as a joke and a rather naïve extortion of 150 francs from our pockets, we had the priggish feeling that it was perhaps patronizing and a kind of insult to make special allowances for these people, simply because they were black. If they chose, as they had, to enter into activity governed by Western values, whether it was conjuring or running a twentieth-century state, they must be done the justice of being expected to fulfil their chosen standards. For the sake of the magician himself and our relation to him as an audience, he must himself give us his 150 francs' worth. We finished our glasses of beer (we had picked up the habit) while the urgent discussion between George, the barman, and the magician went on.

The magician seemed adamant. Almost before George had begun to speak, he was shaking his head, and he did not stop packing away the stuff of his illusions—the cards, the paper flowers, the egg. He drew his lips back from his teeth and answered in the hard tone of flat refusal, again and again. But George and the barman closed in on him verbally, a stream of words that flowed round and spilled over challenges. Quite suddenly the magician gave in, must have given in, on what sounded like a disclaimer of all responsibility, a warning and a reluctant submission more in the nature of a challenge itself.

George turned to us with a happy grin. He bowed and threw up his hands. "I have told him too short. Now he makes some more for you. Some magic." And he laughed, lifting his eyebrows and inclining his head so that his white forage cap nearly fell off, implying that the whole business was simply a miracle to him, as it must be to us.

The magician bowed too. And we clapped him; it was sporting, on both sides. The newly married girl rested her head a moment on the snouty young man's shoulder, and yawned in his ear. Then we were all attention. The assistant, who had taken the opportunity to subside into his chair again, was summoned by the magician and made to stand before him. Then the magician ran a hand along inside the waistband of his trou-

sers, tucking in his shirt in a brief, final, and somehow prepara-
tory gesture, and began to make passes with his hands in front
of the assistant's face. The assistant blinked, like a sleepy dog
worried by a fly. His was a dense, coaly face, bunched towards
the front with a strong jutting jaw, puffy lips, and a broad nose
with a single tattoo mark like a line of ink drawn down it. He
had long, woolly eyelashes and they seemed to sway over his
eyes. The magician's black hands were thin and the yellow-pink
palms looked almost translucent; he might not have had the
words, but he had the gestures, all right, and his hands curled
like serpents and fluttered like birds. The assistant began to
dance. He shuffled away from the magician, the length of the
bar, the slither and hesitation from one foot to another, neck
retracted and arms bent at elbows like a runner, that Africans
can do as soon as they learn to walk, and that they can always
do, drunk or sober, even when they are so old that they can
scarcely walk. A subdued but generous laughter went up. We
were all ready to give the magician good-natured encouragement, now that he was trying. The magician continued to
stand, his hands fallen now at his sides, his slim body modest
and relaxed, hanging from his shoulders in its shabby clean shirt
and too-big grey trousers. He kept his eyes quietly on the assistant, and the man turned and came back to him, singing now as
well as dancing, and in a young *girl's* voice. And here we all
laughed without any prompting wish to seem appreciative. As a
hypnotist the magician had the sense of timing that he lacked
so conspicuously when performing tricks, and before the laughter stopped he had said something curtly to the assistant, and
the man went over to the bar counter and picking up an empty
glass jug that stood there, drank it off in deep, gasping gulps as
if he had been wandering for days in a desert. He was returned
to his inanimate self by one movement of the magician's hands
before his face; he looked at us all without surprise, and then,
finding himself the focus of an attention that did not even
arouse him to any curiosity, sat down in his chair again and
yawned.

"Let's see what he can do with someone else, not his own

man!" one of the Belgians called out good-humouredly, signalling for the barman at the same time. "Yes, come on, someone
else." "Ask him to try someone he doesn't know."

"You want it, yes?" George was grinning. He pointed a finger
at the magician.

"You, George, let's see if he can do you!"

"No, one of *us*." A shiny, tubby-faced man in cocoa research,
who had towards the blacks the chaffing, half-scornful ease of
one of those who knew them well, swung round in his chair.
"That's an idea, eh? Let him have a go at one of us, and see
how he gets on." "Yes, yes." There was a positive chorus of
rising assent; even the honeymooners joined in. Someone said,
"But what about the language? How can he suggest things in
our minds if we don't know the same language?"—but she was
dismissed, and George explained to the magician what was
wanted.

He made no protest; in a swift movement he walked away
towards the bar a few steps and then turned to face us, at bay. I
noticed that his nostrils—he had a fine nose—moved in and out
once or twice as if he were taking slow deep breaths.

We were waiting, I suppose, for him to call upon one of us,
one of the men, of course—the cocoa man and some others
were ready for the right moment, a rough equivalent of the
familiar: Will any kind gentleman or lady please step up onto
the stage? But oddly it did not come. Over the giggles and
nudges and half-sentences, an expectancy fell. We sat looking at
the awkward young black man, searching slowly along our faces,
and we did not know when the performance had begun. Fidget-
ing died out, looking at him, and our eyes surrounded him
closely. He was still as any prey run to ground. And then while
we were looking at him, waiting for him to choose one of us, we
became aware of a sudden smooth movement in our ranks. My
attention was distracted to the right, and I saw the girl—the
honeymoon girl, my girl with the face—get up with a little
exclamation, a faint wondering *tst!* . . . of remembering something, and walk calmly, without brushing against anything, over
to the magician. She stood directly before him, quite still, her
tall rounded shoulders drooping naturally and thrusting forward

a little her head, that was raised to him, almost on a level with his own. He did not move; he did not gaze; his eyes blinked quietly. She put up her long arms and, standing just their length from him, brought her hands to rest on his shoulders. Her cropped head dropped before him to her chest.

It was the most extraordinary gesture. None of us could see her face; there was nothing but the gesture. God knows where it came from—*he* could not have put it into her will, it was not in any hypnotist's repertoire, and she, surely, could not have had the place for something so other, in her female, placidly sensual nature. I don't think I have ever seen such a gesture before, but I knew—they knew—we all knew what it meant. It was nothing to do with what exists between men and women. She had never made such a gesture to her husband, or any man. She had never stood like that before her father—none of us has. How can I explain? One of the disciples might have come before Christ like that. There was the peace of absolute trust in it. It stirred a needle of fear in me—more than that, for a moment I was horribly afraid; and how can I explain that, either? For it was beautiful, and I have lived in Africa all my life and I know them, *us*, the white people. To see it was beautiful would make us dangerous.

The husband sat hunched back in his chair in what was to me a most unexpected reaction—his fist pushed his cheek out of shape and he was frozenly withdrawn, like a parent witnessing a suddenly volunteered performance by a child who, so far as he knew, had neither talent nor ambition. But the cocoa expert, who had dealt with the blacks so long, acted quickly, and jumped up calling, authoritative, loud, but only just controlled, "Hey! No, no, we want him to try his magic with the men, tell him not the ladies. No, no, he must take a man."

The room was released as if it had struck a blow. And at the same moment the magician, before George had begun to translate sharply at him, understood without understanding words and passed his hand across the lower part of his own face in an almost servile movement that bumped the arms of the girl without deliberately touching her, and released her instantly from the gesture. At once she laughed and was dazed, and as her husband came to her as if to escort an invalid, I heard her saying pleasedly, "It's wonderful! You should try! Like a dreamy feeling . . . really!"

She had missed the sight of the gesture; she was the only person at ease in the room.

There was no performance next morning. I suppose the first audience had been too disappointingly small. When my husband asked mildly after the magician, at lunch, George said inattentively, "He has gone." We had not made a stop anywhere, but of course pirogues were constantly coming and going between us and the shore.

The boat began to take on the look of striking camp; we were due at Stanleyville in two days, and some of the Belgians were getting off at the big agricultural research station where we would call a few hours before Stanleyville. Tin trunks with neat lettering began to appear outside the cabins. The honeymoon couple spent hours down on the second barge, cleaning their car—they had rags and a bucket, and they let the bucket down into the Congo and then sloshed the brown water over the metal, that was too hot to touch. The old hand changed a tire on his jeep and announced that he had room for two passengers going from Stanleyville north, towards the Sudan. Only my husband and I and the priest made no preparations; we two had the meagre luggage of air travellers, and the single briefcase of papers for the congress on tropical diseases that we were going to attend, and he was in no hurry to be first off the boat at Stanleyville since, he explained, he would have to wait there several weeks, perhaps, before a car went his way—the mission could not send all that distance specially to fetch him. He had run out of reading matter and allowed himself a cigar in broad daylight as we leaned on the rail together on the morning of our last day aboard, watching passengers struggling ashore from the third-class boat against the stream of visitors and people selling things, coming up the gangplank. We had stopped, with the usual lack of ceremony at such places, at some point in a mile-long village of huts thatched with banana leaves and surrounded by banana plantations that stretched along the river bank. The white boat and the barges stood out in the water at an angle from the shore; the link with it was a tenuous one. But babies and goats and bicycles passed over it, and among them I saw the magician. He looked like any other young black clerk, with his white shirt and grey trousers, and the attaché case. All Africa carries an attaché case now; and what I knew was in that one might not be more extraordinary than what might be in some of the others.

Tenants of the Last Tree-House

First he built a tree-house that summer. His name was Peter Something-or-other, one of those names like Smith or Johnson that take those who share them into a jolly obscurity when they grow up: it would be on the list of the bank's recreation club committee, or the mine's long-service roll. This was the last tree-house of his life, and so really rather too elaborate. It extended L-shaped on the limb of the big jacaranda that stretched out beyond the wire-mesh fence of the house into which his family had recently moved with a mongrel Airedale, two pet geese, and a breeding-cage of budgerigars. When the house in the tree was finished he sat about in it for an afternoon or two, and then said he had made it for his small brother. After that, he entered it only occasionally with an unsafe weight of friends, when they lay up there in the late afternoon to drop peach pips on the heads of the black kitchen boys strolling below with one of their number who played a guitar.

Next door there was a grand house with wooden balconies, a turret with stained-glass windows, and a double flight of steps at the entrance, curling out towards stone urns. Khaki-weed choked the oleander in the garden and in one place the fancy railings were torn apart, the splintered wood sticking up and out round nothing as if someone had just fallen through. The house had lately been a boarding-house, an old people's home, and a nursery school, for shorter and shorter tenancies. It was empty, now, except for the outcast cats that sometimes appeared out of the dark hole that led down into the cellar. Farther up the street, a similar house had been furbished, tended, and repaired; it was let to a minor foreign-trade official. Sixty years ago the first rich men had built on the veld the houses of this neighbourhood—the houses of adventurers and prospectors from England and Germany become chairmen and directors of gold-mining companies. Ordinary suburban bungalows had been put up long ago in their subdivided gardens and the stables were converted into garages; some of the tennis courts were still in use. In one of the big houses, the girl lived with her father—a lawyer—her mother, and several younger children. Her own name was one that her parents had invented to honour some private enthusiasm or commemorate some meaningful event in their own lives, and her surname was an odd one, its obscure origins lost in the misspellings of a country whose white population was the result of cosmopolitan immigration.

Last year, a friendship had flourished between her and the daughter of the foreign-trade official. Then there was the time when she began to go home every day from school with a girl who lived in a suburb eight miles away; her father used to have to pick her up when he came from his chambers, but at least, as her mother said, they knew where she was. Her mother and father had always to know where she was, though she seldom knew where they were.

She rode up and down the street in the brief twilight, standing on the pedals and aware of nothing but the motion of her passage through the air lifting and lowering her hair over her ears. She wore a stiff nylon petticoat under her school dress and one evening she met the daughter of the foreign-trade official, wearing one too. The friendship began again without any awkwardness left over from its failure in the past—they had been two children carrying shoeboxes of dolls' clothes to each other's houses, then—and every afternoon they zigzagged across the asphalt in the streets and left a spoor of tires in the soft red dust of the lanes that ran, under stooping loquat and acacia, between each double row of houses that made a block. These lanes belonged to the children and the servants; the giggles and the exchange of exclamations of the two girls, the gamblers in aprons and gardeners' overalls round the dice, the sagging fence or loose slats through which customers for back-yard beer slipped in and out, the banked privacy of garden rubbish heaps and collapsing outhouses smelling of ash and coolness, did not exist for the master and mistress of the house. Stones flew up from there onto the lawn, sometimes, and cries, drunken or angry, in one of those languages familiar to the ear but not understood; the sad suburban dogs woke from their sleep and flew barking down the garden. The tramp came along there, sometimes, a white tramp rimed and encrusted with filth like a marble statue on an old building. He saw no one, black or white, man or child, and the springy monotony of the guitar, always approaching or receding since it was always played on foot, did not affect that shamble that carried him nowhere.

"What did you do with yourself this afternoon?"

"Oh nothing. Just went about on my bike."

"Cavada, I hope you don't ride around the main road at this time, when all the cars are coming home."

"Oh no, we just go up and down the lane, and our street, that's all."

"Where have you been?"

"Just on my bike."

They were tired from the long day of faces and decisions when they came home, and they sat on the veranda and drank whisky. Their eyes looked as if they were seeing an invisible crowd and trying to watch, to respond—and to catch the furtive movement of a possible pickpocket, as well. After the whisky and the newspaper they were strong enough again to go out, or to entertain friends whose departure might wake sleepers in the night, as the milkman did.

She sat with her legs dangling over the ledge of the veranda for a while and listened to them with an incomprehension that became a kind of passivity. The younger children ignored them, except for the comfort of their physical presence, and were absorbed in games of their own. But she was old enough now for it to be necessary to censor what was said before her. The two of them did this by talking about whatever they wished, but using ellipsis and implications that bobbed towards and away from her like the fir cone on a string with which she sometimes teased the dog until he would turn aside, half hypnotized and forgetting what it was he was supposed to be trying for.

"Oh, you're thinking of the business during the nineteen fifty-nine caucus."

"No, I'm not. I'd call that simply expedient. It's fine if he knows what's good for the party. But does he know what's good for himself? Even in his personal life, I mean. It wasn't too discreet to recuperate in the same hotel as the other one."

"Not the same hotel at all. Why do you exaggerate?"

"Comes to the same thing. Oh I know—Caesar's wife and so on. But only too often she isn't. And people get their confidence in a man like him from a number of things, small things create an image. . . ."

"Look, he'll never have that popular image, anyway. A demagogue never changes his mind unless he knows beforehand how he's going to make the rest change theirs too. Whereas he . . ."

She got up and went into the back yard and took her bicycle. It was pink in the street. The sun had gone down again and again, first beyond this level of trees, then beyond the shape of this house and that. The street was friendly as a room to her. A hand waved; her friend had just turned the corner. They rode together past the house where new people had moved in that summer, and a shower of small stones landed in their hair.

"Think you're funny, don't you?"

They had the fury, the self-righteousness, and bridling disdain of girls of thirteen. But they did not go away. At last the boys came down from the tree-house and the jeers quietened and became more insulting. Two of them were boys they knew, and the third was the new one they'd seen about. He was a tall boy with a slender waist, in long grey pants like a grown-up man, and he said, quietly, "We're only fooling. Forget it, man, can't you forget it."

They carefully avoided the corner where the tree-house was, after that. But on the neutral ground, the no man's land of the lane, they often saw the boys. "Seeing" the boys meant riding slowly, rising and falling measuredly on the pedals, to the place where the boys took to hanging about. They had their bicycles too, propped against the outcrop of rock that ended someone's garden. The girls always remained astride their bicycles while they talked. Hands on the handlebars, one sandal in the dust, the other on a pedal—this attitude of flexed knee and sturdy down-stretched leg was part of the *dressage* by which their relationship to their mounts was codified, and their intentions indicated. It clearly defined, however long they lingered and however friendly they might be, that they accepted nothing of the fraternization that dismounting implies, but remained ready for and at the remove of their own pursuits; they had only to whip up and away. In the meantime, the conversations had the charm of those that never officially begin and so have no end. "And when he leans over to see if the fish is hooked and there's the top of the submarine coming up." "And it pushes his nose back and back, man, and the boat goes over backwards." The younger boys described with full sound effects the films they had seen, imitating jet planes taking off, men gibbering with fear, or women pleading for mercy. Older boys, like the new one from the corner, enjoyed the performance but had lost the knack and employed a straight narrative that had not yet made up in vocabulary what it had lost in grunts and yells. Sometimes people told some tale from home; usually of some possession, a new car, an uncle who had a boat, the promise of a transistor radio. At times the talk submerged and marked time.

"You did say that."

"I did not."

"You did."

"I tell you I did not."

"Liar."

"Liar yourself."

"Look out who you're calling a liar."

"Liar yourself."

Someone would turn suddenly from his contemplation of the dust. "You remember that bit when Dean Martin comes into that office or something—" " 'Snot an office, you dope, it's a sports shop. . . ."

And so conversation would revive.

The boy called Peter and another, Alec, began to ride down to the back gate, when she did not appear, and whistle for her.

"Cavie's boy-friends are calling her," said one of the younger children, one evening.

"Oh rubbish, those kids in the street," she said, laughing and drawn swiftly upright. Her mother put down the newspaper and looked at her.

Now she did not sit with the family in the summer evenings. She sat up in her bedroom on the bookcase made of bricks and planks where there were no books, but a collection of china ornaments and a pile of film magazines that she was grateful to get third-hand from other children. From this perch (which in time she made homely with an old curtain folded up for a cushion, and some pictures of singers stuck on the wall) she could see the tops of people's heads as they passed up the street under the trees. When the whistles came she went downstairs and out of the house, disappearing round corners as quietly as a cat, and shutting doors softly behind her. She leaned against the back gate in a timeless murmur of talk until the servant in the kitchen yelled out of the window to her that dinner was ready, and she turned and came flying into the dim house as if she had come from a long way off.

On the leaves of a group of giant aloes that had been thrown onto someone's rubbish pile and had fallen down the bank of the lane and taken root, someone had carved hearts with the legend: *C loves P.* Some of these had been scored across and between them was scratched: *P fucks C. Go to hell. So what!!!* The smooth surface of the great leaves gave easily to a penknife or a pin and the lesions in the flesh beneath bled a pale lymph that dried and shrank, drawing the cut lines into a scar. Each leaf ended in a witch's fingernail of long polished thorn, and the inscription would be there so long as the aloes lived. An old Zulu whose earlobes were loops where he had once worn inlaid discs, often sat at this spot. He could not read English but he was busy keeping his list of Fah-Fee scores on the lids of cardboard boxes.

The children were discussing him one day. It began with some suppositions about his ears: whether the lobes would grow together again if they were sewn up. Then there was a difference of opinion about the way the numbers game worked. They had all seen the Chinaman come to collect the bets; he came up the lane, sometimes, in a car. The boy Bobby said he had talked to the Chinaman, and knew how the game was run—he was a boy alert to bets and dares as a hovering hawk to prey. They wrangled for a while, the girls contributing nothing but a vague partisanship for what a particular boy said, based not on any knowledge of the subject of gambling, but on personal favour or revenge. One who was small for his age and had a pretty face said that he knew a better game than that, man. Peter said, "Cut it out, Alec," in the stern and private tone that reveals that there has been some association between the one who hovers on the point of an indiscretion, and one who seeks to check him.

"Oh it's stupid, man."

"Well, I bet you never played."

"Gee, I'd like to have a shilling for every time."

"When? Since when? Just tell me—"

"He makes me sick, always talking such big stuff. Why don't you grow up, twerp?"

The girls watched the exchange with nervous attention, half hoping for some knowledge that gossip might let fall.

"Perhaps you've heard of a certain cellar." The pretty face was baiting them all, those who did not want to be reminded of, and those who had not shared whatever was being referred to.

"Cut it out, Alec, man." Peter grabbed the smaller boy by the arm, but the laughing face and the clutch of the boy's other hand on his own free arm seemed to disarm him like the crucial amount of alcohol in a man's blood, and he began to grin too, in spite of himself.

"What's this cellar got to do with it, anyway?"

"What are you talking about? Where is the cellar?"

It was one of those times when voices rose suddenly in the lane like a dust-devil.

On the sidelines, the daughter of the foreign-trade official yelled with sudden deprecation, "Oh I can *guess*! I'll bet they're talking about the cellar in the empty house next to Peter's place! Just a dirty old cellar where the mangy cats live. What's interesting about that, I'd like to know. Alec, you bore me stiff, honestly."

Cavada always watched the effect that her friend's confident words had on the others. She was emboldened to add a gibe of her own. "I suppose he drinks kaffir beer down there with the natives! My father says there's a regular shebeen going on around here, and it's most probably in that house. There're always drunk natives walking past our house at night. He's going to get the police to see about it."

"Old Alec drinks kaffir beer! Alec drinks kaffir beer!"

"Ha-ha. What a sense of humour." Golden eyelashes showed against his cheek as he looked down, getting something out of his pocket. It was a pack of cards. He began dealing them out. He was very efficient. "Every time you lose, you have to take something off."

They were all quiet now. Cavada did not know how to play, but when they said, put this down, pick that one up, she did it. Peter lost and took off a shoe; the other girl, when she lost, made a face and took off her hair ribbon. Alec was barefoot anyway; he took off his shirt. Cavada lost her sandals and then said, "I can't take off anything more." "Oh yes!" "You have to!" "You've got to!" The faces of the boys surrounded her. "Your stiff petticoat, Cav," said her friend in triumph. "Just slip it off from under your dress."

She did so with a flourish, waving it in the air as she stepped out of it. Soon the other girl lost hers. They hung around each other's necks, laughing. "We're going now."

"Oh no. You've got to finish the game," said Bobby, who was not playing.

"We'll finish it off in the cellar," said Alec. "Last week three girls beat us and we had to run for it, man."

"What happens if someone comes down here and sees our petticoats?" said Cavada. She was standing in front of Bobby, who had the bunch of bedraggled net in his hand. It was an appeal to the solidarity of their kind before the front of the grown-up horde. But she did not understand that the rough code of childhood was suddenly torn up.

The daughter of the foreign-trade official was doing better. She darted at Peter and pulled his shirt tails out of his trousers; the boys surrounded her, she slipped away, one caught her. She was squealing and laughing, and every now and then she put her mouth to a scratch that was bleeding on her round upper arm. She grabbed Cavada and the two of them began to run down the lane, tossing their heads, groaning and laughing hysterically. They were carrying their sandals and kept dropping them and snatching at them, and suddenly as they straightened up they found themselves in front of the tramp: his stained rags, the grain of his skin magnified in dirt on his bare neck, his face blacked out with filth in a matted ruff of rippling hair that fell on his shoulders; a pair of green eyes without expression but with the prismatic shapes of light in them that you see in the sightless dreaming eyes of a tiger.

They did not apologize but drew back without a word. He walked on past the group of children and no one thought it necessary to hide the girls' clothing and conceal evidence of the game, from him.

"No thank you, *he* sleeps in the cellar sometimes," one of the smaller boys said in disgust. "I've seen him coming out, on the way to school in the morning."

The girls came slowly to the boys. "Give it back to her," Peter said to Bobby. He took the petticoat from Bobby and handed it to Cavada. The other girl got hers after a halfhearted tussle. They sat on the soft ground and put on their sandals.

"We'll play again tomorrow," said Alec. He and Peter were standing together, but the tall one said nothing.

"I've called and called for you. Where were you?"

Instantly there was that look of open amazement behind which her face hid these days. "Just riding around. When?"

Her mother did not answer, but her father said, "I don't want those boys hanging about the back gate, either."

"Yes, Daddy." Without a pause, she broke into an excited, confidential, good-humoured manner. "Oh we had such a scare this afternoon. We were coming along the lane and we walked straight into the tramp. He glared at us and he's got such eyes, you know, I mean, they're the only clean and shiny things left in his face." Her anecdotal manner fell into an air almost of expectancy, of uncertain hope of reassurance.

"Keep out of his way. And don't ever speak to him, d'you hear." Her mother added, to the father, "It's that damn neglected house. I thought you were going to get someone on to it?"

They found each other in the streets as birds gather, confusedly, for migration. They walked round and round the blocks, past the houses where each of them lived a life about which the pack did not know. Their homes had no meaning for them once they were together; the façades were blank as public buildings. Bobby wheeled his bicycle on the flank of the group and at various points someone would drop out or join them.

"I don't believe a word about that cellar," the foreign-trade official's daughter said, stabbing the warm skin of tarmac on the street with the heel of her shoe. They had paused, for no more reason than, presently, they went on.

"Okay, you don't."

"Hey, I'm not going into Peter's house," said Cavada, pulling back at the gate.

"It's all right, fusspot, everyone's out—Pete?"

The tall boy stood awkwardly, suddenly the helpless host, dubious about the invasion of guests. "Wait—" He disappeared round the back of the house. In a moment he was back; he looked at Alec. "Well, what's the score?" said Alec briskly.

Peter looked at him again; the answer was drawn from him, "No one."

They trooped into the house, across loud worn boards and frayed strips of carpet. They followed Peter and Alec into a lean-to off an old-fashioned pantry. Peter pulled aside a battered tin trunk, a leather suitcase scuffed with lying under the seats of trains, a pile of dahlia bulbs, and a tower of *Women's Weekly*—"This is mad. What you looking for, I'd like to know"—and suddenly they were staring down into a dark place that breathed cold air at them.

Peter held the trapdoor with its beard of cobwebs.

Cavada said, "What is it?" She was appealing to him, but Alec said, "Cellar, of course."

"Is this really the cellar, Peter?" she said.

"Yes."

Her eyes were shining with puzzlement. Alec crouched over the opening, gripped the edge, and let himself down. For a moment he hung from whitening knuckles; they heard a soft thud. "It's jolly nice in here." His voice was flattened and blurred. "Chuck us some matches."

Peter took a matchbox slowly out of his pocket and threw it down. They heard Alec walking about beneath them and then the darkness of the hole thinned, became shadowy, and was hollowed out with light haloed round the bright head of a candle. Alec's foreshortened figure appeared, like another wick. He grinned up at them. The girls drew closer and looked down. The light eddied out under there, trembling and dancing. There was one of those unsteady tables made out of peeled branches that are sold by venders on the highways, a brass pedestal ashtray, several fruit-box stools, a broken leather pouf of the kind that soldiers brought back from the Middle East, and a very old mattress covered by a torn tablecloth and adorned with two cushions. All these things leapt and leaned out of themselves into reaching shadows.

"Jolly nice in here." Alec was grinning.

"Who fixed it up?" said the foreign-trade official's daughter respectfully.

"*Pete*, of course." Bobby nonchalantly threw credit, like a bone, where it was due.

Peter was sitting on the old magazines. "I found the wood for the tree-house down there."

"Come *on*," said Bobby.

It did not seem to the two girls that this was the cellar that talk had returned to again and again. Alec with the pretty face had made the cellar a possibility that day in the lane; it had come to exist out of what people said about it, its walls and being had come up like the thunderclouds of the summer afternoons, in the silence when they were all talking of other things, waiting, helpless, to hear it spoken of again.

With the exception of Alec the boys were quiet.

"Who's going to bite you, d'you think. Aren't you coming?" He was singing, making a show of kicking up a row, there beneath them, and then his head would appear, slightly offended, encouraging.

"Ugh, look at this." Cavada was hooking the cobwebs round the hole onto her shoe. They were heavy with dust, and clung and tore. "I know." Her friend watched her, drawn back as if from a grave.

"Oh, for crying out aloud, who's going to eat you?"

The boys above were curiously inattentive, curiously still.

Cavada turned from the place and walked through the boys. Her walk was careful, awkward, ingratiating, and tight. At the pantry door she broke into a dash that they heard like something falling in quick, broken succession through the house.

In the garden they found her looking for footholds up to the tree-house and several of them began to mob up the tree with her, but Peter said, "Not up there. No one up there," and though they did not listen, the climb turned into horseplay and they scattered, chasing, giggling through the garden, watched by the hissing geese. In the grass beside dusty shrubs they flung themselves down and Bobby began pelting everyone with brittle dead leaves. Jokes and games and scuffles grew one out of the other; the girls, sprawled on the grass, shook with sobbing laughter. Their hair was full of sharp crumbs of leaf and there were brilliant scraps of bougainvillaea flowers on their teeth. The game became a version of the old one, where you pay a penalty if you change the attitude in which you fall. "You're not allowed to move, you're not allowed to move"—and every time one of the girls lifted a helpless hand, or rolled away from a scuffle, some piece of clothing was pulled off her. At last Bobby and Alec carried Cavada, hoarse and drunk, into the half-collapsed summerhouse. Her little girl's body, in all its shameful lack of breasts, stood bared as if in the doctor's waiting room. It had no mark or colour except the shared, sexless variation of fading sunburn. The pale S of the shape from bent shoulders down to buttocks could have been the peeled stem of a plant; the feet, with the toes splayed rigid against the mouldy earth, were the only part of her that cried out: for shame, defiance, bravado. At once, without looking at her, the boys thrust her clothes at her with as much yelling carelessness as they had taken them off.

Everyone was terribly thirsty and they took it in turns to drink with the nozzle of the garden hose in their mouths. When her friend, the daughter of the foreign-trade official, was having her turn, Cavada remembered that she had breasts already and felt a painful, protecting anguish, for her.

Peter did not come to the gate for a few days and then she heard the whistle again. Bobby and Alec were with him; she understood that he could not come without his friends but when she saw Alec she did not want to be reminded of his face. She scarcely spoke to him, but he came again. "Why do you always tag along?" she said. Neither the boy himself nor the other two seemed surprised that he, who belonged, should suddenly be spoken to as an outsider. He became smilingly thick-skinned, like an outsider. "Why has he got to come?" she complained in his presence. "I've *told* him," Peter said. Alec laughed and went on telling jokes. Peter had towards him the attitude of obstinate exasperation that a man will show in his forbearance of an alcoholic he has known in better days.

The three boys came into the house occasionally, and sat up in her room on the bed that she had pummelled and bounced to a hollow as a child of different weights and ages. The day simply came when it was all right to bring them quietly but not furtively up the stairs; no one told her this was so, but it was so, and that was why she did it. The first time, perhaps, her mother was not in, but later there were times when her mother and even her father were in the more public parts of the house. The boys listened to the radio, that had been banished to Cavada's room so that she could follow her serials and jazz programmes without inflicting them on the rest of the family. Eventually her mother and the boys met; the three standing against the passage wall, flung back into gangling, noncommittal childhood. They were taller than the mother was, tall as her husband (except Alec), but she was not a woman to them; that she felt. She went on down the passage after a polite, firm, friendly word or two.

The parents said in the living room now, "Better than hanging about the streets. I suppose at least one knows where she is."

Even when she was alone, she spent most of her time up in her room. The cupboards were nests of lost things: single socks, odd counters from games, dirty clothes that could not be found in the wash. She sat in a litter of paper cuttings and comics worn with thumbing as a monk's breviary, and raised order and beauty: pictures of ballet dancers, dogs, and singers, stuck in a pattern on the wall, and exercise books on which it sometimes took her half an hour to write her name in one of her many elaborate and constantly evolving scripts. Sometimes she suddenly appeared, like the child who has left home to make his way and who returns for one of the visits that are becoming further and further apart—and brought down to the living room some little scrapbook she had prepared for her small brother. They sat on the floor together, lavishly affectionate. He knew no better than that she had come back forever.

At the end of the summer holidays she began her first term at boarding school. When they took her on the appointed day it was clear that she was one of the smallest girls in the dormitory; the girl who had the bed to the right of hers had just taken off high-heeled shoes to change into her school uniform, and the one on the other side was unpacking grown-up dresses. Cavada had gone stripped of all but her official possessions, but the first time she had a Sunday off at home she took back to school her pictures, some china animals, and a large photograph album that had never been filled. Whenever her family saw her now, her hair had been curled and puffed out by an expert among her new friends. A letter beginning "My darling Cavie" was displayed among the cinema tickets and postcards pasted into the album. Underneath it was written: *A letter from Peter.* She herself wrote home once a week. *Dear family . . .* the letters began, and ended *God bless you.* They did not appear to be addressed to anyone at all. Her mother read these letters aloud to the father. After a pause, one or the other would say, "She seems to be shaking down all right." "Thank goodness she's taken it rather well."

One day the father got a call in chambers to come to the school. The headmistress received him in a chintzy study with flowers and water-colours and told him that there were complaints from the parents of several girls who had related a story Cavada had told about a cellar. It was a cellar, the girl told her dormitory mates, where boys undressed girls and some of the girls "had relations" with them. Cavada said that she herself was one of the girls who "had relations." Cavada used the coarsest words when telling the story; the parents of her companions were very disturbed.

The mother said, "She's bragging. She's always been a child who'd stand on her head to get attention. Now she's discovered it's interesting to be wicked. Oh these damned girls' schools."

"But where does she get the cellar idea? There must be some thread she's spun the yarn from."

"The smut she's got from those boys, I suppose."

"She does know everything, though, doesn't she?"

The mother said, "I told her the plain facts of life; but it seems impossible to learn about them like that, in any way that counts."

When she came home on her next half-day they took her into the living room and shut the door. She heard the headmistress's story through in silence; then she seemed to be considering what to do; then, feeling the walls of authority, of defencelessness, of the impossibility of truth, cornering her, she tried for tears. She worked her face as her little brother's worked, but the tears were dry.

"Is there a cellar?"

"Yes."

"Where? In one of your friends' houses?"

She nodded.

"Whose house is it?"

"Peter's. For a club. He fixed it up. But he doesn't take girls in there."

"Have you been in there?"

"No."

Her mother cut in with the directness of one woman challenging another within the code of their class, "Why did you say that you had 'had relations' with a boy? Where do you get such phrases? Don't you understand that to people like us making love isn't something two children do for a game in a cellar? Don't you see all around you that there's more to it than that?"

At once she had a child's instinct to snatch at what righteousness was left to her. "I never said that I had . . . only that other girls . . ."

"Is it true that you haven't been in this cellar, Cavada?"

"Yes, Daddy, I promise you."

"So you've been repeating a story the boys told you."

"Yes." She began to weep easily now. "It's Alec, Alec and some of the others. Once they tried to force us to go in—"

"And Peter? In Peter's house?"

She sobbed. ". . . wasn't even there, he was somewhere else, he wasn't even there. . . ." And it was true, she could not remember him, under the shrubs, among the spiderwebs in the summerhouse when she stood there for a moment, seen by eyes; she could only remember him saying something about the tree-house. "Peter likes to make things, that house in the big tree at the corner of his garden, and he fixed up the cellar for fun—but Alec and the others, they won't listen. He's told Alec hundreds of times, not to come. Even when Alec comes to our house. He's told him, and I'm always telling him . . ."

"The next time he comes here, just tell me, that's all," said her mother.

"Cavada, do you know what 'tart' means?" her father said, determined to go through with it. "I know you know all the so-called rude words connected with the sexual act itself, because I remember from when I was a child that all children know these words, but I wonder whether you know the meaning of some of the other words you used, words that reflect on the honour and decency of the people so described."

"Yes, Daddy," she said respectfully.

"Yes you do, or yes you don't?"

She shook her head.

"You don't know what 'tart' means?"

"No, Daddy."

"It means a woman who earns her living by taking payment in return for sleeping with men."

"—having sexual intercourse with men," said her mother. The fastidious effort at the precision of truth was—at last—an instinct of tenderness. The man and woman hesitated and chose, trying to pick a way for her through the ambiguities and compromises that were about them, comfortably marked by use, like shabby furniture.

Her mother went through the cupboards when everyone was out of the house. She put the crumpled, outgrown clothes in a heap on the floor, as they came. She opened the chocolate boxes of trinkets and plastic charms and closed them again. When she came to a sheet of paper or an old exercise book she stopped and was quite still. *Cavada Patricia Kinschotter:* it defined the limits of a domain like a prison cell. In cursive and italic script, capitals and small letters, backward-sloping, forward-sloping, upright. Across the tops of pages, in the middle of pages—cancelling out a page diagonally. There were notebooks and bridge-scorers and diaries (the kind that tradesmen gave away) as well as exercise books. Most of them were empty, except for the name; the fan of pages opened and fell back again, all the days of the months passing white. In others another name began to appear beside the first—Peter James Smith. I love Peter James Smith—in January, September, April, Tuesdays, Sundays, Fridays, this year, last year, in a month still to come. On the last page of a tartan-covered address book from a Christmas stocking, was scrawled, I love Peter—and adore him—and need him—and want him—forever and ever.

The woman suddenly began to put all the notebooks and diaries back again, hiding them carefully where she had found them. When she had finished she stood in the middle of the room with the air of someone who feels herself watched to see what she will do next. She bundled up the pile of outgrown clothes, after a moment, and went out.

A letter came as usual. *Dear Family. . . . There was a maths test on Thursday and I got 61%. Four girls in the class have gone to the sanatorium with a rash, they thought it was scarlet fever but it isn't. Miss Crossfield sent for me and was very sweet.*

Miss Crossfield sent for me and was very sweet. The head-mistress might have been interviewing her in order to congratulate her on some achievement, rather than to warn her that girls could be expelled for telling tales like hers. Her mother read the sentence again; but her spasm of annoyance had nothing to tighten on: the letter was as calming as all matters of form. Letters continued to arrive regularly, written at the appointed time, on the appointed day of the week. *We played Protea and tied. . . . Dinks says if we don't stop being careless about house-marks, poor old Acacia is going to be last in the whole school. At least no one in 5B has been demoted yet. . . . God bless you all. . . .*

These fits and starts of bald information on activities they knew nothing about made it unnecessary to think of her; one knew where she was. Soon her mother skimmed through the letters in silence, merely remarking, "Cavada must be fetched —half-day on Saturday." "She says you must get a new press for her tennis racquet."

One day when the girl was home for the weekend she heard at the lunch table that a man had been found dead in a cellar that week—the children were full of talk of how the police had been questioning in all the houses of the street. At the word *cellar* her normal comprehension fell apart into the idiotic vacany of one who is caught out. Between one sentence and the next, sitting among her mother and father and brother and sisters at the table, she dropped muffled and gagged into the dark side. Her being lay quite still in the grip of retribution and evil without a name. The threat at her back at night, the fear in lies, the confusion of love and unspeakable shame that were the same and yet dreadfully different—as a man is at once the same man, but alive, and then dead. . . . All this drew abreast of her menacingly. The next moment she understood that it was the cellar of the empty house they were talking about and at a stroke terror went from her like a weird light that passes on and takes distortion with it. She was able to ask with normal curiosity, "Who was it they murdered?"

"D'you know it was the tramp," said her mother, raising her shoulders, crossing her arms over her body, and frowning pityingly. "You remember that tramp who frightened you once when you met him in the lane?"

Good Climate, Friendly Inhabitants

In the office at the garage eight hours a day I wear mauve linen overalls—those snappy uniforms they make for girls who aren't really nurses. I'm forty-nine but I could be twenty-five except for my face and my legs. I've got that very fair skin and my legs have gone mottled, like Roquefort cheese. My hair used to look pretty as chickens' fluff, but now it's been bleached and permed too many times. I wouldn't admit this to anyone else, but to myself I admit everything. Perhaps I'll get one of those wigs everyone's wearing. You don't have to be short of hair, any more, to wear a wig.

I've been years at the garage—service station, as it's been called since it was rebuilt all steel and glass. That's at the front, where the petrol pumps are; you still can't go into the workshop without getting grease on your things. But I don't have much call to go there. Between doing the books you'll see me hanging about in front for a breath of air, smoking a cigarette and keeping an eye on the boys. Not the mechanics—they're all white chaps of course (bunch of ducktails they are, too, most of them)—but the petrol attendants. One boy's been with the firm twenty-three years—sometimes you'd think he owns the place; gets my goat. On the whole they're not a bad lot of natives, though you get a cheeky bastard now and then, or a thief, but he doesn't last long, with us.

We're just off the Greensleeves suburban shopping centre with the terrace restaurant and the fountain, and you get a very nice class of person coming up and down. I'm quite friends with some of the people from the luxury flats round about; they wouldn't pass without a word to me when they're walking their dogs or going to the shops. And of course you get to know a lot of the regular petrol customers, too. We've got two Rolls and any amount of sports cars who never go anywhere else. And I only have to walk down the block to Maison Claude when I get my hair done, or in to Mr. Levine at the Greensleeves Pharmacy if I feel a cold coming on.

I've got a flat in one of the old buildings that are still left, back in town. Not too grand, but for ten quid a month and right on the bus route . . . I was married once and I've got a lovely kid—married since she was seventeen and living in Rhodesia; I couldn't stop her. She's very happy with him and they've got twin boys, real little toughies! I've seen them once.

There's a woman friend I go to the early flicks with every Friday, and the Versfelds' where I have a standing invitation for Sunday lunch. I think they depend on me, poor old things; they never see anybody. That's the trouble when you work alone in an office, like I do, you don't make friends at your work. Nobody to talk to but those duckies in the workshop, and what can I have in common with a lot of louts in black leather jackets? No respect, either, you should hear the things they come out with. I'd sooner talk to the blacks, that's the truth, though I know it sounds a strange thing to say. At least they call you missus. Even old Madala knows he can't come into my office without taking his cap off, though heaven help you if you ask that boy to run up to the Greek for a packet of smokes, or round to the Swiss Confectionery. I had a dust-up with him once over it, the old monkey-face, but the manager didn't seem to want to get rid of him, he's been here so long. So he just keeps out of my way and he has his half-crown from me at Christmas, same as the other boys. But you get more sense out of the boss-boy, Jack, than you can out of some whites, believe me, and he can make you laugh, too, in his way—of course they're like children, you see them yelling with laughter over something in their own language, noisy lot of devils: I don't suppose we'd think it funny at all if we knew what it was all about. This Jack used to get a lot of phone calls (I complained to the manager on the quiet and he's put a stop to it, now) and the natives on the other end used to be asking to speak to Mpanza and Makiwane and I don't know what all, and when I'd say there wasn't anyone of that name working here they'd come out with it and ask for Jack. So I said to him one day, why do you people have a hundred and one names, why don't these uncles and aunts and brothers-in-law come out with your name straight away and stop wasting my time? He said, "Here I'm Jack because Mpanza Makiwane is not a name, and there I'm Mpanza Makiwane because Jack is not a name, but I'm the only one who knows who I am wherever I am." I couldn't help laughing. He hardly ever calls you missus, I notice, but it doesn't sound cheeky, the way he speaks. Before they were allowed to buy drink for themselves, he used to ask me to buy a bottle of brandy for him once a week and I didn't see any harm.

Even if things are not too bright, no use grumbling. I don't believe in getting old before my time. Now and then it's happened that some man's taken a fancy to me at the garage. Every time he comes to fill up he finds some excuse to talk to me; if a chap likes me, I begin to feel it just like I did when I was seventeen, so that even if he was just sitting in his car looking at me through the glass of the office, I would know that he was waiting for me to come out. Eventually he'd ask me to the hotel for a drink after work. Usually that was as far as it went. I don't know what happens to these blokes, they are married, I suppose, though their wives don't still wear a perfect size fourteen, like I do. They enjoy talking to another woman once in a while, but they quickly get nervous. They are businessmen and well off; one sent me a present, but it was one of those old-fashioned compacts, we used to call them flapjacks, meant for loose powder, and I use the solid kind everyone uses now.

Of course you get some funny types, and, as I say, I'm alone there in the front most of the time, with only the boys, the manager is at head office in town, and the other white men are all at the back. Little while ago a fellow came into my office wanting to pay for his petrol with Rhodesian money. Well, Jack, the boss-boy, came first to tell me that this fellow had given him Rhodesian money. I sent back to say we didn't take it. I looked through the glass and saw a big, expensive American car, not very new, and one of those men you recognize at once as the kind who moves about a lot—he was poking out his cheek with his tongue, looking round the station and out into the busy street like, in his head, he was trying to work out his way around in a new town. Some people kick up hell with a native if he refuses them something, but this one didn't seem to; the next thing was he got the boy to bring him to me. "Boss says he must talk to you," Jack said, and turned on his heel. But I said, you wait here. I know Johannesburg; my cash-box was there in the open safe. The fellow was young. He had that very tanned skin that has been sunburnt day after day, the tan you see on lifesavers at the beach. His hair was the thick streaky blond kind, wasted on men. He says, "Miss, can't you help me out for half an hour?" Well, I'd had my hair done, it's true, but I don't kid myself you could think of me as a miss unless you saw my figure, from behind. He went on, "I've just driven down and I haven't had a chance to change my money. Just take this while I get hold of this chap I know and get him to cash a cheque for me."

I told him there was a bank up the road but he made some excuse about it not being worth while for that bit of cash. "I've got to get my friend to cash a cheque for me, anyway. Here, I'll leave this—it's a gold one." And he took the big fancy watch off his arm. "Go on, please, do me a favour." Somehow when he smiled he looked not so young, harder. The smile was on the side of his mouth. Anyway, I suddenly said okay, then, and the native boy turned and went out of the office, but I knew it was all right about my cash, and this fellow asked me which was the quickest way to get to Kensington and I came out from behind my desk and looked it up with him on the wall map. I thought he was a fellow of about twenty-nine or thirty; he was so lean, with a snakeskin belt around his hips and a clean white open-neck shirt.

He was back on the dot. I took the money for the petrol and said, here's your watch, pushing it across the counter. I'd seen, the moment he'd gone and I'd picked up the watch to put it in the safe, that it wasn't gold: one of those Jap fakes that men take out of their pockets and try to sell you on streetcorners. But I didn't say anything, because maybe he'd been had? I gave

him the benefit of the doubt. What'd it matter? He'd paid for
his petrol, anyway. He thanked me and said he supposed he'd
better push off and find some hotel. I said the usual sort of
thing, was he here on a visit and so on, and he said, yes, he
didn't know how long, perhaps a couple of weeks, it all depended, and he'd like somewhere central. We had quite a little
chat—you know how it is, you always feel friendly if you've
done someone a favour and it's all worked out okay—and I
mentioned a couple of hotels. But it's difficult if you don't
know what sort of place a person wants, you may send him
somewhere too expensive, or on the other hand you might rec-
ommend one of the small places that he'd consider just a joint,
such as the New Park, near where I live.

A few days later I'd been down to the shops at lunch hour
and when I came by where some of the boys were squatting
over their lunch in the sun, Jack said, "That man came again."
Thinks I can read his mind; what man, I said, but they never
learn. "The other day, with the money that was no good." Oh,
you mean the Rhodesian, I said. Jack didn't answer but went on
tearing chunks of bread out of a half a loaf and stuffing them
into his mouth. One of the other boys began telling, in their
own language with bits of English thrown in, what I could guess
was the story of how the man had tried to pay with money that
was no good; big joke, you know; but Jack didn't take any
notice, I suppose he'd heard it once too often.

I went into my office to fetch a smoke, and when I was
enjoying it outside in the sun Jack came over to the tap near
me. I heard him drinking from his hand, and then he said, "He
went and looked in the office window." Didn't he buy petrol? I
said. "He pulled up at the pump but then he didn't buy, he
said he will come back later." Well, that's all right, what're you
getting excited about, we sell people as much petrol as they like,
I said. I felt uncomfortable, I don't know why; you'd think I'd
been giving away petrol at the garage's expense or something.

"You can't come from Rhodesia on those tires," Jack said.
No? I said. "Did you look at those tires?" Why should *I* look at
tires? "No-no, you look at those tires on that old car. You can't
drive six hundred miles or so on those tires. Worn out! Down

to the tread!" But who cares where he came from, I said, it's his business. "But he had that money," Jack said to me. He shrugged and I shrugged; I went back into my office. As I say, sometimes you find yourself talking to that boy as if he was a white person.

Just before five that same afternoon the fellow came back. I don't know how it was, I happened to look up like I knew the car was going to be there. He was taking petrol and paying for it, this time; old Madala was serving him. I don't know what got into me, curiosity maybe, but I got up and came to my door and said, how's Jo'burg treating you? "Ah, hell, I've had bad luck," he says. "The place I was staying had another booking for my room from today. I was supposed to go to my friend in Berea, but now his wife's brother has come. I don't mind paying for a decent place, but you take one look at some of them. . . . Don't you know somewhere?" Well yes, I said, I was telling you that day. And I mentioned the Victoria, but he said he'd tried there, so then I told him about the New Park, near me. He listened, but looking round all the time, his mind was somewhere else. He said, "They'll tell me they're full, it'll be the same story." I told him that Mrs. Douglas who runs the place is a nice woman—she would be sure to fix him up. "You couldn't ask her?" he said. I said well, all right, from my place she was only round the corner, I'd pop in on my way home from work and tell her he'd be getting in touch with her.

When he heard that he said he'd give me a lift in his car, and so I took him to Mrs. Douglas myself, and she gave him a room. As we walked out of the hotel together he seemed wrapped up in his own affairs again, but on the pavement he suddenly suggested a drink. I thought he meant we'd go into the hotel lounge, but he said, "I've got a bottle of gin in the car," and he brought it up to my place. He was telling me about the time he was in the Congo a few years ago, fighting for that native chief, whats's name—Tshombe—against the Irishmen who were sent out there to put old whats's name down. The stories he told about Elisabethville! He was paid so much he could live like a king. We only had two gins each out the bottle, but when I wanted him to take it along with him, he said, "I'll come in for it sometime when I get a chance." He didn't say anything, but I got the idea he had come up to Jo'burg about a job.

I was frying a slice of liver next evening when he turned up at the door. The bottle was still standing where it'd been left. You feel uncomfortable when the place's full of the smell of frying and anyone can tell you're about to eat. I gave him the bottle but he didn't take it; he said he was on his way to Vereeniging to see someone, he would just have a quick drink. I had to offer him something to eat, with me. He was one of those people who eat without noticing what it is. He never took in the flat, either; I mean he didn't look round at my things the way it's natural you do in someone else's home. And there was a lovely photo of my kid on the built-in fixture round the electric fire. I said to him while we were eating, is it a job you've come down for? He smiled the way youngsters smile at an older person who won't understand, anyway. "On business." But you could see that he was not a man who had an office, who wore a suit and sat in a chair. He was like one of those men you see in films, you know, the stranger in town who doesn't look as if he lives anywhere. Somebody in a film, thin and burned red as a brick and not saying much. I mean he did talk but it was never really anything about himself, only about things he'd seen happen. He never asked me anything about myself, either. It was queer; because of this, after I'd seen him a few times, it was just the same as if we were people who know each other so well they don't talk about themselves any more.

Another funny thing was, all the time he was coming in and out the flat, I was talking about him with the boy—with Jack. I don't believe in discussing white people with natives, as a rule, I mean, whatever I think of a white, it encourages disrespect if you talk about it to a black. I've never said anything in front of the boys about the behaviour of that crowd of ducktails in the workshop, for instance. And of course I wouldn't be likely to discuss my private life with a native boy. Jack didn't know that this fellow was coming to the flat, but he'd heard me say I'd fix up about the New Park Hotel, and he'd seen me take a lift home that afternoon. The boy's remark about the tires seemed to stick in my mind; I said to him: That man came all the way from the Congo.

"In that car?" Jack said; he's got such a serious face, for a native. The car goes all right, I said, he's driving all over with it now.

"Why doesn't he bring it in for retreads?"

I said he was just on holiday, he wouldn't have it done here.

The fellow didn't appear for five or six days and I thought he'd moved on, or made friends, as people do in this town. There was still about two fingers left in his bottle. I don't drink when I'm on my own. Then he turned up at the garage just at the time I knock off. Again I meant to look at the tires for myself, but I forgot. He took me home just like it had been an arranged thing; you know, a grown-up son calling for his mother not because he wants to, but because he has to. We hardly spoke in the car. I went out for pies, which wasn't much of a dinner to offer anyone, but, as I say, he didn't know what he was eating, and he didn't want the gin, he had some cans of beer in the car. He leaned his chair back with all the weight on two legs and said, "I think I must clear out of this lousy dump, I don't know what you've got to be to get along here with these sharks." I said, you kids give up too easy, have you still not landed a job? "A job!" he said. "They owe me *money*, I'm trying to get *money* out of them." What's it all about, I said, what money? He didn't take any notice, as if I wouldn't understand. "Smart alecks and swindlers. I been here nearly three lousy weeks, now." I said, everybody who comes here finds Jo'burg tough compared with their home.

He'd had his head tipped back and he lifted it straight and looked at me. "I'm not such a kid." No? I said, feeling a bit awkward because he never talked about himself before. He was looking at me all the time, you'd have thought he was going to find his age written on my face. "I'm thirty-seven," he said. "Did you know that? Thirty-seven. Not so much younger."

Forty-nine. It was true, not so much. But he looked so young, with that hair always slicked back longish behind the ears as if he'd just come out of the shower, and that brown neck in the open-neck shirt. Lean men wear well, you can't tell. He did have false teeth, though, that was why his mouth made him look hard. I supposed he could have been thirty-seven; I didn't know, I didn't know.

It was like the scars on his body. There were scars on his back and other scars on his stomach, and my heart was in my mouth for him when I saw them, still pink and raw-looking, but he said that the ones on his back were from strokes he'd had in a boys' home as a kid and the others were from the fighting in Katanga.

I know nobody would believe me, they would think I was just trying to make excuses for myself, but in the morning everything seemed just the same, I didn't feel I knew him any better. It was just like it was that first day when he came in with his Rhodesian money. He said, "Leave me the key. I might as well use the place while you're out all day." But what about the hotel, I said. "I've taken my things," he says. I said, you mean you've moved out? And something in his face, the bored sort of look, made me ask, you've told Mrs. Douglas? "She's found out by now," he said, it was unusual for him to smile. You mean you went without paying? I said. "Look, I told you I can't get my money out of those bastards."

Well, what could I do? I'd taken him to Mrs. Douglas myself. The woman'd given him a room on my recommendation. I had to go over to the New Park and spin her some yarn about him having to leave suddenly and that he'd left the money for me to pay. What else could I do? Of course I didn't tell *him*.

But I told Jack. That's the funny thing about it. I told Jack that the man had disappeared, run off without paying my friend who ran the hotel where he was staying. The boy clicked his tongue the way they do, and laughed. And I said that was what you got for trying to help people. Yes, he said, Johannesburg was full of people like that, but you learn to know their faces, even if they were nice faces.

I said, you think that man had a nice face?

"You see he has a nice face," the boy said.

I was afraid I'd find the fellow there when I got home, and he was there. I said to him, that's my daughter, and showed him the photo, but he took no interest, not even when I said she lived in Lusaka and perhaps he knew the town himself. I said why didn't he go back to Rhodesia to his job but he said the place was finished, he wasn't going to be pushed around by a lot of blacks running the show—from what he told me, it's awful, you can't keep them out of hotels or anything.

Later on he went out to get some smokes and I suddenly thought, I'll lock the door and I won't let him into the flat again. I had made up my mind to do it. But when I saw his shadow on the other side of the frosty glass I just got up and opened it, and I felt like a fool, what was there to be afraid of? He was such a clean, good-looking fellow standing there; and anybody can be down on his luck. I sometimes wonder what'll happen to me—in some years, of course—if I can't work any more and I'm alone here, and nobody comes. Every Sunday you read in the paper about women dead alone in flats, and no one discovers it for days.

He smoked night and day, like the world had some bad smell that he had to keep out of his nose. He was smoking in the bed at the weekend and I made a remark about Princess Margaret when she was here as a kid in 1947—I was looking at a story about the Royal Family, in the Sunday paper. He said he supposed he'd seen her, it was the year he went to the boy's home and they were taken to watch the procession.

One of the few things he'd told me about himself was that he was eight when he was sent to the home; I lay there and worked out that if he was thirty-seven, he should have been twenty in 1947, not eight years old.

But by then I found it hard to believe that he was only twenty-five. You could always get rid of a boy of twenty-five. He wouldn't have the strength inside to make you afraid to try it.

I'd've felt safer if someone had known about him and me, but of course I couldn't talk to anyone. Imagine the Versfelds. Or the woman I go out with on Fridays, I don't think she's had a cup of tea with a man since her husband died! I remarked to Jack, the boss-boy, how old did he think the man had been, the one with the Rhodesian money who cheated the hotel? He said,

"He's still here?" I said no, no, I just wondered. "He's young, that one," he said, but I should have remembered that half the time natives don't know their own age, it doesn't matter to them the way it does to us. I said to him, wha'd'you call young? He jerked his head back at the workshop. "Same like the mechanics." That bunch of kids! But this fellow wasn't cocky like them, wrestling with each other all over the place, calling after girls, fancying themselves the Beatles when they sing in the washroom. The people he used to go off to see about things—I never saw any of them. If he had friends, they never came round. If only *somebody* else had known he was in the flat!

Then he said he was having the car overhauled because he was going off to Durban. He said he had to leave the next Saturday. So I felt much better; I also felt bad, in a way, because there I'd been, thinking I'd have to find some way to make him go. He put his hand on my waist, in the daylight, and smiled right out at me and said, "Sorry; got to push on and get moving sometime, you know," and it was true that in a way he was right, I couldn't think what it'd be like without him, though I was always afraid he would stay. Oh he was nice to me then, I can tell you; he could be nice if he wanted to, it was like a trick that he could do, so real you couldn't believe it when it stopped just like that. I told him he should've brought the car into our place, I'd've seen to it that they did a proper job on it, but no, a friend of his was doing it free, in his own workshop.

Saturday came, he didn't go. The car wasn't ready. He sat about most of the week, disappeared for a night, but was there again in the morning. I'd given him a couple of quid to keep him going. I said to him, what are you mucking about with that car in somebody's back yard for? Take it to a decent garage. Then—I'll never forget it—cool as anything, a bit irritated, he said, "Forget it. I haven't got the car any more." I said, wha'd'you mean, you mean you've sold it?—I suppose because in the back of my mind I'd been thinking, why doesn't he sell it, he needs money. And he said, "That's right. It's sold," but I knew he was lying, he couldn't be bothered to think of anything else to say. Once he'd said the car was sold, he said he was waiting for the money; he did pay me back three quid, but he borrowed again a day or so later. He'd keep his back to me when I came into the flat and he wouldn't answer when I spoke to him; and then just when he turned on me with that closed, half-asleep face and I'd think, this is it, now this is it—I can't explain how finished, done-for I felt, I only know that he had on his face exactly the same look I remember on the face of a man, once, who was drowning some kittens, one after the other in a bucket of water—just as I knew it was coming, he would burst out laughing at me. It was the only time he laughed. He would laugh until, nearly crying, I would begin to laugh too. And we would pretend it was kidding, and he would be nice to me, oh, he would be nice to me.

I used to sit in my office at the garage and look round at the car adverts and the maps on the wall and my elephant ear growing in the oil drum and that was the only place I felt: but this is nonsense, what's got into me? The flat, and him in it—they didn't seem real. Then I'd go home at five and there it would all be.

I said to Jack, what's a '59 Chrysler worth? He took his time, he was cleaning his hands on some cotton waste. He said, "With those tires, nobody will pay much."

Just to show him that he mustn't get too free with a white person, I asked him to send up to Mr. Levine for a headache powder for me. I joked, I'm getting a bit like old Madala there, I feel so tired today.

D'you know what that boy said to me then? They've got more feeling than whites sometimes, that's the truth. He said, "When my children grow up they must work for me. Why don't you live there in Rhodesia with your daughter? The child must look after the mother. Why must you stay here alone in this town?"

Of course I wasn't going to explain to him that I like my independence, I always say I hope when I get old I die before I become a burden on anybody. But that afternoon I did something I should've done long ago, I said to the boy, if ever I don't turn up to work, you must tell them in the workshop to send someone to my flat to look for me. And I wrote down the

address. Days could go by before anyone'd find what had become of me; it's not right.

When I got home that same evening, the fellow wasn't there.
He'd gone. Not a word, not a note; nothing. Every time I heard
the lift rattling I thought, here he is. But he didn't come.
When I was home on Saturday afternoon I couldn't stand it
any longer and I went up to the Versfelds and asked the old
lady if I couldn't sleep there a few days, I said my flat was being
painted and the smell turned my stomach. I thought, if he
comes to the garage, there are people around, at least there are
the boys. I was smoking nearly as much as *he* used to and I
couldn't sleep. I had to ask Mr. Levine to give me something.
The slightest sound and I was in a cold sweat. At the end of the
week I had to go back to the flat, and I bought a chain for the
door and made a heavy curtain so's you couldn't see anyone
standing there. I didn't go out, once I'd got in from work—not
even to the early flicks—so I wouldn't have to come back into
the building at night. You know how it is when you're nervous,
the funniest things comfort you: I'd just tell myself, well, if I
shouldn't turn up to work in the morning, the boy'd send
someone to see.

Then slowly I was beginning to forget about it. I kept the
curtain and the chain and I stayed at home, but when you get
used to something, no matter what it is, you don't think about
it all the time, any more, though you still believe you do. I
hadn't been to Maison Claude for about two weeks and my hair
was a sight. Claude advised a soft perm and so it happened that
I took a couple of hours off in the afternoon to get it done. The
boss-boy Jack says to me when I come back, "He was here."

I didn't know what to do, I couldn't help staring quickly all
round. When, I said. "Now-now, while you were out." I had
the feeling I couldn't get away. I knew he would come up to me
with that closed, half-asleep face—burned as a good-looker life-
saver, burned like one of those tramps who are starving and
lousy and pickled with cheap booze but have a horrible healthy
look that comes from having nowhere to go out of the sun. I
don't know what that boy must have thought of me, my face.

He said, "I told him you're gone. You don't work here any more. You went to Rhodesia to your daughter. I don't know which place." And he put his nose back in one of the newspapers he's always reading whenever things are slack; I think he fancies himself quite the educated man and he likes to read about all these blacks who are becoming prime ministers and so on in other countries these days. I never remark on it; if you take any notice of things like that with them, you begin to give them big ideas about themselves.

That fellow's never bothered me again. I never breathed a word to anybody about it—as I say, that's the trouble when you work alone in an office like I do, there's no one you can speak to. It just shows you, a woman on her own has always got to look out; it's not only that it's not safe to walk about alone at night because of the natives, this whole town is full of people you can't trust.

Vital Statistics

Ismelda was one of the Catholic children the convent taught for nothing, making it up (as Protestant parents complained among themselves) on the fees charged for non-Catholics. Not all Catholics were free pupils, of course—only those whose parents were hard up—but it was pretty easy to spot them. Annie Badger, for instance, was obviously too poor to attend a paying school; it was Annie Badger who was sent home with a note, that time, because of her hair—and everyone knew that Reverend Mother had found things in it—ugh! Reverend Mother's face was all there seemed to be of her, a relic exhibited in the swaddling of coif and habit as if she were already a saint. She wore a tiny white dog in her sleeve, supported by a thin yellow hand bound in a white knitted mitten. All the children were paralysed in the general guilt of schoolchildren as she entered. Her gaze went over Ismelda like a wing. "Annie Badger, come here, child."

Sister Eulalia (a Flamande) said, "You are keeping Reverend Muzzer waiting!"

Ismelda saw Annie drag at her black stockings as she went past innocently, with her dirty, spiky hair sticking up where it was tied with a bit of ribbon. Poor Annie Badger! Ismelda wildly wanted to laugh. The gaze came down to concentrate its intensity on Annie Badger. "You will come with me, my child . . ." The minute sharp muzzle of the dog appeared at the opening of the sleeve; the entire classroom of faces was reflected in the convex of each of its shiny black eyes while Annie Badger went out before Reverend Mother.

"Reverend Mother washed it herself, with special stuff!" "I'm itching all over, poof!" Next day the sensation swept the class giggling and blurting into an enjoyable hysteria. "Shame, she's poor, she can't help it. . . ." said a jolly little Jewish girl, offering round some cookies—"Come on! My mom made them." But as Ismelda took the cake she experienced a terrible sense of relief, as if she took along with it the understanding that she had been in great danger. And while she and the other girls wrangled in a rivalry of pity and ridicule over Annie Badger, Ismelda was aware for the first time both that they did not know that *she* was one of the free pupils, and also that to be one was something dangerous. To be one meant that you could get insects in your hair, and be found out with them; such a thing could never happen to the others.

Ismelda was not really much of a Catholic—not more than was sufficient to keep her in the school. Her father, Dowd, came from a Catholic family that had lost its religion along with its Irishness and the prefix O apostrophe to its name, through generations of intermarriage in South Africa, a Protestant country. After a brief period of extravagantly pious admiration for the pink and white plaster baby Jesus and his blue-robed mother, and important pleasure in the ownership of one of the rosaries that Sister Maria took from the box marked "1 Gross 2/-ea." Ismelda had settled down to religious observance as part of the routine of school. She was second youngest in the family. By the time she was twelve her sister Edith had had various jobs in shops, and Eddie, the elder brother, was at trades school. Their mother worked in a suburban dairy depot, and her sister, Aunt Doreen, who lived with the family, worked at the dry cleaners. When Ismelda and the littlest one, Wilfred, came home from school in the afternoons there was no one in the house but the old man, their grandpa. He sat all day on the red granolithic stoep that faced the street, and he never went out except to attend gatherings of the MOTHS. People thought of him as an invalid, and it was a surprise to see him, every year on the eleventh of November, marching down the main street with his Shellhole cronies behind the municipal band. After the ceremony at the war memorial the Shellhole had a celebration of its own; the old man usually came home, as Ismelda's mother said, "full of pots"—but that was nothing, when you remembered what a drinker he had been. She spoke of this with a kind of calm pride, at this distance from her youth and the knocking about she and Doreen used to get from him in his drinking days. The Dowd children thought of these drinking days in exactly the same context as those other distant events for which the same tone was employed—the grandfather's exploits in that war, long ago, at a place called Ee-praise or something. The old man had been an electrician and also, in his spare time, a piano tuner, and he sometimes reproached Edith and Ismelda because they could not play the piano. There was no piano for them to learn to play; but Mrs. Dowd would say, always eager to seize a chance to bring him up to date, "Well, that's how kids are, Dad. It's nothing but the wireless, and running to see film stars. It's not like it was in your day. All *that's* finished and over."

The father, Dowd, was an engine driver on one of the gold mines that had brought the town into existence. He was very interested in household matters and he liked to go up to the Portuguese greengrocers' to buy vegetables and fruit, carrying the bag made of squares of red and green oil-baize that was kept hanging behind the kitchen door. He was proud of his familiarity with the Portuguese who ran the place, and would "chaff" them. "*Caramba*, you making money today, Lopes, man? You cleaning it up." He would enter a room, a shop, a post office, as if everywhere he was expected and had some important information to impart. When he was young he had talked a lot about getting his Red Ticket (a certificate of physical fitness to work as a miner underground) and when he was older he talked of what he might have done if he had ever got his Red Ticket, but the fact was that he had remained an engine driver and a surface worker, poorly paid.

Eddie failed at trades school and left to be apprenticed to a garage; "They want to earn a bit of money and enjoy life, these days," his mother said. "You've got to move with the times." At the garage Eddie acquired a second-hand motor scooter, and at first took Ismelda and Wilfred for rides, but soon he acquired a black leather lumber jacket as well, and roared about with a group of others like himself, whom shiftlessness, just as regimentation does, made appear identical. Edith was going steady with a salesman from the furniture shop; Wilfred was at the stage when girls, even his own sister, embarrassed him and he spent his evenings running around the blocks of the neighbourhood in training for school athletics. Ismelda, between the two, once in touch with both, was thrown entirely upon the resources of girls her own age.

These girls had dropped childhood, with its bond of physical dependency on parents, behind them. They had forgotten what they had been, and they did not know that they would become what their parents were. For the brief hiatus they occupied themselves with preparations for a state of being very different —a world that would never exist. It was furnished with the grown-up make-believe of advertising: truth was the money-back guarantee on a face cream, achievement was the million-dollar contract given to the teenage singer, love was the fifth and most highly publicized marriage of a favourite film star. The sole daily aim in school was to oppose life tangible in shrunken serge and the lumpy hassock under your knees, with the symbols of this other life: teased hair, plucked eyebrows, and all the other signs by which its denizens were recognized. Out of school the girls dressed alike and hung about outside the radio and electrical goods shop, where the latest hits were going full blast.

There were boys to be met at the Greek tearoom near the station, among the stands of dog-eared comics. But the only real closeness, the sense of clinging together in identity, was between the girls. Sister Maria told Ismelda that if she stayed on at school she would certainly pass her matric, although it was assumed that she would leave at the end of the year, once she had turned sixteen, as Edith had done. "You could become a teacher, even. There are scholarships for the Normal College."

A teacher. Ismelda knew no one, except the nuns, who was a teacher; she was dimly drawn towards the attraction of being singled out; but for what? She felt no connection with the possibilities Sister Maria outlined for her: the other girls were going to start work.

When she told her mother what the nun had suggested, her

mother said, "It's only half-day, of course, and there's all those long holidays." Aunt Doreen took the cigarette out of her mouth and screwed up one eye against the smoke that poured from her nostrils. "I don't know if it's worth the studying and all. Unless you're the old-maid type. Not for a nice-looking girl, you only work a few years until you get married. We've got a girl straight out of school just come to the works, and she's getting twenty-two-ten to start."

Ismelda wandered back to the room she and Edith shared with Aunt Doreen. Aunt Doreen got all her dry cleaning done at cost price; as usual, two or three dresses, still wrapped in plastic and bearing the cleaner's labels, hung behind the door giving off her smell of benzine. Edith's trousseau chest looked very new in the room. Ismelda threw her schoolcase down hard on her bed, and the lid flew open on the haphazard contents, at once familiar and alien, like school itself. Lunch-tin with the picture of a girl smiling seductively among artificial lilacs, books, orange peel, nail file in a plastic case, notes scribbled on bits of paper, borrowed movie magazine with a man holding another smiling girl by the shoulders so that her breasts rose pressed together out of her dress. . . . She took up a book in a brown paper cover scuffed furry that had a slip of paper in it marking the place for homework. Page 96. The Renaissance in Italy: Florence. Lorenzo the Magnificent. Caterina Sforza. A famous writer of the period, Pandolfini. . . . "Round about Florence lie many villas . . . amid cheerful scenery, and with a splendid view . . . many are like palaces, many like castles costly and beautiful to behold."

She read the words; on the opposite page there was a blurred picture: View of Florence, 1530 by Giorg—somebody-or-other. Sometimes she liked to hear about these things; but it had all happened long ago; the places were far away. A schoolteacher learns about them, and passes on what was over long ago, in places she's never seen. There was a town hall, behind the monument where her grandpa went with the others to lay the wreath every year. A kind of palace . . . she didn't know. She wasn't a little kid any more, who thought of a fairy palace. As with so many words, she felt the emptiness of having no image to fit it. She took out the movie magazine. Someone had said she looked like the girl in one of the advertisements inside; she turned to it. Tripe. Rubbish. Except perhaps she would, if her hair were longer, and done like that, and she was dressed up.

She was at a friend's house one afternoon and they were steaming their faces over the bathroom basin—the magazines said that it opened the pores. Ida Parks said, "You should enter, why don't you? The photo's taken free. And you should see what some of them look like!"

"I know—Edith told me she saw the pictures in a shop window, and Gloria Slack's one of them!"

"Well, why don't you?"

"Don't be nuts."

"But you're pretty. All the girls think so; honest, man, I'm not kidding."

Ismelda made a rude noise and they both laughed, lifting streaming red faces. But Ida set her hair for her (she had grown it, during the last six months) and she looked with critical appraisal at the result: with her eyebrows plucked and darkened, her long colourless lashes stiffly coated with mascara, and her lips coloured and wet-looking with Ida's new lipstick, she wasn't a bad copy of the face she saw so often in the cinema. "Oh *go on*, Ismelda, man. Just for kicks."

Ismelda pulled a face at herself.

Two days later she said to Ida, "I've done it."

"You having me on."

"Truly."

"What'll happen if Reverend Mother finds out?"

"Who's going to tell her?" said Ismelda in a derisive whine.

"If one of the farts sees the picture and says something—Annie Badger and that creeping crowd?"

"Not all the photos go into Brady's window; only the ones that're picked out."

"There you are! I knew you were having me. You never did it!"

"Okay, then."

But by Saturday Ismelda's photograph was on display in the

shop window among the entrants for the Combined Swimming
and Water Polo Club's Christmas Belle Contest. Her sister
Edith was the first to see it, on her way home from work. "I
nearly had a fit! *Ismelda,* I'm telling you . . . there's Ismelda. . . . When'd you have it taken? Your hair looks gor-
geous! If you *don't* mind! I'm telling you, Mom. . . . But
when'd you have it taken?"

"This I must see!" yelled Aunt Doreen past the cigarette in
her mouth, putting on an act of her own. She thrust her thick,
bluish bare feet into the Blancoed white sandals she wore.
"Come on, Vera, on your bicycle."

They did not go just then, but directly after lunch. Nothing
would persuade Ismelda to accompany them—Edith, Aunt
Doreen, and her mother—although Aunt Doreen told her she
was a spoilsport, and Edith said, "I'd be getting a kick out of it,
if I was you—my photo in the window." On the way out of the
house her mother paused, went up to the grandfather, and said
loudly, "Well, wha'd'you think of your granddaughter, *Oupa*
—she fancies herself a beauty." He had been present during the
meal when they had all been talking about the photograph, but
their manner of speaking was generally incomprehensible to
him and so they treated him as if he were deaf.

Ismelda stood on the stoep, not near him, watching them go
off down the street, the harassed stump of her mother and Aunt
Doreen on either side of Edith's quick, high-heeled wobble.
Ismelda had been playing basketball that morning and she was
still in her gym, black stockings, and dirty canvas shoes. On her
child's face the lift of the plucked eyebrows looked like something that would wash off, like the lines she sometimes inked on
her palms.

"I wouldn't call her a beauty; not to my mind," the old man
said suddenly, in the hoarse voice of someone who speaks
seldom. It had still the trace of some English regional accent.
The girl smiled embarrassedly and was unable to go away, fid-
dling with a plant that put up a single coarse leaf from a corm
that stuck out of a tin of red soil. "Well, her young man does, I
suppose, and that's what matters," he added. Ismelda felt suddenly lighthearted and happy, as if the whole adult world had

nothing to do with her, and she played for half an hour, completely absorbed, with a beetle that must have fallen from the light that had attracted it the night before, and was now trying to find its way off the granolithic floor of the stoep. It was perhaps the last half-hour of her childhood and she never remembered it.

She went to look at the photograph, alone. It was five o'clock on a weekday afternoon and plenty of people, mostly girls and women, stopped to gaze at the window. There was the face, slightly inclined towards the simpering hand placed by the photographer, the eyes turned ecstatically on nothing, the lips curved symmetrically round the teeth, the arrangement of each strand of hair clear as if it had been drawn on. There was no mistaking it; she recognized the face of beauty, as she knew it from magazines and the huge faces that bloated the screen. She was wearing one of the broad shiny belts through which the waists of beauty queens can be threaded like the apocryphal cloth through a wedding ring, and her hair was puffed and tousled more or less in the way it had been done for the photograph, but no one noticed her, standing there among them; she felt the barrier, more than glass, more than anonymity, between ordinary people and those on the other side, on whom the gaze of ordinary people is fixed.

When the photograph in the window was talked of at home she giggled and said contemptuously, "It's just for a dare, that's all." But right from the moment she had been acknowledged, through the picture in the window, it was as if she had already won, and to her it was only a confirmation when she actually did win the contest. The announcement was made in the local weekly paper shortly before the school term—her last—broke up for the Christmas holidays. The girls were swept into an extravagant, swaggering pride in and emotion towards her, and Annie Badger cried and hugged her—poor Annie Badger, as she came close her hair smelled of cooking oil.

The Christmas Belle was to be crowned at a Christmas Eve dance in the town hall, and Ismelda was going to wear the bridesmaid's dress that was already in preparation for her sister

Edith's wedding. Her mother and Aunt Doreen sat in the littered kitchen where the dressmaker worked, their eyes on the figure of Ismelda standing on the table under the light of a dangling bulb. When she breathed in, her long waist narrowed almost to nothing, and the pins in the dressmaker's mouth bristled, dismayedly alert to the possibility that the bodice might need taking in *again*.

The two women gazed out of the slumped and sagging bodies that had accumulated around them. Between yellow fingers, Aunt Doreen put another cigarette on her lower lip. "You could get your hands round it, look at that—"

Presently the mother said, "You remember that outfit I had. The photo with the hat. The living image. Of course, no one knows that when they ask who she takes after."

Reverend Mother sent for Ismelda. It was not unusual; all girls who were leaving school had this half-hour with Reverend Mother through which they sat, already out of reach of the threat of her quiet voice and the once-intimidating green walls of that room.

It was strange to be sitting down when you had never before sat in her presence; the chair was a basket chair with a tied-on cushion embroidered by the nuns. . . . Reverend Mother was talking about the Christmas Belle contest! Ismelda's face filled with blood that died down again patchily. ". . . a Catholic girl . . . a sorrow to your parents if they had known. . . ." In the silence in which Reverend Mother waited for her to answer, she said, "But you see, if you're over sixteen you're allowed to enter."

The old woman sat back behind her desk and looked straight at Ismelda. When she began to speak again it was not the distant murmur directed somewhere at her frail hands in their white knitted mittens (the dog was dead) but deliberate speech that showed the small worn nodules of yellowed ivory in her open mouth as she paused a moment, holding it so, for emphasis. "My child. If one is given the grace of beauty it is a gift from God, it is sacred and is not for display or gain. You must not make the terrible mistake of using a pretty face as if it were a talent. Can you understand? It is not like being able to play the piano. Or being able to sing. A talent or an ability is something one must develop and use, for the benefit of other people and to the glory of our Lord. But beauty of face and body—that is how God made you, if you use it for gain—if you get money for displaying it simply as such—d'you understand what I mean?—you are putting *yourself* up for sale, you are selling the vessel of your soul in the market-place. I am not talking now of the sin against God, but of the sin against yourself."

"Yes, Mother."

The ancient face searched, waited.

"Yes, Mother."

After a moment Reverend Mother folded the hands attached somewhere in the folds of linen and flannel and murmured tiredly, "What is it you are going to do now that your school-days are over?"

"I'm not sure, Mother. I might take typing. Or my aunt might know of a job for me, she's with the dry cleaners."

". . . God bless you, my child. We shall pray for you . . . always remember you are a convent girl. . . ."

". . . and blah-blah, I'll pray for you my child." Ismelda rolled her eyes as the girls gathered round her in the playground. "She knew about me and the contest," she said.

"Wh-a-a-t!"

"D'she blow you up? What' she *say*? Yrrr!"

Ismelda giggled, half embarrassed, half conscious of owing it to them. "I dunno. All about a gift of God, and sin and so on."

"Oh, the usual jaw. Well, we finished with all that tripe now, thank goodness."

Through the connections of Aunt Doreen, Ismelda went to work at a small blouse factory as an office-girl-cum-receptionist. Part of her prize had been a complete summer outfit, given by a department store, and when she wore the pink two-piece that they had seen earmarked in the store's windows, the coloured machinists would call out to each other, "Girls! Come see, man! She gawt it on!"

Aunt Doreen said to people with a boastful groan, "Plenty of talent round our place these days, you bet!" Edith had had boy-friends in her time, but she was the kind who quickly settled for one and started collecting her trousseau. The boys who came around after Ismelda were mostly those whom she had known at the Greek tearoom; also, some of Eddie's crowd began to wolf-whistle after her. Everyone knew she'd won a beauty contest. Then in September, when she was nearly seventeen, she entered the Rotarians' Spring Queen Contest, and won it. This was a different class of thing from the Swimming Club contest; the prize was money, a thirty-guinea ball dress and fur cape, and a month's modelling course in Johannesburg, and the crowning was held at the Annual Rotary Ball in the country club. The shopkeepers, doctors, lawyers, dentists of the town belonged to the country club, also the senior officials of the mines; no en-gine driver was ever a member. In an article in the local press about the Spring Queen's home life, the old man was described as an ex-war-hero pioneer of the town, and Dowd was quoted: "Having been unable to obtain the Red Ticket, he has given 40 years of service to the surface."

At the country club Ismelda sat with the Rotary president and the mayor and mayoress. It was there, wearing long white gloves, that she danced with Bob Findlay. He was not so far removed from her as the estate agent's son, who was studying law, or the doctor's son, who was almost an architect, although he was dressed like them in a dinner jacket with silk lapels; he was working underground and studying mining engineering at night. He was the only man she danced with who did not mention the beauty contest; he was not shy, but rather calm and serious. They went about a lot together because (so far as she thought about it) he had a car and was handsome. Also, she knew he thought a lot of her—that is, he thought she was beautiful, although he never paid her compliments like the others. He would say to her watchfully, "That bit of hair's standing up at the back," or, "When you walk in those shoes your ankles keep going over."

After her month's course at the modelling school in Johan-nesburg she had not returned to her job. She was given the chance of a few small modelling commissions (advertising a chocolate bar and a cold cure) and she went back and forth to the city by train. When these petered out she looked for a job in the small town again, but she had no qualification for anything, or, as her mother put it, there was "nothing for her, in a place like this."

Already, sitting beside Bob Findlay in the cinema, or standing on the station platform, she looked different from any other girl in the town. She had picked up the stylized gait and gestures of one whose movements are not natural and expressive, but professional. Sometimes one of the girls she had gone about with at school would rush up to give an effusive greeting that faded quickly into awkwardness: Ismelda's clothes, her stance with one leg elegantly before the other, the whole tended artifice of face and body put her at the distance of that world that they had invented briefly, with her, in the last year of school—that heavenly world of appearances which they had already forgotten. Local boys indulged in detailed sexual speculation about her among themselves, but individually they took her out purely for prestige; no one would have dreamt of making a pass at that terrific doll whom one had displayed to the admiration of all eyes at the dance or cinema. Bob Findlay knew, from the kisses she had returned under his mouth, that she felt, suffered even, desire. But he too was inhibited by the curious feeling that she could be damaged—like the shell figurines, hand-done, in his mother's china cabinet. It obviously took her so much time to turn out as she did; how could you mess it all up?

Once on a Sunday afternoon when he stopped the car in the mine plantation and he did manage to get her all hot, she said afterwards, "Look at the shadows under my eyes now. Tomorrow I've got to be photographed for a close-up." It was not vanity—the fear of plainer girls, when they hastened to put lipstick on lips kissed pale, that they might appear unattractive to the man. He had an unexpected fellow feeling for her in this moment as she examined her face in the car mirror, recognizing the way he felt when he knew that the beers he had drunk with some chaps after work would mean that he would appear less intelligent at the mine manager's class in the evening.

But Ismelda went home and covered her face carefully with

cream, like a hospital nurse efficiently and unsentimentally tending a wound. She lay down on her bed in the dark and she heard Wilfrid revving Eddie's old motor scooter in the yard, her father's voice, wails above the soothing incantations of her mother and Aunt Doreen. Edith and her husband were there for Sunday. Edith had an ailing infant of five months and another on the way; the wedding and the honeymoon in Durban had given way to sleepless nights and the new furniture scheme smelling of baby's sick. Ismelda got up and soaked two chunks of cotton wool in witch hazel. With these on her eyes cold as the pennies on a dead man's, she slept.

This time she won a national beauty contest. An airline flew her to Paris; a textile company had her photographed with the designer of a minor fashion house; an arranged escort—one of the youthfully plump-faced, smooth-haired, not-young men whom she was beginning to be able to recognize as the garment trade, whatever incomprehensible tongue they spoke—took her to a famous night club. She met girls from other countries and although they could not exchange a word with each other, they knew each other by the identity of their photograph-triggered smiles and the clothes, not of their own choice but given them as a form of advertising by mass manufacturers. In their improbable shoes they were trailed in an improbable crocodile up the Eiffel Tower, and in the furs they had won they were herded into the Folies Bergère.

When Dowd went up to the Portuguese vegetable shop now he might see one of the Sunday-paper pictures of Ismelda in the pile of newspapers kept for wrapping fruit and vegetables, and he would bang his fist down on it and call through the busy shop, "Know who that is, Lopes, man?"

"Please?" The Portuguese was hacking the tops off a customer's beet roots.

"D'you mean to say you don't recanize that face? He doesn't even know a little thing used to come in to buy tickey bananas! It's my girl! That's my daughter, man, the one used to come in here"—and his hand measured a height a few feet from the floor.

It was about this time, when Ismelda's picture was in all the papers, that the old man, the grandfather, died. Over his obituary in the local weekly, the MOTHS had supplied a picture of him in his uniform taken during their war. Though no one thought to make the comparison, it was clear, then, where the beauty queen had got her looks from.

After Ismelda returned from Europe she did not enter for beauty contests any more, and she raised her eyebrows at the tinted picture of herself, from that first Christmas Belle thing, that was kept hanging on a gilt wire in the sitting room. She had long abandoned the cinch-waisted dresses and the mountainous piled curls, also the calendar-girl smile. The real style was something quite different. She looked so well in loose-topped black dresses that showed off her long waist and clung over her slim behind that she was in demand to model "sophisticated" fashions. Sometimes she was photographed in a paste tiara with her hair drawn up on top of her head, the insignia of a fashion-magazine duchess.

She shared a flat in town with a girl who was an air hostess on an international run; about twice a month, when the girl and her pilot boy-friend both happened to be in Johannesburg at the same time, it was only fair for Ismelda to get out of the way. Then she would come home for a few days to the small town, stepping off the train onto the familiar platform like a stranger, in her beautiful clothes. Bob Findlay was doing well. He was a shift-boss and he owned a fibreglass boat that he sailed on the Vaal Dam every weekend. It was said he had been seen with the younger daughter of the mine manager himself, but when Ismelda was back it was she who sat beside him as they whizzed along to the dam, seeing, in the mirror in which Ismelda had once discovered a blemish under her eyes, the boat on its trailer following them closely.

He said one day, "I'm off to the Free State for a few months. Going to dig a very deep hole, far in the ground, and bring you back a diamond as big as that."

She knew that he meant he was going shaft-sinking on a new mine. She smiled, friendlily interested. "A diamond mine?"

"No, but you can buy things with that pay-packet." Shaft-sinking on a gold mine was a very highly paid short-term job, with bonuses for record time, and a certain dash and glamour involved as a result.

She held his hand and told him she wouldn't feel like coming back to the town while he was away, and she meant it. But curiously, at the same time as she was warming towards him there was forming firmly and finally within her, hard as a diamond: no, no. It was all very nice that he had the boat and they went sailing and so on. He was not like the others, like Eddie and Edith's husband and the rest, and he would be a salaried official on the mine, one of the people she and her family, the family of a weekly-paid engine driver, never knew, when she was a kid. But was it good enough, now, for her—for her face? Wouldn't it be a waste, to let that face carry her only so far, to break off, as it were: it was all she had; who knew what it was finally worth?

She knew a lot of men in Johannesburg. In time she even knew some who belonged in New York, London, Paris, and Johannesburg, going from one to the other almost as ordinary people catch a bus to work each day: she had bottles of perfume from duty-free airport shops from Reykjavik to Nairobi. The younger men looked middle-aged, and the older ones looked middle-aged; in fact, they made it seem that for men there was only one age, an indeterminate one in which one was kind, free with money, popular with *maîtres d'hôtel*, and prided oneself on knowing how to treat a girl. Wherever you went with them, doors opened, faces smiled, backs were slapped, there were artificial breezes in summer and artificial warmth in winter. Walking only between vestibule and car door, your feet scarcely touched the ground. The older ones told jokes against themselves to show their liveliness, and taking from her what was to them "chicken feed," trebled it for her on the stock exchange. Sample Paris models, Italian shoes—all these things came her way: were the due of her face, always reflecting the current image of fabricated beauty. She called these men "darling" just as they did her, but although they all at some time or another wanted to get into bed with her, they protected themselves against rebuff by (again) treating themselves rather as a joke; she was young, with her looks she could pick and choose. The younger ones were more importunate and, anyway, once or twice she herself was overcome by a peculiarly helpless passion for one or another; the affair was all that she could have wanted, from the point of view of the expensive night clubs, the penthouses, the candlelit dinners with which it was staged, but what was not meant to be part of the vision was the secret panic that woke up and ran from dark to dark inside her—listening painfully, beating from within at that exterior that heard nothing, simply went on painting and combing and arranging itself. Just when face and body were receiving the most fervent homage, she secretly felt they had failed her; how she could not have said, but she knew it was so because she was afraid. And her fears took the only form and sought the only reassurance possible for her—she tinted her hair a new colour; she lay and found surcease in the pummelling of the masseuse who was supposed to have worked for Elizabeth Taylor.

One of the young men she had an affair with had a boat; but it was a small sailing boat with a cabin, you could sleep and live in it. When she woke up there beside him in the morning she watched the sunlight hovering in reflection of the water, across the ceiling, and was happy. Once she crept out and loosed the mooring, so that when he woke up they had drifted out into open water. "Hey—what's the idea?" She lay back in bed against him, laughing. "I'm crazy when I'm in love."

In the next few years she often earned in a day what her father had earned in a whole month shunting his mine train with its trucks of shale, and sounding the whistle as he went over the level crossing between the compound and the shaft-head with a load of black men being carried to their shift underground. He had reached the retiring age and had his pension, but her mother still worked at the dairy. Before others the mother was arrogantly proud of her daughter's success—she often said to Aunt Doreen "let them have their noses rubbed in it a bit"—but in the actual presence of her daughter she got shyer and shyer as she grew older. When her daughter (she was known as Mel, now, it was a smart, terse name for a model) wanted to give her the fox fur cape, still perfectly good, that had been a prize in the beauty contest years ago, she was suddenly bewildered and wouldn't look in the mirror, but sat with the cape on and her feet planted straight before her, drawing in her chin now and then to squint down distressfully at the thick fur. She contemplated it with longing in the cupboard for three weeks and then gave it to Edith, who put it away in mothballs.

Mel Dowd had a black caracul coat made of prize skins that had been part payment for modelling South West African caracul in England and America. In time, when it became the insignia of the rich and notorious, she had a leopard coat; one of the men among the crowd of garment factory owners and furriers she knew let her have it at cost price. She had not married. Several times she was brought to the point; but always, she remembered—this, then, would be the chosen limit? And always, she decided against it. It was the same with the offers of married men who wanted to set her up permanently in expensive flats; first one of the textile chaps, old enough to be her father, but sweet, she was very fond of him; and then the director of some finance corporation, only forty-two. But again —should she settle for either? Having come thus far? Could she allow the shape of her body and the disposition of her face to be enjoyed by one man when these things were not her private possession but her stock-in-trade? As for the young ones she had been crazy about; it turned out that they had a secret estimate of their stock-in-trade, too. When it came to marriage and children there was a calculation love for her didn't enter into, and she didn't know about. One married the daughter of a stockbroker. The other, the one with the sailing boat, was a Jew and although *he* didn't care about this, his family expected him to, so he consoled himself by marrying the good-looking daughter of old friends of the family.

Mel Dowd had not been back to the small town for a long time. When she did go, the local paper announced the visit of "Former Local Girl Now Top Model." Aunt Doreen kept a scrapbook of such cuttings and she at once brought it out. While she was sticking down this latest addition to the collection, the girl's eyes went critically over the quickly yellowing pictures of herself in various outfits and postures: ". . . a robe worthy of Madame Récamier," "the *gamin* look for winter": all the words, the names, the palaces for which she had had no image were filled, now, by the image of herself in certain clothes —and suddenly she saw a girl who was not herself. No, certainly not herself, in that ordinary-looking wedding dress. And on the arm of a man. As she recognized him she was also saying, "What's this doing here?" He was Bob Findlay. "Married a Kimberley girl last month," said Aunt Doreen.

She understood; part of the record of her life. "I thought he would have been married ages ago," she said.

"Of course, you was the one he had his eye on," said her mother, with a shrug for him. The two older women took un-ease from one another. Aunt Doreen looked down at Bob Findlay and dismissed him with her smoker's laugh that always turned into an attack of coughing. When she could speak through it, she said, "Him of all people. Why, he should've had the sense; she can have anything."

She did not need consolation for the marriage of Bob Findlay, for she was thinking not of him, but of the other one with whom she had gone sailing, and then she was not thinking of him, either, but that she needed to know, for the first and last time, exactly what she could get.

Something for the Time Being

He thought of it as discussing things with her, but the truth was that she did not help him out at all. She said nothing, while she ran her hand up the ridge of bone behind the rim of her child-sized yellow-brown ear, and raked her fingers tenderly into her hairline along the back of her neck as if feeling out some symptom in herself. Yet her listening was very demanding; when he stopped at the end of a supposition or a suggestion, her silence made the stop inconclusive. He had to take up again what he had said, carry it—where?

"Ve vant to give you a tsance, but you von't let us," he mimicked; and made a loud glottal click, half angry, resentfully amused. He knew it wasn't because Kalzin Brothers were Jews that he had lost his job at last, but just because he had lost it, Mr. Solly's accent suddenly presented to him the irresistibly vulnerable. He had come out of prison nine days before after spending three months as an awaiting-trial prisoner in a political case that had just been quashed—he was one of those who would not accept bail. He had been in prison three or four times since 1952; his wife Ella and the Kalzin Brothers were used to it. Until now, his employers had always given him his job back when he came out. They were importers of china and glass and he was head packer in a team of black men who ran the dispatch department. "Well, what the hell, I'll get something else," he said. "Hey?"

She stopped the self-absorbed examination of the surface of her skin for a slow moment and shrugged, looking at him.

He smiled.

Her gaze loosened hold like hands falling away from a grasp. The ends of her nails pressed at small imperfections in the skin of her neck. He drank his tea and tore off pieces of bread to dip in it; then he noticed the tin of sardines she had opened, and sopped up the pale matrix of oil in which ragged flecks of silver were suspended. She offered him more tea, without speaking.

They lived in one room of a three-roomed house belonging to someone else; it was better for her that way, since he was often likely to have to be away for long stretches. She worked in a textile factory that made knitted socks; there was no one at home to look after their one child, a girl, and the child lived with a grandmother in a dusty peaceful village a day's train journey from the city.

He said, dismissing it as of no importance, "I wonder what chance they meant? You can imagine. I don't suppose they were going to give me an office with my name on it." He spoke as if she would appreciate the joke. She had known when she married him that he was a political man; she had been proud of him because he didn't merely want something for himself, like the other young men she knew, but everything, and for *the people*. It had excited her, under his influence, to change her awareness of herself as a young black girl to awareness of herself as belonging to the people. She knew that everything wasn't like something—a hand-out, a wangled privilege, a trinket you could hold. She would never get something from him.

Her hand went on searching over her skin as if it must come soon, come anxiously, to the flaw, the sickness, the evidence of what was wrong with her; for on this Saturday afternoon, all these things that she knew had deserted her. She had lost her wits. All that she could understand was the one room, the child growing up far away in the mud house, and the fact that you couldn't keep a job if you kept being away from work for weeks at a time.

"I think I'd better look up Flora Donaldson," he said. Flora Donaldson was a white woman who had set up an office to help political prisoners. "Sooner the better. Perhaps she'll dig up something for me by Monday. It's the beginning of the month."

He got on all right with those people. Ella had met Flora

Donaldson once; she was a pretty white woman who looked just like any white woman who would automatically send a black face round to the back door, but she didn't seem to know that she was white and you were black.

He pulled the curtain that hung across one corner of the room and took out his suit. It was a thin suit, of the kind associated with holiday-makers in American clothing advertisements, and when he was dressed in it, with a sharp-brimmed grey hat tilted back on his small head, he looked a wiry, boyish figure, rather like one of those boy-men who sing and shake before a microphone, and whose clothes admirers try to touch as a talisman.

He kissed her good-bye, obliging her to put down, the lowering of a defence, the piece of sewing she held. She had cleared away the dishes from the table and set up the sewing machine, and he saw that the shapes of cut material that lay on the table were the parts of a small girl's dress.

She spoke suddenly. "And when the next lot gets tired of you?"

"When that lot gets tired of me, I'll get another job again, that's all."

She nodded, very slowly, and her hand crept back to her neck.

"Who was that?" Madge Chadders asked.

Her husband had been out into the hall to answer the telephone.

"Flora Donaldson. I wish you'd explain to these people exactly what sort of factory I've got. It's so embarrassing. She's trying to find a job for some chap, he's a skilled packer. There's no skilled packing done in my workshop, no skilled jobs at all done by black men. What on earth can I offer the fellow? She says he's desperate and anything will do."

Madge had the broken pieces of a bowl on a newspaper spread on the Persian carpet. "Mind the glue, darling! There, just next to your foot. Well, anything is better than nothing. I suppose it's someone who was in the Soganiland sedition case.

Three months awaiting trial taken out of their lives, and now they're chucked back to fend for themselves."

William Chadders had not had any black friends or mixed with coloured people on any but master-servant terms until he married Madge, but his views on the immorality and absurdity of the colour bar were sound; sounder, she often felt, than her own, for they were backed by the impersonal authority of a familiarity with the views of great thinkers, saints, and philosophers, with history, political economy, sociology, and anthropology. She knew only what she felt. And she always did something, at once, to express what she felt. She never measured the smallness of her personal protest against the establishment she opposed; she marched with Flora and five hundred black women in a demonstration against African women's being forced to carry passes; outside the university where she had once been a student, she stood between sandwich-boards bearing messages of mourning because a bill had been passed closing the university, for the future, to all but white students; she had living in her house for three months a young African who wanted to write and hadn't the peace or space to get on with it in a Location. She did not stop to consider the varying degrees of usefulness of the things she did, and if others pointed this out to her and suggested that she might make up her mind to throw her weight on the side of either politics or philanthropy, she was not resentful but answered candidly that there was so little it was possible to do that she simply took any and every chance to get off her chest her disgust at the colour bar. When she had married William Chadders, her friends had thought that her protestant activities would stop; they underestimated not only Madge, but also William, who, although he was a wealthy businessman, subscribed to the necessity of personal freedom as strictly as any bohemian. Besides he was not fool enough to want to change in any way the person who had enchanted him just as she was.

She reacted upon him, rather than he upon her; she, of course, would not hesitate to go ahead and change anybody. (But why not? she would have said, astonished. If it's to the good?) The attitude she sought to change would occur to her as something of independent existence, she would not see it as a cell in the organism of personality, whose whole structure would have to regroup itself round the change. She had the boldness of being unaware of these consequences.

William did not carry a banner in the streets, of course; he worked up there, among his first principles and historical precedents and economic necessities, but now they were translated from theory to practice of an anonymous, large-scale, and behind-the-scenes sort—he was the brains and some of the money in a scheme to get Africans some economic power besides their labour, through the setting up of an all-African trust company and investment corporation. A number of Madge's political friends, both white and black, thought this was putting the middle-class cart before the proletarian horse, but most of the African leaders welcomed the attempt as an essential backing to popular movements on other levels—something to count on outside the unpredictability of mobs. Sometimes it amused Madge to think that William, making a point at a meeting in a boardroom, fifteen floors above life in the streets, might achieve in five minutes something of more value than she did in all her days of turning her hand to anything— from sorting old clothes to duplicating a manifesto or driving people during a bus boycott. Yet this did not knock the meaning out of her own life, for her; she knew that she had to see, touch, and talk to people in order to care about them, that was all there was to it.

Before she and her husband dressed to go out that evening, she finished sticking together the broken Chinese bowl, and showed it to him with satisfaction. To her, it was whole again. But it was one of a set, that had belonged together, and whose unity had illustrated certain philosophical concepts. William had bought them long ago, in London; for him, the whole set was damaged forever.

He said nothing to her, but he was thinking of the bowls when she said to him as they drove off, "Will you see that chap, on Monday, yourself?"

He changed gear deliberately, attempting to follow her out of his preoccupation. But she said, "The man Flora's sending. What was his name?"

He opened his hand on the steering wheel, indicating that the name escaped him.

"See him yourself?"

"I'll have to leave it to the works manager to find something for him to do," he said.

"Yes, I know. But see him yourself, too?"

Her anxious voice made him feel very fond of her. He turned and smiled at her suspiciously. "Why?"

She was embarrassed at his indulgent manner. She said, frank and wheedling, "Just to show him. You know. That you know about him and it's not much of a job."

"All right," he said, "I'll see him myself."

He met her in town straight from the office on Monday and they went to the opening of an exhibition of paintings and on to dinner and to see a play, with friends. He had not been home at all, until they returned after midnight. It was a summer night and they sat for a few minutes on their terrace, where it was still mild with the warmth of the day's sun coming from the walls in the darkness, and drank lime juice and water to quench the thirst that wine and the stuffy theatre had given them. Madge made gasps and groans of pleasure at the release from the pressures of company and noise. Then she lay quiet for a while, her voice lifting now and then in fragments of unrelated comment on the evening—the occasional chirp of a bird that has already put its head under its wing for the night.

By the time they went in, they were free of the evening. Her black dress, her earrings, and her bracelets felt like fancy dress; she shed the character and sat on the bedroom carpet, and, passing her, he said, "Oh—that chap of Flora's came today, but I don't think he'll last. I explained to him that I didn't have the sort of job he was looking for."

"Well, that's all right, then," she said, inquiringly. "What more could you do?"

"Yes," he said, deprecating. "But I could see he didn't like the idea much. It's a cleaner's job; nothing for him. He's an intelligent chap. I didn't like having to offer it to him."

She was moving about her dressing table, piling out upon it the contents of her handbag. "Then I'm sure he'll understand. It'll give him something for the time being, anyway, darling. You can't help it if you don't need the sort of work he does."

"Huh, he won't last. I could see that. He accepted it, but only with his head. He'll get fed up. Probably won't turn up tomorrow. I had to speak to him about his Congress button, too. The works manager came to me."

"What about his Congress button?" she said.

He was unfastening his shirt and his eyes were on the evening paper that lay folded on the bed. "He was wearing one," he said inattentively.

"I know, but what did you have to speak to him about it for?"

"He was wearing it in the workshop all day."

"Well, what about it?" She was sitting at her dressing table, legs spread, as if she had sat heavily and suddenly. She was not looking at him, but at her own face.

He gave the paper a push and drew his pyjamas from under the pillow. Vulnerable and naked, he said authoritatively, "You can't wear a button like that among the men in the workshop."

"Good heavens," she said, almost in relief, laughing, backing away from the edge of tension, chivvying him out of a piece of stuffiness. "And why can't you?"

"You can't have someone clearly representing a political organization like Congress."

"But he's not there *representing* anything, he's there as a workman?" Her mouth was still twitching with something between amusement and nerves.

"Exactly."

"Then why can't he wear a button that signifies his allegiance to an organization in his private life outside the workshop? There's no rule about not wearing tie-pins or club buttons or anything, in the workshop, is there?"

"No, there isn't, but that's not quite the same thing."

"My dear William," she said, "it is exactly the same. It's nothing to do with the works manager whether the man wears a Rotary button, or an Elvis Presley button, or an African National Congress button. It's damn all his business."

"No, Madge, I'm sorry," William said, patient, "but it's not the same. I can give the man a job because I feel sympathetic toward the struggle he's in, but I can't put him in the workshop as a Congress man. I mean that wouldn't be fair to Fowler. That I can't do to Fowler." He was smiling as he went towards the bathroom but his profile, as he turned into the doorway, was incisive.

She sat on at her dressing table, pulling a comb through her hair, dragging it down through knots. Then she rested her face on her palms, caught sight of herself, and became aware, against her fingers, of the curving shelf of bone, like the lip of a strong shell, under each eye. Everyone has his own intimations of mortality. For her, the feel of the bone beneath the face, in any living creature, brought her the message of the skull. Once hollowed out of this, outside the world, too. For what it's worth. It's worth a lot, the world, she affirmed, as she always did, life rising at once in her as a fish opens its jaws to a fly. It's worth a lot; and she sighed and got up with the sigh.

She went into the bathroom and sat down on the edge of the bath. He was lying there in the water, his chin relaxed on his chest, and he smiled at her. She said, "You mean you don't want Fowler to know."

"Oh," he said, seeing where they were, again. "What is it I don't want Fowler to know?"

"You don't want your partner to know that you slip black men with political ideas into your workshop. Cheeky kaffir agitators. Specially a man who's just been in jail for getting people to defy the government!—What was his name; you never said?"

"Daniel something. I don't know. Mongoma or Ngoma. Something like that."

A line like a cut appeared between her eyebrows. "Why can't you remember his name." Then she went on at once, "You don't want Fowler to know what you think, do you? That's it? You want to pretend you're like him, you don't mind the native in his place. You want to pretend that to please Fowler. You don't want Fowler to think you're cracked, or Communist, or whatever it is that good-natured, kind, jolly rich people like old Fowler think about people like us."

"I couldn't have less interest in what Fowler thinks outside our boardroom. And inside it, he never thinks about anything but how to sell more earth-moving gear."

"I don't mind the native in his place. You want him to think you go along with all that." She spoke aloud, but she seemed to be telling herself rather than him.

"Fowler and I run a factory. Our only common interest is the efficient running of that factory. Our *only* one. The factory depends on a stable, satisfied black labour force, and that we've got. Right, you and I know that the whole black wage standard is too low, right, we know that they haven't a legal union to speak for them, *right*, we know that the conditions they live under make it impossible for them really to be stable. All that. But the fact is, so far as accepted standards go in this crazy country, they're a stable, satisfied labour force with better working conditions than most. So long as I'm a partner in a business that lives by them, I can't officially admit an element that represents dissatisfaction with their lot."

"A green badge with a map of Africa on it," she said.

"If you make up your mind not to understand, you don't, and there it is," he said indulgently.

"You give him a job but you make him hide his Congress button."

He began to soap himself. She wanted everything to stop while she inquired into things, she could not go on while a remark was unexplained or a problem unsettled, but he represented a principle she subscribed to but found so hard to follow, that life must go on, trivially, commonplace, the trailing hem of the only power worth clinging to. She smoothed the film of her thin nightgown over the shape of her knees, again and again, and presently she said, in exactly the flat tone of statement that she had used before, the flat tone that was the height of belligerence in her, "He can say and do what he likes, he can call for strikes and boycotts and anything he likes, outside the factory, but he mustn't wear his Congress button at work."

He was standing up, washing his body that was full of scars; she knew them all, from the place on his left breast where a piece of shrapnel had gone in, all the way back to the place under his arm where he had torn himself on barbed wire as a child. "Yes, of course, anything he likes."

Anything except his self-respect. Pretend, pretend. Pretend he doesn't belong to a political organization. Pretend he doesn't want to be a man. Pretend he hasn't been to prison for what he believes. Suddenly she spoke to her husband. "You'll let him have anything except the one thing worth giving."

They stood in uncomfortable proximity to each other, in the smallness of the bathroom. They were at once aware of each other as people who live in intimacy are only when hostility returns each to the confines of himself. He felt himself naked before her, where he had stepped out onto the towelling mat, and he took a towel and slowly covered himself, pushing the free end in round his waist. She felt herself in intrusion and, in silence, went out.

Her hands were tingling. She walked up and down the bedroom floor like someone waiting to be summoned, called to account. I'll forget about it, she kept thinking, very fast, I'll forget about it again. Take a sip of water. Read another chapter. Let things flow, cover up, go on.

But when he came into the room with his wet hair combed and his stranger's face, and he said, "You're angry," it came from her lips, a black bird in the room, before she could understand what she had released—"I'm not angry. I'm beginning to get to know you."

Ella Mgoma knew he was going to a meeting that evening and didn't expect him home early. She put the paraffin lamp on the table so that she could see to finish the child's dress. It was done, buttons and all, by the time he came in at half past ten.

"Well, now we'll see what happens. I've got them to accept, *in principle*, that in future we won't take bail. You should have seen Ben Tsolo's face when I said that we lent the government our money interest-free when we paid bail. That really hit him. That was language he understood." He laughed, and did not seem to want to sit down, the heat of the meeting still upon him. "*In principle*. Yes, it's easy to accept in principle. We'll see."

She pumped the primus and set a pot of stew to warm up for him. "Ah, that's nice"—he saw the dress. "Finished already?" And she nodded vociferously in pleasure; but at once she noticed his forefinger run lightly along the line of braid round the neck, and the traces of failure that were always at the bottom of her cup tasted on her tongue again. Probably he was not even aware of it, or perhaps his instinct for what was true —the plumb line, the coin with the right ring—led him absently to it, but the fact was that she had botched the neck.

She had an almost Oriental delicacy about not badgering him, and she waited until he had washed and sat down to eat before she asked, "How did the job go?"

"Oh that," he said. "It went." He was eating quickly, moving his tongue strongly round his mouth to marshal the bits of meat that escaped his teeth. She was sitting with him, feeling, in spite of herself, the rest of satisfaction in her evening's work. "Didn't you get it?"

"It got *me*. But I got loose again, all right."

She watched his face to see what he meant. "They don't want you to come back tomorrow?"

He shook his head, no, no, no, to stem the irritation of her suppositions. He finished his mouthful and said, "Everything very nice. Boss takes me into his office, apologizes for the pay, he knows it's not the sort of job I should have and so forth. So I go off and clean up in the assembly shop. Then at lunch time he calls me into the office again: they don't want me to wear my ANC badge at work. Flora Donaldson's sympathetic white man, who's going to do me the great favour of paying me three pounds a week." He laughed. "Well, there you are."

She kept on looking at him. Her eyes widened and her mouth

tightened; she was trying to prime herself to speak, or was trying not to cry. The idea of tears exasperated him and he held her with a firm, almost belligerently inquiring gaze. Her hand went up round the back of her neck under her collar, anxiously exploratory. "Don't do that!" he said. "You're like a monkey catching lice."

She took her hand down swiftly and broke into trembling, like a sweat. She began to breathe hysterically. "You couldn't put it in your pocket, for the day," she said wildly, grimacing at the bitterness of malice towards him.

He jumped up from the table. "Christ! I knew you'd say it! I've been waiting for you to say it. You've been wanting to say it for five years. Well, now it's out. Out with it. Spit it out!" She began to scream softly as if he were hitting her. The impulse to cruelty left him and he sat down before his dirty plate, where the battered spoon lay among bits of gristle and potato eyes. Presently he spoke. "You come out and you think there's everybody waiting for you. The truth is, there isn't anybody. You think straight in prison because you've got nothing to lose. Nobody thinks straight, outside. They don't want to hear you. What are you all going to do with me, Ella? Send me back to prison as quickly as possible? Perhaps I'll get a banishment order next time. That'd do. That's what you've got for me. I must keep myself busy with that kind of thing."

He went over to her and said, in a kindly voice, kneading her shoulder with spread fingers, "Don't cry. Don't cry. You're just like any other woman."

Message in a Bottle

There are days when the world pauses, gets stuck senselessly, like one of those machines that ought to give cigarettes or make balls bump round but simply becomes an object that takes kicks, shakes, unyieldingly. You drop out of step with the daily work or habit that carries you along and stare about. Halt, halt! It's fatal. This is not Sunday, with cows beside winter willows and dried-up streams, and white egrets catching up with their own forward-jerking necks. I notice a face in the strip of mirror attached with crystal knobs to the pillar in the coffee shop. An uneven face, looks as if it's been up all night for years: my own. Once I had no face to speak of, only a smile, bright eyes, and powdered cheeks, nicely arranged. I order two coffees, one for myself, one for the child—"Would you like a cup of coffee?": it is a piece of clumsy flattery, a status I confer upon her because she has just been to a doctor and suffered a painful treatment. She accepts it, her token smile knowing its worth.

She shivers a little, from shock, in her dusty school clothes; at this time of the morning, she ought to be doing mental arithmetic. I am in my work clothes too, interrupted by necessity. I do not know what to talk to the child about because she has plumbed cheerful, jollying reassurances over months of pain, and efforts at distraction she takes as a kind of insult. She resents my sympathy because I have not her pain; my solicitously gentle voice is easy enough for me, it does not help her, she has discovered. So we don't talk, and I eat a piece of cheesecake, not so much because I want it, but to show her that life must go on. By such moves and signals do we conduct the battle that is waged between the sick and the well.

I eat the cheesecake and look again at the only other custom-

ers in the place at this time on a Wednesday morning. I half-
saw them when we came in, but my awareness was merely of a
presence that brought to light my old trousers and cardigan. An
oldish man and a blond girl out of a fashion magazine. She is
tall as they always are and she sits not with her knees under the
table but with the length of her body from behind to head
turned diagonally towards him and supported by her elbow on
the table. From the door, without detail, they fell into an image
of a girl making up to a man. But she is weeping. Tears fill and
refract marvellously the one eye I can see, and then run slowly
down the pale beige cheek. She stretches the muscles of her
face to hold them and puts up the forefinger of a clenched hand
to catch them. One distinctly runs over the finger and drops to
the tablecloth. There will be a little splotch there, where it
fell.

I look away but when I look back again the tears are still
coming, in slow twos and threes down the powdered and perfect cheek. She is talking all the time to the man, not looking at
him but talking without a sound that I can hear, directly to his
ear with the dark shadow in it that must be a tuft of hair. That
tense tendon in her neck may become permanent when she is
older, but there is no reason why she will be so unhappy often.
It looks like the kind of misery one grows out of.

She is a beautiful girl dressed from head to foot in pale beige
that matches her face and hair. He would be ugly if he were a
poor man, sucked dry, at his age, and leathery; but his crowded
features, thin ridged nose and eyes and line of mouth, are filled
out, smoothly built up, deal by deal, as a sculptor adds clay
daub by daub, by ease and money-making. He has never been a
good-looking young man, never. While she talks he looks out
across the room. He does not look at her but at the waiters
passing, the door opening, the woman at the cash register ringing up the sale of a packet of cigarettes. It is a face that has put
love into making money. Yes, he is ugly, but I do not know
whether I imagine that she already has the look of one of those
lovely creatures whose beauty—that makes them feel they may
have any man—brings them nothing but one of these owners of

textile factories; while we others, who are ignored by the many, carry off the particular prizes, the distinguished, the gentle, the passionately attractive, the adventurous. Is she pleading with him not to break off an affair? The one remark I do hear belies this: ". . . what about that boy-friend of yours, doesn't he . . ." The very tone of his voice, raised plainly above the confidential, is that of the confidant importuned, stonily turning nasty and wanting to give up his privilege to anyone who seems under a more valid obligation to deal with the situation. Yet I don't know. She is still pleading, clearly going over and over what she had said a dozen times before. How beautifully she weeps, without a bloated nose; why should one feel not moved by her just because she is beautiful, why, in spite of everything, is there the obstinate cold resentment that her face is more than she deserves?

The man's eyes (he is obviously keenly long-sighted) follow the passing of someone on the other side of the glass barrier, in the street. As he changes focus we meet, my piece of cheesecake halfway to my mouth. We know each other, this morning, above the heads of the child and the weeping one. I should never have thought it; but you don't always choose the ones you know. The girl has not paused in her desperate monologue and the child, beside me, has her one uncovered eye screwed up, nuzzling toward brightness without seeing, like a mole.

I pay and the child and I walk out just behind the other two. There is a big black car outside the door and a black chauffeur, fat henchman, opens the door for them. One feels the girl likes this, it turns up the fragment of a fairy tale. She steps inside elegantly, with a certain melancholy pleasure, balanced like a brimming glass.

I drive out of the city to an address where the child is to have a culture made from the infected tissues in her eyelids. The doctor has drawn a little map for me; through suburbs, past country clubs and chicken farms, everywhere the sun shines evenly through a bloom of blue smoke that marks the position of the city, from far off, like the spout of a whale. The research institute is spread out pleasantly on a rise, there are gardens, and horses standing in a field. We get out of the car and it's as if a felt-lined door has been shut—the sound of life in the city comes only as a slight vibration under one's feet. I take her by the arm and we cross some grass, city people in the sunlight, and wander from building to building. They are white inside and although we hear voices through frosted doors, all desks are empty. We see an African in a white coat blocking the light at the end of a corridor. He directs us to another building. He has a kind of trolley full of small cages with dark shapes in them that don't move. Out of the clean buildings, round the goldfish ponds (she is too old to want to linger beside them any more), we come into a courtyard full of grey monkeys in cages. She forgets about her eye and breaks away from me, finding her way. "Oh aren't they sweet!" They swing from grey tails, they have black masks through which amber eyes shine with questions. They have patches where the fur has been shaved and the skin has been punctured again and again and painted with medicaments; oh why, but why? She pulls back from my arm when I tell her. There are rats, crouched guinea pigs, piles of empty cages in yards. The horses, that were standing so peacefully in the field, have glazed eyes and the hopelessness of working animals who have come out of the shafts for good. On their rumps and necks are the shaved and painted patches. Their stalls are being swilled out and scrubbed by men in rubber boots; it is so clean, all this death and disease.

"Now we're going to try and grow these nasty goggas from your eye, dear, we're going to grow them in an egg and see whether we can make you well." The woman in the white coat talks soothingly as she works on the eye. While she is out of the laboratory for a moment we listen to a kettle that is singing up to the boil and I say, "Don't rub it." The child says after a silence, "I wish I could be the one who sits and watches." Pain is taking her innocence, she is getting to know me. But if she indicts, she begins at the same time to take on some of the guilt. "They will grow mine in an egg? Only in an egg?" The sun is high; we do not know what time it is, driving back. She tells time by the school bell, I by the cardboard file growing thinner.

My husband has a story to tell when he comes home in the evening. An acquaintance, who took him out shooting last weekend, has committed suicide. He does not tell it baldly like this but starts slowly at what led up to the beginning, although we can tell almost from the beginning what is coming. "He was in wonderful form. I stood next to him and watched him bring down four birds with five cartridges. Alba worked so well and he asked me whether I couldn't ask Jack Strahan to sell him one of the next litter. He couldn't get over the way Alba worked; he said he'd never seen a dog like it, for range. And he asked when I was going to bring you on a shoot again, when're you going to bring your wife out here with you, he said, he remembered that time last year when we had such a good time in the camp."

The man kissed his wife, dropped his children at their school, telephoned his office to say he would be a little late, and then drove out into the veld. "Shut himself in the boot of the car and shot himself through the head." I scarcely knew the man, met him only that once at the camp, but at this detail of the manner of his death, I suddenly think of something. "But don't you remember, he used to shut his hunting dogs in the boot? He did it that day, and when I picked him out about it he said it wasn't cruel and they didn't mind being shut up in there!"

Nobody knows why he killed himself, he has gone without a word to anyone—except this. The stranger who cannot remember clearly what he looked like is the one into whose hands his last message has fallen. What can I do with it? It's like a message picked up on the beach, that may be a joke, a hoax, or a genuine call of distress—one can't tell, and ends by throwing the bottle back into the sea. If it's genuine, the sender is beyond help already. Or someone else may pick it up and know what it's all about.

If I keep it perhaps I might crack the code one day? If only it were the sort of code that children or spies use, made out of numbers or lines from the Bible. But it is made of what couldn't be equated or spelled out to anyone in the world, that could leave communication only in the awkward movement of his body through the air as he scrambled into the smell of dust and petrol, where the dogs had crouched, and closed the lid over his head.

For no reason at all, my mind begins to construct a dialogue with the girl—that girl in the coffee shop. I see her somewhere, years later. She is laughing, she is conscious of her beauty. I say to her quite abruptly, "What happened that morning, anyway? You know, he has developed hardened arteries and his teeth are giving him trouble. He's on a strict diet—no wine, no red meat —and his old wife cooks for him again. He never goes out."

The child comes in and stands squarely before me. She has put her dark glasses on and I can't see her eyes. "And if the egg should hatch," she says, "if the egg hatches?"

Native Country

Among the things in Anita's bedroom there was a clock as well as a Renaissance chair with a bit of string tied between its arms so that no one could sit in it. It was a mantel clock with only one hand and until she grew old enough to be taught at school to tell the time she had always thought that other people's clocks were strange. "I didn't know there was something wrong with ours," she told her father. "There is nothing 'wrong' with ours," he said in the tone of distant disgust with which he approached the subject of the people among whom they lived. He was a very pale man with eyes as pale, though blue, as his fine skin and thick silky white hair that waved back high all round from temples and brow. "It is a seventeenth-century clock and at that time they were made with only one hand, to mark the hours, only of course these people know nothing about such things. They know the tin alarm clock that wakes them up in the morning."

Other children's parents were young and red-armed; they played golf and tennis and dug in the garden. In their houses they had only furniture whose purpose was obvious, beds to sleep in and chairs to sit in, and everything was new. They had smart standing ashtrays that swallowed cigarette stubs down into a chromium column when you pressed a button.

Anita had never known the Europe which, as she knew from her parents' own house and the friends who came in and out of it, was an interior peopled and furnished quite differently. The sun was kept out from objects like faces. The chairs, tables, bureaux, and commodes had each their inlay, carving, or encrustation of coloured lacquer just as Dr. Manides, Mr. Gruntz, the Terbegens, and the Crespignys had their different accents. The lisps and intonations in their English kept present other tongues, ancient civilizations, philosophies growing into political systems, and political systems growing one out of the other; the objects kept present concepts of beauty laid one upon the other, the skill of guilds that had evolved and disappeared, and the proportions of other rooms. So Anita knew from an early age that the strange faded beast in which her father sat with his hands resting on its two snarling heads, belonged somewhere. When a child she had brought home with her from the neighbouring streets was struck dumb before the presence of her father and Mr. Gruntz sitting in silence over the chess table, and gazed round in a growing oppression that almost entirely inhibited breathing as the gaze reached the harpsichord, Anita would whisper, "A kind of piano."

The street outside into which she and the friend then burst was white with blazing afternoon sunlight. Black nannies yelled gossip where they congregated restlessly with their white charges. Barefoot boys cycled to buy milk or bread from the Greek shop on the corner. Sometimes the older children played cricket with an upended fruit box for wicket, or *bok-bok*, a wild game rougher than leapfrog, from which Anita would emerge with her fringe drenched in sweat. Every Saturday afternoon she went with her school friends to the cinema down the road, where they traded American comics with each other, blew bubble gum, and stopped their ears when the schoolboys whistled between their teeth at the love scenes. After rain, she and the other children in their street paddled in the swirling gutters of warm brown water and teased black delivery men by throwing bunches of wet leaves at them as they rode by. Now and then there were fights; a party of jeering boys would provoke the girls. Anita always came back into the house with an exhilarated face that slowly took on the indoor calm of heavy curtains and the smell of coffee brewing.

"Anita has been enjoying herself." Her father would push his chair away from the table, as if inviting the guests to contemplate her. "And where she has been?" Frau Gruntz gave singing lessons (ex-Vienna opera) and at sixty, in a smart linen costume, she offered the white bosom and wide painted smile of the moment when the first note of an aria is about to be sounded. Dr. Manides, who regarded it as an affront to his esteemed friend Gruntz that she should be married to him, said, "Is Anita's business."

Her mother said, "Your hair . . ." with resigned acceptance and a certain timidity towards this apparition from activities not so much unthinkable as discounted.

"Oh Mommy, man!" Anita spoke as the other children did.

But these were elderly city people who had spent a large part of their lives talking in cafés and the interruption of Anita was hardly more than a pause; quickly and absently passed over.

The family was living in a working-class suburb of bungalows out towards the mine dumps on the south side of Johannesburg. After the war they moved to the crush of flat buildings squeezing out older houses of the town's beginnings on the ridge of the north side. There were many more people like themselves, now; Italians, Hollanders, half the Polish aristocracy. Later came Germans; and after 1956, the Hungarians were to follow. There were delicatessen shops, an audience for chamber music, *espresso*, and even one or two cafés where the newspapers hung from wooden spines. Anita's father's bookkeeping job (he had been in the family bank, at home) gave way to something better, though he did not rise to a new prosperity, as some of the others did—the German Jews in the clothing industry, the Italians in engineering and building. Into the shabby double-story house he brought the things he began to pick up; Persian rugs, a *guéridon*, gilt clocks, *gesso* frames, a single English lead wineglass that one of the local "antique" dealers had known no better than to include in a job lot of modern Czechoslovakian rubbish. The new waves of refugees and immigrants had brought, like the sand that is found among clothes when one unpacks after a holiday at the sea, some residue of Europe. Professor Terbegen went to auctions too, and there was an endless rivalry pursued in the discussion of chipped and gilded objects, now doubly removed, in latitude as well as time, from their inspiration.

Once, while they were still living in the humble suburb, Anita's father had shown another round his treasures—but not

an immigrant, not a refugee with the dust of interrupted conversation in a long-bombed café hanging in his mind. He was a
man with the self-assured handsomeness that good looks take
on at the end of the thirties, and at that time he was in he
uniform of a colonel of one of the "free" forces of an occupied
country, attached to British Intelligence. A staff car waited outside; he talked to Anita's mother and father in their own tongue
and brought alive animation and laughter, a draught of their
world in common. In him it was not a memory; he was Europe,
living and present, the special dry humour of the capital, the
logical mind of a particular university, the eyes and hands
sensually accustomed to marble and chestnut trees in bloom.
Anita, fifteen years old, knew only the South African privates
with baggy khaki trousers strapped down over their clumsy
boots, who came home to the neighbourhood houses on weekend leave. She followed her father and this visitor round, keeping out of the way and studying him in secrecy and amazement.

Axelrod was in South Africa for over a year and he came to
the house often. He was the son of friends in the old Europe,
whom Anita had never met, but who belonged to the best
period of her parents' lives. He was an expert on German
porcelain and French furniture, English silver and Italian
glass—in fact all the furnishings and ornaments of that interior
which Anita had never inhabited. Although he became an intimate, his visits (sometimes he spent the weekend) were always
an event. Anita knew every seam and braid of his uniform. She
knew his phrasing in French; his play on words in German. He
got her a special seat at a military tattoo and he paid her mock
grown-up compliments like giving her French perfume on her
birthday—a celebration at which he held all the attention and
provided all the fun. While he was in the house he made it his
own, but he would leave at a time confirmed by a quick glance
at his watch, so that the high note of his presence was main-
tained by the sudden sense of the width of his life, opening out
here and there and everywhere, beyond them, and yet at
the same time taking them up into it. He would come back
with the same smile of lively participation with which he had

gone out; he had been to a party, or with a woman. In the meantime, Anita was asked by one of the young South African soldiers to go to a dance in the Scout Hall, but she was too afraid to ask permission from her parents. The boy said, "But why can't you even try, man?" His lips came together humbly as waiting hands.

After the war Axelrod came out from Europe on a visit because he had the idea that he might acquire some African pieces—there was a small band of collectors who were interested in Benin bronzes and old wooden sculpture from West Africa. He and Anita's father stood looking at two crouching figures unwrapped upon the plush cloth on her mother's table. The heavy black wood was covered with a clinging spiderweb of the spores of dried mould. The protuding navel stood out like a Cyclopean eye. The gash of the female sex, the third limb of the male were statements beyond the age of chivalry or the prurience of a Marquis de Sade. One had, tied on its belly, a small cloth bundle stiff with a dried, still reddish stain. A piece of tarnished mirror set into its chest showed your face rotting and falling away like something dug up from a grave.

Axelrod smiled with the corners of his mouth dipped comically; her father looked at the things with his head instinctively drawn back, sourly sideways out of his pale eyes. They appraised each other in the way of people who knew each other's thoughts, and in a moment, began to laugh. "Don't try to make a fool of me, Axelrod."

"No, Felix, these are good pieces. At least a hundred and fifty years old. Mrs. van Rose will go mad about them."

They laughed delightedly at each other's disgust, Axelrod shaking his head and holding the older man's shoulder.

It was extraordinary to have Axelrod in the house again. Now it was the house in Hillbrow, of course. His voice downstairs when he talked on the telephone. The smell of his cigarettes. His expensive English suits being carried upstairs after Beauty, the servant girl, had pressed them. Anita was nearly eighteen and she emerged from the chrysalis of her room, awkward, hot-faced under her wild-falling short hair. She was present as she had been, following them round as a child; but now she accompanied them to restaurants and shared the wine at dinner, silently listening and following with her eyes not only the guest's face, but the invisible contours of his conversation. There was always something out-of-breath about her; now and then they would turn to her with a parenthetic smile or remark, as to a child who has just run in.

When she was back in her room she would stand at the window like a person who has lost his memory. The scene that she knew intimately, down there in the yard between the flat buildings, was unrecognizable to her, as if she had never been there before. And yet how much of her time did she spend, watching the life that moved in and out the slanting bifurcation of shade that, cast by high buildings, travelled like the arm of a compass round the well of bright sunlight. Black men and women who were cleaners and maids in the flats lived there; they slept in dormitories on the roofs, and their life zigzagged up and down the iron fire escapes, and rebounded in shouts of anger and laughter from wall to wall. The men gambled on their haunches at lunchtime. At night they drank the brew that, she knew so well, was kept hidden in the electrical-installation kiosk. They argued, barbered each other's hair, put their hands on the lovely backsides of the girls, and, on their respective days off, went up to the roof in kitchen-boy garb and came down again as bold, well-dressed men with brushed hats and polished shoes. Down there, the servant, Beauty, had another being than that of Anita's parents' house.

But with Axelrod's presence in the rooms behind her, Anita heard and saw nothing that was before her eyes. She was alive in the streets whose names he let fall in his anecdotes ("near the rue de Courcelles," "in the Quaistrasse") and in the houses, hidden in winter rain, among the elaborate objects he and her father admired and understood.

One of the pleasantries with which Axelrod took his leave at the airport was "And Anita? You must send her when she finishes school. Elisabeth will look after her." There had been a wife at some time, but they were parted; Elisabeth was an old family retainer he had taken with him when he set up house in London.

Like all such pleasantries, it was smiled at and meant nothing, yet when Anita was taken by her mother to Europe for the
first time, just after her eighteenth birthday, it was Axelrod who
showed them the Wallace Collection ("my favourite place in
London") and, in the British Museum, swept them past rooms
they mustn't waste their time with, to stand in homage before
certain selected objects. Anita was left by her mother to spend a
year with relatives in Lausanne and to attend some secretarial
school there. But when Axelrod, passing through on business,
took her out to lunch like an uncle giving a niece a treat and
found her mutely miserable, he disposed of her homesickness in
a sentence—"I'll take you to London." He added, "That's the
place for you. You can learn your typewriting with some nice
young ladies from Kensington."

"I want to go home."

Axelrod smiled with absent adult indulgence, and said, "Oh
there. I shouldn't think Felix and your mother would stick it
out much longer. They'll be here soon, too, I'm sure."

He wrote to Felix and without even waiting for an answer,
packed the girl into his car and drove her round Switzerland for
a week before taking her to London. Installed in his house, with
Elisabeth to keep her company when she came home from her
secretarial college, she saw little of Axelrod. She soon discovered
that he was having an affair with a pianist; that had been his
reason for being in Switzerland: so long as the affair lasted, he
combined business with his preoccupation and followed his
mistress round Europe while she fulfilled concert engagements.
Later he was in love with the beautiful wife of Lord T——
(Anita got to know the lovely croaky voice over the telephone),
and there were others. He began to look older but never less
attractive, with deep lines accentuating the strength of his
mouth and his youthful slenderness turned to leanness. When
Anita finished her secretarial course, he took her to her first
night club. She was telling him her experiences as applicant for
several jobs. They laughed about them and he said, "What
about applying to me?" She made some joking remark; but his
careless, impulsive suggestions were part of his acquisitive flair,
and as he spoke the joke became perfectly sensible: "I need a

secretary at home as well as at the rooms. Someone to pick up the bits of paper I scrawl important things on, eh? Someone to write down what I think before I forget it. Someone to follow me round . . ." While he was talking she was following him in a different way, on the dim concourse of the dance floor. Her legs and body moved with his, in all its assurance of the love of women.

Her mother and father came over on a visit that year and stayed in the house in London. There were important sales of seventeenth-century furniture and rare glass and above various objects the eyes of the old man and Axelrod met in the passion of assessment and appreciation. At dinner, at the theatre, over morning coffee, the talk was of nothing but rarities. Anita knew the difference between a *tazza* and *caqueteuse*, now—she had been working with Axelrod among such things for some months, and she could place them, like the strange faces of foreigners once one has seen their counterparts in their home countries. Her father looked at her with pride, as he would at some *objet d'art* that had emerged well from its saleroom obscurity. "There is nothing there for anybody. A lot of blacks and the white people are worse—agh!"

Axelrod, on his travels about the collections and salerooms of the world, continued to send her the kind of grown-up presents that flatter a child. From Japan came an absurd tinned oyster, guaranteed to contain a cultured pearl. He himself always carried in his pocket, the rosary of his religion of beautiful objects, an oblong alexandrite to fondle while he thought or talked. His letters were as amusing as his gifts: *My little amanuensis, Meet me in Paris, Thursday—M. Jarnoux has some bargains to show me and I need someone to conspire with against him. You will be wanting to replenish your wardrobe anyway; the spring showings are on. . . .* It was a joke with him to pretend that she was not a shy girl who wore nothing but skirts and jerseys. In the open-air cafés of Rome and Paris they looked like a handsome youngish father and his suddenly shot-up daughter, who find they get on tremendously well together. She had a few young friends, a boy or two, but Axelrod—a job like hers, that was, took up one's life completely: how could a young man with a couple of tickets for the cinema compete with a sudden summons to meet Axelrod in Paris?

In Vienna he made love to her for the first time, in a hotel that delighted him in its perfect restoration to the rococo splendour that he remembered from before the war. They had had a most successful few days, there; a treasure of wonderful porcelain that had emerged from some hiding place, one of the most important collections he had acquired in years—and it was in the sweet buoyancy of success that he gave in to her: for, of course, it was plain as the nose on her face that she was in love with him. "It's incest, eh?" he said tenderly, honestly. "But I know you are a big girl. Yes? You have been a big girl with me for a long time, now."

But she misunderstood the extent of the indulgence.

When they got back to London, he said, "Write to them and tell them the news about their bachelor friend. We are going to be married. You can't compromise me in this way, my darling Anita. What about my reputation?" Coming from Axelrod, it was a declaration beyond her wildest fantasies: the single fantasy that had been begun out of the seams of his uniform, the smell of his cigarettes when she was fifteen years old. Her parents had no qualms; Axelrod was the son they might have had if they had not had Anita, child of their exile and old age, born, like the people around them who were strangers to them, in a strange land. In a way, he would always be more a son of theirs than Anita would ever be a daughter. Yet by the fact of Axelrod's marrying her, she became more of a daughter than she had been.

Married to Axelrod, she changed remarkably little. She was there at the head of the table at his brilliant dinner parties, of course, and on her hand were his rings—for one crazy moment she had thought he would give her his alexandrite as her engagement ring, but no, it was still in his pocket, and she was thankful she had said nothing. She bore three children, and gained confidence among his friends and in her indispensability to him in his work—as time went by she was able to take all practical matters, including complicated financial transactions from country to country, off his hands. Yet her appearance, even in her thirties, continued to have something about it of the awkward schoolgirl: this, after all, was what Axelrod had married. He took her to Italy to buy her clothes (Paris, he said, was not her style); her suède skirts and raw silk blouses were really only more expensive versions of the old jerseys and skirts.

As she grew towards maturity, and he towards age (there were twenty-five years between them) their relationship evened out somewhat. She accepted without her former humbleness his affairs with women. Her gauche appearance became her style; and rather stylish. She was no longer conscious of a certain helplessness before other women's beautifully manicured hands, skilfully raised breasts, and those deliberately fake faces that Axelrod enjoyed as much as he did the enamelled ones on his favourite French miniatures. He had still, unchanged, what people thought of as his charm—for her, the old affectionate amusement with which he had treated her all her life. He was a better lover than ever, and they had the one ground on which, at least, they had been equals from the start: their interest and pleasure in their children. If she had never had from him the one proof—and that she had never had it was confirmed by the fact that she did not know what form it would take—if she had never had the one proof that he loved her, then at least she had made her life with him just as if that proof had been in the house all the time, along with all the other treasures that belonged there.

In the spring of his fifty-eighth year Axelrod went away for a few days on one of his usual quick trips. He telephoned from Rome to the country house in Berkshire they had had for some years, to say that he would be back on Monday at lunchtime; the sun was shining and the leaves were out, already, in the Pincio Gardens—he wished they were all there with him. Anita and her eldest child, Daniel, spent the weekend beside the fire, in a furious chess battle. On Monday morning she drove the children back to town in time for school and as she opened the front door she saw Axelrod's partner and the secretary from the offices standing up to confront her. Axelrod had collapsed and died of a heart attack in a terrace café.

There was a seat booked for her on a plane and she went

without telling anyone, not even their closest friends. She sat alone in the plane looking at the condensed moisture vibrating on the window as she had done all the other times she had gone to join Axelrod. She went to him at the mortuary and saw that he had not known he would die; his death had taken him on impulse while the pleasure of some new acquisition was still on his face. She walked about the streets of Rome and past the café where they had told her he had died and the absurd expression that one's heart could be "sore" became true for her, she felt a rough soreness inside her as if some organ were being manhandled. Then she followed the way, by fountain, by marble triton and square, along the chestnuts coming into new leaf, back to his hotel, and packed his things. And as she put her hand blindly, for comfort, into the pocket of his trousers in the gesture with which he always felt for the jewel that he fingered there, she touched a small hard box. She took out a jeweller's case. In it was Axelrod's oblong alexandrite, made up into a ring.

The air blotched before her eyes and her ears began to sing; she sat on the bed and thrust her head down over her knees, her hands raked up into her hair.

The blood flowed back to her brain and she was able to get up again. She took the ring out of its slot in the velvet pad and put it on her third finger; it was just a little tight; unless a jeweller had the actual finger from which to take his measurements, it was difficult to be accurate to a millimetre. This very week, on the Thursday, they would have been married fourteen years. Every year on the anniversary Axelrod brought her a present, one of the objects she had learned from him were beautiful and precious, but the truth was that of all the lovely things with which their house was filled she had coveted only one—the jewel that Axelrod played with in his pocket. And she could never ask him for it; had long ago accepted that although he knew she wanted it, he delicately saved her the humiliation of his admitting this since he knew he could never give it to her.

She hid her face in her hands with a panting gasp. Joy buffeted her body unfamiliarly, she turned her head this way and that; a blazing pride of fulfilment shocked and delighted her. Sorrow came back; but it was not the sediment of old sorrow, that had been dissolved in her veins.

With the summer, some months later, she began to feel that the ring really was too tight. She took it to a jeweller. While he was taking the correct measurement of her finger on a bunch of metal rings, she thought suddenly as if someone spoke out loud: Was the ring meant for her?

Why had she never thought of this before?

What reason was there to have assumed that Axelrod had had the alexandrite made up for her? The coming anniversary had not been a special landmark. He had never been ill before that first and fatal blood clot and he was the last sort of person to have any romantic premonition of death.

What on earth had made her so sure? After fourteen years, might the ring not just as well have been made for some other woman? All his life Axelrod had had his love affairs just as he had his childhood memories of the Guignol in Paris parks, and his passionate familiarity with the objects that had piled up through the centuries as if in some junk room of the trappings of empires and principalities, before the Wall, waiting for the Bomb—that life of Europe to which he belonged and which it had never been expected, either by her parents or by him, she would ever really understand as one born to it. She found herself thinking of the crude afternoon sun in the street where she had played *bok-bok*. The soldier with his sunburnt, razor-nicked face and issue boots, who had wanted to take her to a dance. The black men in the ridiculous shorts and tunics who gambled and talked and drank and made love with their women in the bare well between the buildings, where there was nothing but strong sun, and strong shade marking the passage of the sun like the hand of a clock: she thought of the single hand of the clock that had stood in her room in Africa. Oh why had she come in from the street? Why had she not gone to the dance with the clumsy young soldier? Why had she not gone down there among the black men and women and learned what they were laughing at and tasted what they tasted when they tipped the jam tin and the beer went down their throats?

Long ago, that time, Axelrod and her father had looked with ridicule on the heavy black wooden figures with bellies and breasts and sex plainly stated. She tried to remember the figures but it was too far away, and she could not. And yet she had cared for nothing of the things *they* had valued. Nothing.

Only the alexandrite.

Some Monday for Sure

My sister's husband, Josias, used to work on the railways but then he got this job where they make dynamite for the mines. He was the one who sits out on that little iron seat clamped to the back of the big red truck, with a red flag in his hand. The idea is that if you drive up too near the truck or look as if you're going to crash into it, he waves the flag to warn you off. You've seen those trucks often on the Main Reef Road between Johannesburg and the mining towns—they carry the stuff and have DANGER—EXPLOSIVES painted on them. The man sits there, with an iron chain looped across his little seat to keep him from being thrown into the road, and he clutches his flag like a kid with a balloon. That's how Josias was, too. Of course, if you didn't take any notice of the warning and went on and crashed into the truck, he would be the first to be blown to high heaven and hell, but he always just sits there, this chap, as if he has no idea when he was born or that he might not die on a bed an old man of eighty. As if the dust in his eyes and the racket of the truck are going to last forever.

My sister knew she had a good man but she never said anything about being afraid of this job. She only grumbled in winter, when he was stuck out there in the cold and used to get a cough (she's a nurse), and on those times in summer when it rained all day and she said he would land up with rheumatism, crippled, and then who would give him work? The dynamite people? I don't think it ever came into her head that any day, every day, he could be blown up instead of coming home in the evening. Anyway, you wouldn't have thought so by the way she took it when he told us what it was he was going to have to do.

231

I was working down at a garage in town, that time, at the petrol pumps, and I was eating before he came in because I was on night shift. Emma had the water ready for him and he had a wash without saying much, as usual, but then he didn't speak when they sat down to eat, either, and when his fingers went into the mealie meal he seemed to forget what it was he was holding and not to be able to shape it into a mouthful. Emma must have thought he felt too dry to eat, because she got up and brought him a jam tin of the beer she had made for Saturday. He drank it and then sat back and looked from her to me, but she said, "Why don't you eat?" and he began to, slowly. She said, "What's the matter with you?" He got up and yawned and yawned, showing those brown chipped teeth that remind me of the big ape at the Johannesburg zoo that I saw once when I went with the school. He went into the other room of the house, where he and Emma slept, and he came back with his pipe. He filled it carefully, the way a poor man does; I saw, as soon as I went to work at the filling station, how the white men fill their pipes, stuffing the tobacco in, picking out any bits they don't like the look of, shoving the tin half shut back into the glove box of the car. "I'm going down to Sela's place," said Emma. "I can go with Willie on his way to work if you don't want to come."

"No. Not tonight. You stay here." Josias always speaks like this, the short words of a schoolmaster or a boss-boy, but if you hear the way he says them, you know he is not really ordering you around at all, he is only asking you.

"No, I told her I'm coming," Emma said, in the voice of a woman having her own way in a little thing.

"Tomorrow." Josias began to yawn again, looking at us with wet eyes. "Go to bed," Emma said. "I won't be late."

"No, no, I want to . . ." He blew a sigh. "When he's gone, man—" He moved his pipe at me. "I'll tell you later."

Emma laughed. "What can you tell that Willie can't hear." I've lived with them ever since they were married. Emma always was the one who looked after me, even before, when I was a little kid. It was true that whatever happened to us happened to us together. He looked at me; I suppose he saw that I was a

man, now: I was in my blue overalls with *Shell* on the pocket
and everything.

He said, "They want me to do something . . . a job with
the truck."

Josias used to turn out regularly to political meetings and he
took part in a few protests before everything went underground,
but he had never been more than one of the crowd. We had
Mandela and the rest of the leaders, cut out of the paper,
hanging on the wall, but he had never known, personally, any
of them. Of course there were his friends Ndhlovu and Seb
Masinde who said they had gone underground and who occasionally came late at night for a meal or slept in my bed for a
few hours.

"They want to stop the truck on the road—"

"Stop it?" Emma was like somebody stepping into cold dark
water; with every word that was said she went deeper. "But how
can you do it—when? Where will they do it?" She was wild, as
if she must go out and prevent it all happening right then.

I felt that cold water of Emma's rising round the belly because Emma and I often had the same feelings, but I caught
also, in Josias's not looking at me, a signal Emma couldn't
know. Something in me jumped at it like catching a swinging
rope. "They want the stuff inside . . . ?"

Nobody said anything.

I said, "What a lot of big bangs you could make with that,
man," and then shut up before Josias needed to tell me to.

"So what're you going to do?" Emma's mouth stayed open
after she had spoken, the lips pulled back.

"They'll tell me everything. I just have to give them the best
place on the road—that'll be the Free State road, the others're
too busy . . . and . . . the time when we pass. . . ."

"You'll be dead." Emma's head was shuddering and her
whole body shook; I've never seen anybody give up like that.
He was dead already, she saw it with her eyes and she was
kicking and screaming without knowing how to show it to him.
She looked like she wanted to kill Josias herself, for being dead.
"That'll be the finish, for sure. He's got a gun, the white man in
front, hasn't he, you told me. And the one with him? They'll

kill you. You'll go to prison. They'll take you to Pretoria jail and hang you by the rope. . . . Yes, he's got the gun, you told me, didn't you—many times you told me—"

"The others've got guns too. How d'you think they can hold us up? They've got guns and they'll come all round him. It's all worked out—"

"The one in front will shoot you, I know it, don't tell me, I know what I say. . . ." Emma went up and down and around till I thought she would push the walls down—they wouldn't have needed much pushing, in that house in Tembekile Location—and I was scared of her. I don't mean for what she would do to me if I got in her way, or to Josias, but for what might happen to her: something like taking a fit or screaming that none of us would be able to forget.

I don't think Josias was sure about doing the job before but he wanted to do it now. "No shooting. Nobody will shoot me. Nobody will know that I know anything. Nobody will know I tell them anything. I'm held up just the same like the others! Same as the white man in front! Who can shoot me? They can shoot me for that?"

"Someone else can go, I don't want it, do you hear? You will stay at home, I will say you are sick. . . . You will be killed, they will shoot you. . . . Josias, I'm telling you, I don't want . . . I won't . . ."

I was waiting my chance to speak, all the time, and I felt Josias was waiting to talk to someone who had caught the signal. I said quickly, while she went on and on, "But even on that road there are some cars?"

"Roadblocks," he said, looking at the floor. "They've got the signs, the ones you see when a road's being dug up, and there'll be some men with picks. After the truck goes through they'll block the road so that any other cars turn off onto the old road there by Kalmansdrif. The same thing on the other side, two miles on. There where the farm road goes down to Nek Halt."

"Hell, man! Did you have to pick what part of the road?"

"I know it like this yard. Don't I?"

Emma stood there, between the two of us, while we discussed

the whole business. We didn't have to worry about anyone hearing, not only because Emma kept the window wired up in that kitchen, but also because the yard the house was in was a real Tembekile Location one, full of babies yelling and people shouting, night and day, not to mention the transistors playing in the houses all round. Emma was looking at us all the time and out of the corner of my eye I could see her big front going up and down fast in the neck of her dress.

". . . so they're going to tie you up as well as the others?"

He drew on his pipe to answer me.

We thought for a moment and then grinned at each other; it was the first time for Josias, that whole evening.

Emma began collecting the dishes under our noses. She dragged the tin bath of hot water from the stove and washed up. "I said I'm taking my off on Wednesday. I suppose this is going to be next week." Suddenly, yet talking as if carrying on where she let up, she was quite different.

"I don't know."

"Well, I have to know because I suppose I must be at home."

"What must you be at home for?" said Josias.

"If the police come I don't want them talking to *him*," she said, looking at us both without wanting to see us.

"The police—" said Josias, and jerked his head to send them running, while I laughed, to show her.

"And I want to know what I must say."

"What must you say? Why? They can get my statement from me when they find us tied up. In the night I'll be back here myself."

"Oh yes," she said, scraping the mealie meal he hadn't eaten back into the pot. She did everything as usual; she wanted to show us nothing was going to wait because of this big thing, she must wash the dishes and put ash on the fire. "You'll be back, oh yes.—Are you going to sit here all night, Willie?—Oh yes, you'll be back."

And then, I think, for a moment Josias saw himself dead, too; he didn't answer when I took my cap and said, so long, from the door.

I knew it must be a Monday. I notice that women quite often don't remember ordinary things like this, I don't know what they think about—for instance, Emma didn't catch on that it must be Monday, next Monday or the one after, some Monday for sure, because Monday was the day that we knew Josias went with the truck to the Free State mines. It was Friday when he told us and all day Saturday I had a terrible feeling that it was going to be *that* Monday, and it would be all over before I could—what? I didn't know, man. I felt I must at least see where it was going to happen. Sunday I was off work and I took my bicycle and rode into town before there was even anybody in the streets and went to the big station and found that although there wasn't a train on Sundays that would take me all the way, I could get one that would take me about thirty miles. I had to pay to put the bike in the luggage van as well as for my ticket, but I'd got my wages on Friday. I got off at the nearest halt to Kalmansdrif and then I asked people along the road the best way. It was a long ride, more than two hours. I came out on the main road from the sand road just at the turn-off Josias had told me about. It was just like he said: a tin sign KALMANSDRIF pointing down the road I'd come from. And the nice blue tarred road, smooth, straight ahead: was I glad to get onto it! I hadn't taken much notice of the country so far, while I was sweating along, but from then on I woke up and saw everything. I've only got to think about it to see it again now. The veld is flat round about there, it was the end of winter, so the grass was dry. Quite far away and very far apart, there was a hill, and then another, sticking up in the middle of nothing, pink colour, and with its point cut off like the neck of a bottle. Ride and ride, these hills never got any nearer and there were none beside the road. It all looked empty and the sky much bigger than the ground, but there were some people there. It's funny you don't notice them like you do in town. All our people, of course; there were barbed-wire fences, so it must have been white farmers' land, but they've got the water and their houses are far off the road and you can usually see them only by the big dark trees that hide them. Our people had mud houses and there would be three or four in the same place made bare by goats and people's feet. Often the huts were near a kind of crack in the ground, where the little kids played and where, I suppose, in summer, there was water. Even now the women were managing to do washing in some places. I saw children run to the road to jig about and stamp when cars passed, but the men and women took no interest in what was up there. It was funny to think that I was just like them, now, men and women who are always busy inside themselves with jobs, plans, thinking about how to get money or how to talk to someone about something important, instead of like the children, as I used to be only a few years ago, taking in each small thing around them as it happens.

Still, there were people living pretty near the road. What would they do if they saw the dynamite truck held up and a fight going on? (I couldn't think of it, then, in any other way except like I'd seen hold-ups in Westerns, although I've seen plenty of fighting, all my life, among the Location gangs and drunks—I was ashamed not to be able to forget those kid-stuff Westerns at a time like this.) Would they go running away to the white farmer? Would somebody jump on a bike and go for the police? Or if there was no bike, what about a horse? I saw someone riding a horse.

I rode slowly to the next turn-off, the one where a farm road goes down to Nek Halt. There it was, just like Josias said. Here was where the other roadblock would be. But when he spoke about it there was nothing in between! No people, no houses, no flat veld with hills on it! It had been just one of those things grown-ups see worked out in their heads: while all the time, here it was, a real place where people had cooking fires, I could hear a herdboy yelling at a dirty bundle of sheep, a big bird I've never seen in town balanced on the barbed-wire fence right in front of me. . . . I got off my bike and it flew away.

I sat a minute on the side of the road. I'd had a cold drink in an Indian shop in the dorp where I'd got off the train, but I was dry again inside my mouth, while plenty of water came out of my skin, I can tell you. I rode back down the road looking for the exact place I would choose if I were Josias. There was a stretch where there was only one kraal consisting of two houses, and that quite a way back from the road. Also there was a dip where the road went over a donga. Old stumps of trees and nothing but cows' business down there; men could hide. I got off again and had a good look round.

But I wondered about the people, up top. I don't know why it was, I wanted to know about those people just as though I was going to have to go and live with them, or something. I left the bike down in the donga and crossed the road behind a Cadillac going so fast the air smacked together after it, and I began to trek over the veld to the houses. I know most of our people live like this, in the veld, but I'd never been into houses like that before. I was born in some Location (I don't know which one, I must ask Emma one day) and Emma and I lived in Goughville Location with our grandmother. Our mother worked in town and she used to come and see us sometimes, but we never saw our father and Emma thinks that perhaps we didn't have the same father, because she remembers a man before I was born, and after I was born she didn't see him again. I don't really remember anyone, from when I was a little kid, except Emma. Emma dragging me along so fast my arm almost came off my body, because we had nearly been caught by the Indian while stealing peaches from his lorry: we did that every day.

We lived in one room with our grandmother but it was a tin house with a number and later on there was a streetlight at the corner. These houses I was coming to had a pattern all over them marked into the mud they were built of. There was a mound of dried cows' business, as tall as I was, stacked up in a pattern, too. And then the usual junk our people have, just like in the Location: old tins, broken things collected in white people's rubbish heaps. The fowls ran sideways from my feet and two old men let their talking die away into ahas and ehês as I came up. I greeted them the right way to greet old men and they nodded and went on ehêing and ahaing to show that they had been greeted properly. One of them had very clean ragged trousers tied with string and sat on the ground, but the other,

sitting on a bucket seat that must have been taken from some
scrapyard car, was dressed in a way I've never seen—from the
old days, I suppose. He wore a black suit with very wide
trousers, laced boots, a stiff white collar and black tie, and on
top of it all, a broken old hat. It was Sunday, of course, so I
suppose he was all dressed up. I've heard that these people who
work for farmers wear sacks most of the time. The old ones
didn't ask me what I wanted there. They just peered at me with
their eyes gone the colour of soapy water because they were so
old. And I didn't know what to say because I hadn't thought
what I was going to say, I'd just walked. Then a little kid slipped
out of the dark doorway quick as a cockroach. I thought perhaps
everyone else was out because it was Sunday but then a voice
called from inside the other house, and when the child didn't
answer, called again, and a woman came to the doorway.

I said my bicycle had a puncture and could I have some
water.

She said something into the house and in a minute a girl,
about fifteen she must've been, edged past her carrying a
paraffin tin and went off to fetch water. Like all the girls that
age, she never looked at you. Her body shook under an ugly old
dress and she almost hobbled in her hurry to get away. Her head
was tied up in a rag-doek right down to the eyes the way old-
fashioned people do, otherwise she would have been quite
pretty, like any other girl. When she had gone a little way the
kid went pumping after her, panting, yelling, opening his
skinny legs wide as scissors over stones and antheaps, and then
he caught up with her and you could see that right away she
was quite different, I knew how it was, she yelled at him, you
heard her laughter as she chased him with the tin, whirled
around from out of his clutching hands, struggled with him;
they were together like Emma and I used to be when we got
away from the old lady, and from the school, and everybody.
And Emma was also one of our girls who have the big strong
comfortable bodies of mothers even when they're still kids,
maybe it comes from always lugging the smaller one round on
their backs.

A man came out of the house behind the woman and was friendly. His hair had the dusty look of someone who's been sleeping off drink. In fact, he was still a bit heavy with it.

"You coming from Jo'burg?"

But I wasn't going to be caught out being careless at all, Josias could count on me for that.

"Vereeniging."

He thought there was something funny there—nobody dresses like a Jo'burger, you could always spot us a mile off—but he was too full to follow it up.

He stood stretching his sticky eyelids open and then he fastened on me the way some people will do: "Can't you get me work there where you are?"

"What kind of work?"

He waved a hand describing me. "You got a good work."

" 'Sall right."

"Where you working now?"

"Garden boy."

He tittered, "Look like you work in town," shook his head.

I was surprised to find the woman handing me a tin of beer, and I squatted on the ground to drink it. It's mad to say that a mud house can be pretty, but those patterns made in the mud looked nice. They must have been done with a sharp stone or stick when the mud was smooth and wet, the shapes of things like big leaves and moons filled in with lines that went all one way in this shape, another way in that, so that as you looked at the walls in the sun, some shapes were dark and some were light, and if you moved, the light ones went dark and the dark ones got light instead. The girl came back with the heavy tin of water on her head making her neck thick. I washed out the jam tin I'd had the beer in and filled it with water. When I thanked them, the old men stirred and ahaed and ehêed again. The man made as if to walk a bit with me, but I was lucky, he didn't go more than a few yards. "No good," he said. "Every morning, five o'clock, and the pay—very small."

How I would have hated to be him, a man already married and with big children, working all his life in the fields wearing sacks. When you think like this about someone he seems something you could never possibly be, as if it's his fault, and not just the chance of where he happened to be born. At the same time I had a crazy feeling I wanted to tell him something wonderful, something he'd never dreamed could happen, something he'd fall on his knees and thank me for. I wanted to say, "Soon you'll be the farmer yourself and you'll have shoes like me and your girl will get water from your windmill. Because on Monday, or another Monday, the truck will stop down there and all the stuff will be taken away and they—Josias, me; even you, yes—we'll win forever." But instead all I said was, "Who did that on your house?" He didn't understand and I made a drawing in the air with my hand. "The women," he said, not interested.

Down in the donga I sat a while and then threw away the tin and rode off without looking up again to where the kraal was.

It wasn't that Monday. Emma and Josias go to bed very early and of course they were asleep by the time I got home late on Sunday night—Emma thought I'd been with the boys I used to go around with at weekends. But Josias got up at half past four every morning, then, because it was a long way from the Location to where the dynamite factory was, and although I didn't usually even hear him making the fire in the kitchen which was also where I was sleeping, that morning I was awake the moment he got out of bed next door. When he came into the kitchen I was sitting up in my blankets and I whispered loudly, "I went there yesterday. I saw the turn-off and everything. Down there by the donga, ay? Is that the place?"

He looked at me, a bit dazed. He nodded. Then: "Wha'd' you mean you went there?"

"I could see that's the only good place. I went up to the houses, too, just to see . . . the people are all right. Not many. When it's not Sunday there may be nobody there but the old man—there were two, I think one was just a visitor. The man and the women will be over in the fields somewhere, and that must be quite far, because you can't see the mealies from the road. . . ." I could feel myself being listened to carefully, getting in with him (and if with him, with *them*) while I was talking, and I knew exactly what I was saying, absolutely clearly, just as I would know exactly what I was doing. He began to question me; but like I was an older man or a clever one; he didn't know what to say. He drank his tea while I told him all about it. He was thinking. Just before he left he said, "I shouldn't't've told you."

I ran after him, outside, into the yard. It was still dark. I blurted in the same whisper we'd been using, "Not today, is it?" I couldn't see his face properly but I knew he didn't know whether to answer or not. "Not today." I was so happy I couldn't go to sleep again.

In the evening Josias managed to make some excuse to come out with me alone for a bit. He said, "I told them you were a hundred-per-cent. It's just the same as if I know." "Of course, no difference. I just haven't had much of a chance to do anything . . ." I didn't carry on: ". . . because I was too young"; we didn't want to bring Emma into it. And anyway, no one but a real kid is too young any more. Look at the boys who are up for sabotage. I said, "Have they got them all?"

He hunched his shoulders.

"I mean, even the ones for the picks and spades . . . ?"

He wouldn't say anything, but I knew I could ask. "Oh, boetie, man, even just to keep a lookout, there on the road. . . ."

I know he didn't want it but once they knew I knew, and that I'd been there and everything, they were keen to use me. At least that's what I think. I never went to any meetings or anything where it was planned, and beforehand I only met the two others who were with me at the turn-off in the end, and we were told exactly what we had to do by Seb Masinde. Of course, neither of us said a word to Emma. The Monday that we did it was three weeks later and I can tell you, although a lot's happened to me since then, I'll never forget the moment when we flagged the truck through with Josias sitting there on the back in his little seat. Josias! I wanted to laugh and shout there in the veld; I didn't feel scared—what was there to be scared of, he'd been sitting on a load of dynamite every day of his life for years now, so what's the odds. We had one of those tins of fire and a bucket of tar and the real ROAD CLOSED signs from the PWD and everything went smooth at our end. It was at the Nek Halt end that the trouble started when one of these AA patrol bikes had to come along (Josias says it was something new, they'd never met a patrol on that road that time of day, before) and get suspicious about the block there. In the meantime the truck was stopped all right but someone was shot and Josias tried to get the gun from the white man up in front of the truck and there was a hell of a fight and they had to make a getaway with the stuff in a car and van back through our block, instead of taking over the truck and driving it to a hiding place to offload. More than half the stuff had to be left behind in the truck. Still, they got clean away with what they did get and it was never found by the police. Whenever I read in the papers here that something's been blown up back at home, I wonder if it's still one of our bangs. Two of our people got picked up right away and some more later and the whole thing was all over the papers with speeches by the chief of Special Branch about a master plot and everything. But Josias got away okay. We three chaps at the roadblock just ran into the veld to where there were bikes hidden. We went to a place we'd been told in Rustenburg district for a week and then we were told to get over to Bechuanaland. It wasn't so bad; we had no money but around Rustenburg it was easy to pinch pawpaws and oranges off the farms. . . . Oh, I sent a message to Emma that I was all right; and at that time it didn't seem true that I couldn't go home again.

But in Bechuanaland it was different. We had no money, and you don't find food on trees in that dry place. They said they would send us money; it didn't come. But Josias was there too, and we stuck together; people hid us and we kept going. Planes arrived and took away the big shots and the white refugees but although we were told we'd go too, it never came off. We had no money to pay for ourselves. There were plenty others like us in the beginning. At last we just walked, right up Bechuanaland and through Northern Rhodesia to Mbeya, that's over the border in Tanganyika, where we were headed for. A long walk; took

Josias and me months. We met up with a chap who'd been given a bit of money and from there sometimes we went by bus. No one asks questions when you're nobody special and you walk, like all the other African people themselves, or take the buses, that the whites never use; it's only if you've got the money for cars or to arrive at the airports that all these things happen that you read about: getting sent back over the border, refused permits, and so on. So we got here, to Tanganyika at last, down to this town of Dar es Salaam where we'd been told we'd be going.

There's a refugee camp here and they give you a shilling or two a day until you get work. But it's out of town, for one thing, and we soon left there and found a room down in the native town. There are some nice buildings, of course, in the real town—nothing like Johannesburg or Durban, though—and that used to be the white town, the whites who are left still live there, but the Africans with big jobs in the government and so on live there too. Some of our leaders who are refugees like us live in these houses and have big cars; everyone knows they're important men, here, not like at home where if you're black you're just rubbish for the Locations. The people down where we lived are very poor and it's hard to get work because they haven't got enough work for themselves, but I've got my standard seven and I managed to get a small job as a clerk. Josias never found steady work. But that didn't matter so much because the big thing was that Emma was able to come to join us after five months, and she and I earn the money. She's a nurse, you see, and Africanization started in the hospitals and the government was short of nurses. So Emma got the chance to come up with a party of them sent for specially from South Africa and Rhodesia. We were very lucky because it's impossible for people to get their families up here. She came in a plane paid for by the government, and she and the other girls had their photograph taken for the newspaper as they got off at the airport. That day she came we took her to the beach, where everyone can bathe, no restrictions, and for a cool drink in one of the hotels (she'd never been in a hotel before), and we walked up and down the road along the bay where everyone

walks and where you can see the ships coming in and going out
so near that the men out there wave to you. Whenever we
bumped into anyone else from home they would stop and ask
her about home, and how everything was. Josias and I couldn't
stop grinning to hear us all, in the middle of Dar, talking away
in our language about the things we know. That day it was like
it had happened already: the time when we are home again and
everything is our way.

Well, that's nearly three years ago, since Emma came. Josias
has been sent away now and there's only Emma and me. That
was always the idea, to send us away for training. Some go to
Ethiopia and some go to Algeria and all over the show and by
the time they come back there won't be anything Verwoerd's
men know in the way of handling guns and so on that they won't
know better. That's for a start. I'm supposed to go too, but
some of us have been waiting a long time. In the meantime I go
to work and I walk about this place in the evenings and I buy
myself a glass of beer in a bar when I've got money. Emma and
I have still got the flat we had before Josias left and two nurses
from the hospital pay us for the other bedroom. Emma still
works at the hospital but I don't know how much longer. Most
days now since Josias's gone she wants me to walk up to fetch
her from the hospital when she comes off duty, and when I get
under the trees on the drive I see her staring out looking for me
as if I'll never turn up ever again. Every day it's like that. When
I come up she smiles and looks like she used to for a minute but
by the time we're ten yards on the road she's shaking and
shaking her head until the tears come, and saying over and over,
"A person can't stand it, a person can't stand it." She said right
from the beginning that the hospitals here are not like the
hospitals at home, where the nurses have to know their job.
She's got a whole ward in her charge and now she says they're
worse and worse and she can't trust anyone to do anything for
her. And the staff don't like having strangers working with
them anyway. She tells me every day like she's telling me for the
first time. Of course it's true that some of the people don't like
us being here. You know how it is, people haven't got enough

jobs to go round, themselves. But I don't take much notice; I'll
be sent off one of these days and until then I've got to eat and
that's that.

The flat is nice with a real bathroom and we are paying off
the table and six chairs she liked so much, but when we walk in,
her face is terrible. She keeps saying the place will never be
straight. At home there was only a tap in the yard for all the
houses but she never said it there. She doesn't sit down for
more than a minute without getting up at once again, but you
can't get her to go out, even on these evenings when it's so hot
you can't breathe. I go down to the market to buy the food
now, she says she can't stand it. When I asked why—because
at the beginning she used to like the market, where you can
pick a live fowl for yourself, quite cheap—she said those little
rotten tomatoes they grow here, and dirty people all shouting and she can't understand. She doesn't sleep, half the time,
at night, either, and lately she wakes me up. It happened only
last night. She was standing there in the dark and she said, "I
felt bad." I said, "I'll make you some tea," though what good
could tea do. "There must be something the matter with me,"
she says. "I must go to the doctor tomorrow."

"Is it pains again, or what?"

She shakes her head slowly, over and over, and I know she's
going to cry again. "A place where there's no one. I get up and
look out the window and it's just like I'm not awake. And every
day, every day. I can't ever wake up and be out of it. I always
see this town."

Of course it's hard for her. I've picked up Swahili and I can
get around all right; I mean I can always talk to anyone if I feel
like it, but she hasn't learnt more than *ahsante*—she could've
picked it up just as easily, but she *can't*, if you know what I
mean. It's just a noise to her, like dogs barking or those black
crows in the palm trees. When anyone does come here to see
her—someone else from home, usually, or perhaps I bring the
Rhodesian who works where I do—she only sits there and
whatever anyone talks about she doesn't listen until she can
sigh and say, "Heavy, heavy. Yes, for a woman alone. No
friends, nobody. For a woman alone, I can tell you."

Last night I said to her, "It would be worse if you were at home, you wouldn't have seen Josias or me for a long time."

But she said, "Yes, it would be bad. Sela and everybody. And the old crowd at the hospital—but just the same, it would be bad. D'you remember how we used to go right into town on my Saturday off? The people—ay! Even when you were twelve you used to be scared you'd lose me."

"I wasn't scared, you were the one was scared to get run over sometimes." But in the Location when we stole fruit, and sweets from the shops, Emma could always grab me out of the way of trouble, Emma always saved me. The same Emma. And yet it's not the same. And what could I do for her?

I suppose she wants to be back there now. But still she wouldn't be the same. I don't often get the feeling she knows what I'm thinking about, any more, or that I know what she's thinking, but she said, "You and he go off, you come back or perhaps you don't come back, you know what you must do. But for a woman? What shall I do there in my life? What shall I do here? What time is this for a woman?"

It's hard for her. Emma. She'll say all that often now, I know. She tells me everything so many times. Well, I don't mind it when I fetch her from the hospital and I don't mind going to the market. But straight after we've eaten, now, in the evenings, I let her go through it once and then I'm off. To walk in the streets when it gets a bit cooler in the dark. I don't know why it is, but I'm thinking so bloody hard about getting out there in the streets that I push down my food as fast as I can without her noticing. I'm so keen to get going I feel queer, kind of tight and excited. Just until I can get out and not hear. I wouldn't even mind skipping the meal. In the streets in the evening everyone is out. On the grass along the bay the fat Indians in their white suits with their wives in those fancy coloured clothes. Men and their girls holding hands. Old watchmen like beggars, sleeping in the doorways of the shut shops. Up and down people walk, walk, just sliding one foot after the other because now and then, like somebody lifting a blanket, there's air from the sea. She should come out for a bit of air in the evening, man. It's an old, old place this, they say.

Not the buildings, I mean; but the place. They say ships were coming here before even a place like London was a town. She thought the bay was so nice, that first day. The lights from the ships run all over the water and the palms show up a long time even after it gets dark. There's a smell I've smelled ever since we've been here—three years! I don't mean the smells in the native town; a special warm night-smell. You can even smell it at three in the morning. I've smelled it when I was standing about with Emma, by the window; it's as hot in the middle of the night here as it is in the middle of the day, at home—funny, when you look at the stars and the dark. Well, I'll be going off soon. It can't be long now. Now that Josias is gone. You've just got to wait your time; they haven't forgotten about you. Dar es Salaam. Dar. Sometimes I walk with another chap from home, he says some things, makes you laugh! He says the old watchmen who sleep in the doorways get their wives to come there with them. Well, I haven't seen it. He says we're definitely going with the next lot. Dar es Salaam. Dar. One day I suppose I'll remember it and tell my wife I stayed three years there, once. I walk and walk, along the bay, past the shops and hotels and the German church and the big bank, and through the mud streets between old shacks and stalls. It's dark there and full of other walking shapes as I wander past light coming from the cracks in the walls, where the people are in their homes.